Praise for

LOST IN THOUGHT

"Deborah Serra can spin a tale. Every character jumps off the page. Ilana's journey as an accomplished young woman trying to figure out who she is, is compelling, unexpected, and also heartbreaking. This novel captured me."

—Delia Ephron, screenwriter, author of *Left on Tenth*

"This book is about a character navigating matters of self-control and real choices. It is an interesting hybrid—a cross between sheer storytelling and storytelling where the impact of a scientific idea is profound and underlies the entire work. It is gripping."

—Patricia S. Churchland, author, neuro-philosopher, professor

"Great characters, exceptional dialogue. I loved the backstage anecdotes about the opera world. I laughed out loud a couple of times."

—Jerry Mayer, Emmy-nominated writer, international playwright

"*Lost in Thought* will take you on a fascinating journey between your heart and your mind, your conscious and your unconscious. You won't stop thinking about what it means for your own life."

—Lawrence Kasanoff, film producer, *True Lies*; president, Threshold Entertainment; production manager, *Platoon*, *Dirty Dancing*

"The story was rich and engrossing and took so many unexpected turns. Truly funny and incredibly empathetic, the writing was often captivatingly beautiful."

—Roni Feinstein, PhD, author, curator, art historian

"*Lost in Thought* is a magical blend of stellar prose, philosophical and scientific curiosity, and characters that are entirely unique yet highly relatable. Emotionally charged, intellectually bold, and beautifully rendered, this story will compel readers to reconsider their own motivations, decision-making, and visions for their future selves."

—Anastasia Zadeik, award-winning author of *Blurred Fates*, *The Other Side of Nothing*

"Ilana Barrett is flawed, wry, and loveable. Her curiosity is a window to ourselves; her truth is a universal question we all confront: who am I, and why am I? In Deborah Serra's beautiful prose, we realize with Ilana the silent gravitational pull of decisions made by others. *Lost in Thought* reminds us that free will is transient. Highly recommend."

—Elisabeth St. John, acclaimed author of *The Lydiard Chronicles*

Lost in Thought
by Deborah Serra

© Copyright 2024 Deborah Serra

979-8-88824-456-2

All rights reserved. No part of this publication may be reproduced, stored in a retrieval system, or transmitted in any form or by any means—electronic, mechanical, photocopy, recording, or any other—except for brief quotations in printed reviews, without the prior written permission of the author.

This is a work of fiction. All the characters in this book are fictitious, and any resemblance to actual persons, living or dead, is purely coincidental. The names, incidents, dialogue, and opinions expressed are products of the author's imagination and are not to be construed as real.

Published by

◄köehlerbooks™

3705 Shore Drive
Virginia Beach, VA 23455
800-435-4811
www.koehlerbooks.com

LOST IN THOUGHT

a novel by

Deborah Serra

VIRGINIA BEACH
CAPE CHARLES

Does your mind wander?
Where does it go without you?

For Dad

Ilana held her briefcase with her right hand and slipped her left into the pocket of her tan blazer. She felt the sharp slice of a paper cut from the pointed corner edge of the train ticket inside. How could such a small slice hurt? Was it a premonition about tomorrow? Certainly not, she didn't believe such things. There it was, though, proof of her intent for the following day. She felt around the contours of the ticket. No matter what, she would be on that train tomorrow. She opened the glass door to her office building and walked in. Sinking into thought, she was annoyed by the earworm that was there when she woke up: the one line of a song that repeated incessantly in her mind. Over and over. Why couldn't she make it stop? She pressed the button for the elevator.

When the doors slid open, Ilana noted that elevators still looked like opened mouths, gummy with other people's germs. She looked inside and was relieved to find the eight-by-eight-foot traveling container empty. If her office were not on the twelfth floor, she would take the stairs, but she found that impossible after the initial four attempts that delivered her up panting. Now, she was searching for a viable method for the elevator. She had tried holding her breath for the twelve floors, but that success depended on how many stops the rising petri dish would make along the way. The gasping when she ran out of breath around floor eight felt significantly worse. She was currently practicing a shallow breathing technique. The virus had changed her behavior in a few ways that had stuck.

She stepped in and used her elbow to press the button. Three floors later, the elevator slowed to a stop. She looked up. The ding, then the illuminated number four.

Damn.

She breathed shallowly. The jaws opened, and a young professional woman limped in. Then, in a moment of regrettable friendliness, Ilana asked, "Oh, hurt foot, huh?"

The woman looked back at her plainly. "MS."

Oh, shit.

Ilana's face got hot, and her body froze simultaneously. It was a paradox of physicality. She mumbled something unintelligible that she hoped sounded sympathetic but not patronizing, and then she stood properly erect and looked forward uneasily. She felt guilty for her capable body, which she took for granted. Her intentions were good, but it made for a starkly quiet ride. She smiled awkwardly at the woman as she exited the elevator, and then she listened to her brain screw her over all day long.

Oh, hurt foot, huh? Idiot. Couldn't smile silently? Nod pleasantly. Say something civilized about the weather?

Her mind always did this. Her mind was not reliably on her side. Contrary to her self-assured gait and cynically raised left eyebrow, Ilana knew she was always teetering on the edge of mortal embarrassment while her front was flawless, and others envied her cool command. She hated being conspicuous more than anything. She headed down the corridor toward her office, running her index finger over the Amtrak ticket in her pocket. During quarantine, she'd had time to wonder. What if the people who had the answers about her, the people who knew how she came to be, disappeared? Not only bodies slipped into the box that shuts forever, but also memories, truths, and secrets effectively kept. The wondering had laid hands on her and began to squeeze. Her sleep was disrupted by a recurring dream of opening a diary on her wooden coffee table and then flipping frenetically through the pages to find them blank, blank, blank. And as the crown-headed virus stripped away lives indiscriminately, she realized she did want to know. What if, someday, she needed to know? What if everyone who did know was gone? This wondering became relentless when every night, the New York City body count rose unimaginably, and if a friend didn't return your phone call in an hour, you became jittery with alarm. After all, you knew they were home. Ilana was locked down when her mother became gravely ill, and that tragedy seeped into the core of her. She could feel the unwelcome pump of cortisol throughout her body day after day. She would stare out of the window from her Perry Street apartment, where her hours were as vacant as the sidewalks. One afternoon, for a solid hour, she watched a dandelion that had pushed its way up through the crack in the cement now that all the trampling had stopped. *A little sprig of life*, she thought, *Gaia stretching*.

Inside her apartment, Ilana, like everyone else, waited. There was nothing to remember about any day because nothing happened: weeks went by, and she couldn't say a single thing about them. She read *Angle of Repose* by Wallace Stegner, and he wrote "No life goes past so swiftly as an eventless one, no clock spins like a clock whose days are all alike." She had time to think about that. It was true that every day blended into the next; it was true that she couldn't remember much about it. It was one vast blank.

A cloud cover of dark vulnerability hung over Manhattan. When she had to go out, other people looked like weapons with worried eyes behind blue disposable masks. It was all disposable: the nights, the days, the casual friendships. Even now, she had a closet full of toilet paper, and she looked forward to the day when some kid would ask her why.

So, in some of those long, vacant hours, she did the research, found what she was looking for, and bought the train ticket. Adam had invited friends to dinner at her apartment, which is where they were most nights. If it came up, she felt confident that she could present the trip sensibly. She was well-known as the sensible one. She would chalk it up to curiosity. People were deferential to curiosity, quietly impressed by it. We'd all been told curiosity was the sign of an active mind, that curiosity was good, of course, except when it wasn't. People were killed by curiosity every day of the week, and people were satisfied by it. One never knew.

Tomorrow, I go.

As the production manager for the Lyric Opera House, everything was Ilana's responsibility. A crushing volume of details defined her world. All five feet, four inches of her lithe frame could direct the towering stagehands and stare down the labor unions. Those who worked under her supervision would be shocked to learn it was an authority she didn't own naturally. She never stopped feeling like she needed to earn it. Insecurity hid in the folds of her fashionable suit.

Ilana settled into her office to work the numbers for the future production of *The Magic Flute*. She loved the challenge of the puzzle and the interdependence of the pieces. Every piece of her production relied on every other piece to keep its place, or else it collapsed into ruin. She manipulated the different departments: sets, costumes, wigs, stage crew, director, designers, and lighting; she moved the disparate pieces of each area around the production like a board game. What to rent? What to build? For *Flute*, she wanted to build new sets but rent the costumes. Now there was no money to build. Scrimp. Scrimp. Creativity in her job had never been more important. She would contact the San Diego Opera. She remembered that the designer Zandra Rhodes created some extravagant costumes for their production of *Flute*. She could get a reasonable price. She started making calls, and once she sank back in, the day took off, and she was startled when her office door swung open so violently that it left an impression in the drywall.

Lucia di Lammermoor entered in full makeup, full costume, and full attitude.

Ilana rose and stepped toward her. "Ms. Vacatelli, shouldn't you be backstage?"

"I told that juvenile director, and by the way, he still has teenaged acne. Really, where do you find these people?"

"You're piqued about the director's skincare?"

"I told him that I would not take the stage if he refused to replace the two supers behind me."

"Has someone in the background offended you?"

"Those two skinny bitches standing directly behind me, on purpose! Get them off my stage." Vacatelli reached out, grabbed Ilana's arm, and read her watch. "You don't have much time to replace them."

Ilana did not jump and run as the diva expected, even though it was what she was used to from other production managers. She hadn't worked with Ilana before; someone should have warned her. Ilana was velvet. She left the drama to the stage. She believed that in business, emotion was a sign of defeat, and she never showed weakness, no matter how she felt. The soprano found Ilana's ethereal calm provoking.

"Oh, I see." Ilana slowly sat back down at her desk thoughtfully. A long, silent moment passed. "Mmmm . . ."

The diva confronted her. "If you don't hurry, you will have to hold the curtain."

"Hold the curtain?" Ilana coolly regarded the soprano. "Well, I certainly hope not."

Disproportionately unglued, the diva flung her arms out in a livid thrashing, and Ilana imagined her as an oversized feral stork. She kept this image but knew not to grin.

Vacatelli accused, "Oh, I know what you're doing. Don't think that I don't understand that because I'm foreign and—"

"You're from Cleveland."

"But I *studied* on the continent."

"Which continent?"

"You know perfectly, oh, oh, I see." The diva was so hot, her makeup was melting. Ilana was maddeningly calm. "You intend to blame me! You'll blame me for holding the curtain. You'll all blame me in the press, and I'll look like I'm unreasonable, or ah"—she gasped—"unprofessional. Well, I am not going to do that. I'll change my own blocking so I'm nowhere near either one of those skinny bitches." The soprano whipped around and furiously blew out of the room with her full costume skirt creating enough wind to shimmy the papers on Ilana's desk.

Ilana rose, walked over, closed her office door, and then hit the call button on her stage walkie-talkie. It beeped.

The stage manager, Vincent, answered, sounding bored, "Nut factory. This is cashew."

"Lucia just left my office. She's pissed the supers are thinner than her."

"Should've seen that coming," he said with a sarcastic edge.

"So, she's threatening to change her blocking. Without rehearsal, without notice to tech or the other performers."

"Surprises give me hives, Ilana."

"Talk to lighting. Tell them during her arias to drop down the upstage lights and heat up her spot, then no matter where she moves, put the spot where she is supposed to be. Do not follow her. No way she'll voluntarily walk out of that spotlight."

A pause, and then, he said dryly, "I'm in love with you."

"Yeah? Get in line." She switched off the walkie-talkie.

Opera singers lived on the edge, and Ilana felt sorry for them. She couldn't imagine how terrifying it would be to stand in front of a critical audience like this one, open your mouth, and hope the flawlessly formed, faultlessly pitched note floated out and fed the appetite of the judgmental black monster. That's what they called it—the black monster—because on stage, the footlights blinded them, and so for the performers, there was only blackness out there, but they could feel it, hear it breathing, coughing, and—the worst—getting up from their seat. While the opera audience appreciated an inspirational experience, the prospect of ruin was so much more alluring. In the back of their minds, they yearned for the theatrical catastrophe because they craved the drama. Everyone secretly wished they had been in the audience that night at the Paris Opera when Maria Callas missed the high C in *Norma*. Shockingly, Callas stopped singing. She held up her hand to the orchestra. They stopped. There was a moment of confused silence. A confrontational and insulting whistle rang out from the black monster. Callas glared. Then, regally, she signaled for the conductor to begin again. The maestro straightened and raised his eyebrows, the musicians' jaws dropped, and the audience inched forward in their seats. This did not happen. Ever. If Callas started again and missed again, well, that would be the end of her career. The risk was too great. Continuing on as though it hadn't happened and then making a credible excuse to the newspapers the next day, an excuse that sounded heroic for even trying, was the only sensible course, and everyone knew this—everyone. Callas had engendered passionate conflict her entire life, both personally and professionally.

The audience was evenly split between intense defenders and even more intense haters of Callas. This was drama. This was career suicide. A steady, uncompromising stare from the immovable diva, and the maestro nodded, raised the baton, and began the aria again. The audience was riveted as she approached the high C. The orchestra was electrified. And then, the note. She hit it loud and confidently and held it. Flawless. The place exploded! It caused a riot in the audience, fist fights, and yelling. The French Republican Guard had to be called to the opera house to restore order.

Drama is energy. The greater the drama, the greater the satisfaction. The opera stars knew this. They knew that while a transcendent performance would be much admired, a catch in the throat, a wayward gnat in the mouth, or a simple postnasal drip could release a note that made headlines, and people would crowd around retelling, reveling, gloating parasites, sucking energy for themselves from the drama of it, from the drama of tragic, public demise. That terror turned soloists into lunatics. Nevertheless, Ilana did not let it affect her job. She was really good at her job. Usually, she would stay until curtain, but tonight she had a dinner party, and tomorrow occupied her mind.

The six o'clock subway car was like the sale rack at Macy's, with arms hooked around poles and seat rails, humans jammed next to each other. It was an opaque thicket of commuters who swayed as a pack. She had argued that after the sickness, the masks, the gloves, the sanitizers, the dread, after it all, people would be less sanguine about crowding into, well, anywhere. The caution lasted, but too briefly. People slipped back into their lifelong habits, and although some still wore masks, it was far from the norm now. Looking around this packed train tonight, her blood pressure rose. What the hell was she doing in this packed tube?

Too close. Too tight.

She realized that she had walked to the subway unconsciously. She had no recollection of entering Rockefeller Center or of taking the busy cement stairs that led down to the F train. She doesn't remember waiting on the platform or noticing the F train when it thundered in. She doesn't remember stepping into the car. She fell into her old route home without a single conscious moment. How odd to feel as though she woke up with no clue how she got there. Now, inside this train, instantly aware, she saw it as a sausage, a stuffed mammal intestine, a long line of links like the ones she saw hanging in the Italian grocery market, each car connected thinly to the next and overstuffed with people-meat. She promised herself that this was her last time on this subway. She would not be lazy, hurried, or distracted; from now on, she would leave earlier and walk to Midtown in the morning and then back to her apartment every day. It would be good and invigorating. She would wear her comfy Allbirds sneakers with her Armani suit and leave her good pumps at the office in her drawer. Plenty of other professional women in the city did this.

Ilana shifted her weight from her right foot to her left, which was all that was possible in the way of adjustment. She fought the anxiety aroused by the crowd. Her skin was getting clammy, she felt the muscles of her jaw tighten uncomfortably, and she was forcibly trying to relax, but with little results. Something wispy brushed her bare leg. And even though subway riders were skilled at looking but not seeing each other, she had to see. Her eyes strayed left. A gray-haired man in short shorts grinned at her. The wiry long leg hair on his calf tickled her leg an inch below her knee.

Ugh.

She cringed and wondered what would possess a seventy-year-old man to wear shorts. Why is he not in big-boy pants? He's on public transit. She hadn't worn shorts or sat down on public transit for fifteen years, not since she was fourteen years old. It was unacceptably gross, like the word moist.

A bleating voice from somewhere within the crush of standing bodies yelled out, "I hid what mattered to me most in between the toes of my right foot."

Sometimes, Ilana loved Manhattan. This was the other time.

The spoken word poet continued at the top of her lungs inside the train. "I put my pride between my pinkie toe and my fourth toe. I tucked it there so I would always feel it when I moved. Pride makes you feel like you're someone you aren't, or like you deserve something. I really felt my life would've turned out so much better if only my shoulders had been square. Maybe then they would have led me, led me somewhere!"

"Off this train works for me," someone yelled back. People smiled but kept their eyes down. *There it is*, she thought, *that's the Manhattan I love.*

Ilana tilted her face up, reaching for a breath of freshness. She knew that she was breathing in human exhaust, used air, other commuter's discarded oxygen. She ran the numbers because running numbers was comforting to her: the air was 20.95 percent oxygen, and when she breathed in, she kept about 4 percent and exhaled about 16 percent. In this crowded metal tube, the air she took in had been inside someone else's lungs.

Eww.

She bent her neck all the way forward, dropping her head and trying to nestle her nose inside her suit jacket. Would that be some kind of filter? This was absolutely the last time she would be on this subway.

The train stopped, and the doors slid open with a ding, accompanied by the usual garbled announcement. Hundreds of passengers shifted places as some stepped onto the platform. Ilana darted out and ran up the stairs to the open-sky world above.

Her phone rang. She pulled it out of her pocket and saw the time. Four minutes late? Isn't that maddening? Everyone's sense of time has collapsed. Technology turned us into an entire nation of people tapping their feet.

Ilana answered the call. "Hi, Adam. Almost there."

"Yes, good, because there's a well-dressed and attractive neuroscientist standing on your doorstep and balancing a heavy grocery bag because he forgot the key you gave him."

"Oh? I thought I chose a smart guy."

They had been together for three years. It was only recently that she felt an annoying invisible piece of foreign matter between them. It was like a sesame seed stuck between her molars; she couldn't dislodge it, and she couldn't accept it. It was unnerving because she had always felt certain of Adam. If the pandemic hadn't shut everything down, they would probably be married by now. But, instead, well, they're not. She wondered if her restlessness was related to her questions about her past and the trip tomorrow. Was it related to the unmoored feeling that had emerged along with the curiosity? This kind of incertitude was unlike her. She felt the only way to ward off making mistakes in life was to be certain and walk with purpose. Her dad always told her, "If you walk with purpose, people will step aside." Even as a young girl, with her hair blowing in the breeze from all the opened doors before her, she was always sure that she must appear certain at all times. While her friends were on their tiptoes, stepping cautiously around the groundwater that seeped up from their doubts,

Ilana walked on successfully ignoring her dampening feet.

She picked up her pace. "Adam, I don't want to be up too late. Perhaps we should reconsider this dinner. Is it too late to cancel? I've got a lot going on tomorrow."

"I've got all the food. Guests are coming. And this trip is silly."

"Silly?"

"Maybe not silly, but unnecessary," he said.

"For you."

"Ilana."

"Adam."

"Let me go with you."

"No."

"I want to."

"No."

"You want to discuss it?"

"No."

"You seem certain."

"Yes."

He paused, then said, "How uncharacteristic."

She heard the smile in his voice. Of course, he knew her. She turned onto West Fourth Street.

Muggy, the perfect description; she felt mugged as summer laid its sweaty fingers on her skin. She turned uptown and hurried toward her apartment, stepping over the eruptions on the cement face of the sidewalks. Along West Fourth Street, the trees were buried up to their necks in cement but still thriving; she liked that. She liked what that said about New York. She turned right onto Perry Street. The industrial breezes from cars and buses and subway vents blew hot into her face, grabbed her silk skirt, and whipped the loose strands of her hair. The beat of the street pumped into the soles of her black heels, and she felt it as she walked, the city rumba. She lived with ease inside these rhythms. Being anywhere else was like being unplugged. While it may be temporarily relaxing, it was not her normal state; it was a broken state. She was not bothered by the smells of aging cheeses or the waft of pungent winos, or by the angry taxi horns, or the man who screamed his love every night to a boarded-up window. She walked past the chanting Jamaican woman who sold voodoo dolls on the corner, never noticing her, and yet, she would miss her if one day she were gone. She turned into the brownstone.

She always thought of her mom when she arrived home. It had been five long months since she threw the handful of dirt on the oblong box that held the painted doll crust of her mother. Her mother, who was on a ventilator for three months and finally gave in. Forbidden from entering the hospital, Ilana watched her mom die on an iPad. She understood, but she could not forgive. She had showered twice every day since then, trying to wash it all away. The washing felt essential; it was her essential work. Essential was now inextricably attached to a particular place and a desperate time. Was it good or bad to be essential during a crisis? So many of her friends considered themselves essential—and announced they were essential—but they weren't. They angered her. She committed to cutting down to one shower per day, even though inside the shower was the only time her brain didn't replay the *beep beep beep* that had played incessantly through her iPad from the ICU. Always there, softly in the background, *beep beep beep*. She swung open the door to her building and stepped inside.

Up the stairs, Adam waited on the landing outside her door. He blamed his impatience on the city. He missed the verdant hills, the autumn blaze maple, the pink and white flowering dogwoods, of his Pennsylvania home. Manhattan was gray and bland, and it smelled like bus fumes and wet newspaper. The screensaver on his computer flashed the jade and ruby leaves from his youth. Saying goodbye to that beauty was sad, but Columbia offered him a lab at the neuroscience facility, so he'd packed up, and then, after he met Ilana, it all made sense. He had made all the right choices. He laughed at himself as he thought this because he knew he didn't really make choices, not in a deliberative way, the way most people think they do. He didn't make a choice to love Ilana; it was decided on a chemical level, certainly not by deliberation. Adam understood choice better than the average person, better than the average scientist. Finally, Adam was making his mark. His research on decision-making had made him a player in his field, and his research had proven, to his satisfaction, that humans were deluding themselves. Sapiens were not the thoughtful, analytical creatures they liked to believe they were. Never tiring of explaining this to people, he did wonder if all his excited talk about his research and the blurry shifting line between conscious deliberation and unconscious decision-making had fed Ilana's desire to take this trip tomorrow. He had a bad feeling about the trip. He didn't like the idea one bit.

Leaning his slim, long back against the door molding, he pulled out his phone and opened his email. A request surfaced for him to blurb a colleague's upcoming book, and he replied yes because he was a member of the cabal of intelligentsia that blurbed each other's books, sometimes as a friend, sometimes as an expert, sometimes as a pay-it-forward for one's own upcoming book; some of them even blurbed without reading to keep their own name in print. Yes, it was a racket. All the games and egos that the general public assumed the academics were above played out with vicious stealth behind the scenes. Adam always read the book. It was true, though, that sometimes he chose the words for his reviews with conspicuous ambiguity. For instance, he might say a book was "thought-provoking" because that could go either way and really said nothing at all; a nursery rhyme was thought-provoking, and a blueberry could be thought-provoking. When he found himself on a panel with other scientists (many of whom hated each other in private and all of whom were trying to out-cold-blood each other), he used his passion to connect with the audience. He wanted to reach people. He knew his field of neuroscience was on the cusp of revolutionizing world thought. His prestige was growing in the scientific community, and the burden to prove himself was loosening its grip around his throat. People were listening to him.

He felt at the top of his game. Now he only needed to stay there to research, publish, speak, and stay relevant.

He heard her shoes clicking up the stairs toward the landing. He knew the sound of her step. Her shoulder-length loose hair would be swishing back and forth as she rounded the top of the stairs. It would expose her neck a bit and reminded him of the white heron that would stand in ethereal composure at the edge of the pond behind his childhood home. Ilana would be slightly damp from the humidity. He knew exactly how she would smell. He knew the arch of her left eyebrow, and he could feel his palm flat on the sexy concave small of her back. He liked being with a woman who was so clearly herself, who knew who she was and what she wanted. He reveled in her candidness toward life. He knew to his very core what a good match they were.

As Ilana reached the top of the stairs and saw Adam, she knew they were destined for yet another conversation about her trip to Albany. Why was he so focused on this? Why couldn't he just let it go? So what if she thought it might give her answers to questions that, until recently, she didn't know were bothering her? Still, they were answers that she had every right to. She wanted to know if there was a box, like a coffin, with a secret inside aching for a breath of air, a secret kept and at risk of being buried forever. A secret about her? In all likelihood, she knew that it would turn out to be a prosaic disappointment, but she had to try.

"Sorry," Ilana said quickly as she joined him at the door to her apartment. She opened the door, and they went in. They turned right and headed for the small kitchen. "Crazy day. We lost our baritone to laryngitis, and so there was a casting scramble."

"Were you able to fill it?"

"Yes, I cast you in that role."

"That would be dramatic—atonal but dramatic. Are you getting tired of all the aggravation there?"

"Are you kidding? When I do my job, several thousand formally dressed people applaud wildly." She grinned at him. "Hard to beat it."

"I could see that."

Ilana did feel insanely privileged that in her job, the black ink on her spreadsheet was accompanied by wild applause. She loved the relentless pressure of the eight o'clock curtain and the hunger of the seated crowd. Eagerly, each night, as the curtain rose, she held her breath. She saw the curtain like an eyelid in that last moment before waking, a shudder and then up to reveal a whole new world of color, of anguish, and of joy—the opera.

"I did find the missing chair for the new cellist lodged inside a stall in the restroom."

"Who did that?"

"You know it's the brass section. It's always the horns."

Adam pulled two tomatoes out of the bag. "I need something for these."

"Yup."

Ilana reached into the cabinet and pulled out an empty Tupperware container. Her eyes fell hard on the lid, and everything stopped. Adam's voice receded. The refrigerator's hum intensified and overtook the room. Her vision clouded. She stopped breathing. All she saw was the lid of this used container. What once had been written boldly, by black marker, across the top, was now only a few barely discernible faded gray lines, unreadable to anyone, anyone but her. Her throat fisted, and her renowned composure was stripped away by a Tupperware lid and the crash of a vivid memory. She saw her mother walking into the kitchen a year ago, carrying this exact container.

"Chinese food," Mom said. "For you and Adam, because you don't eat properly and you work too hard, but I'm sick and tired of you never returning my Tupperware." (Ilana had dropped her head to smile. Of course, her mother was right; she never did return it.) "And so, I wrote my name across the lid. Now there's no confusion." And that she had, in brazen black, bold letters, with a marker across the lid: **MOM**. It was exactly the sort of thing her mother would do. They could afford as much Tupperware as she could ever possibly desire, but there was something about lifted Tupperware that peeved her.

"Okay, Mom." And Ilana knew it wouldn't matter. She still wouldn't return it. And she hadn't. It was in her hands.

The writing on the Tupperware lid had faded. It washed away casually, little by little, the way grief washes out of us one sad cell at a time. Each time she took the lid out of the dishwasher, it was a bit more faded. Standing there now in the kitchen, gripping the lid, the tips of her fingers were bloodless. She was lost to the soft, broken, indiscernible gray lines that had once said MOM and were now only a smudge. Suddenly frantic, she yanked open the junk drawer with such force that things scattered. She pulled out a black marker and rewrote boldly across the lid in thick dark lines **MOM**. She took in a quick gulp of air, unaware she had stopped breathing. She looked at the lid, and her stomach calmed.

Better. Yes, better. There.

She felt a tender touch on her arm. She looked up and saw Adam. They stood a moment in utter stillness. Then, slowly, he reached out, took the black marker, put the top back on, and gently returned it to the junk drawer. She handed him the Tupperware, and they went back to preparing dinner in the silence that comes when no words will do.

Later that evening, Ilana and Adam lounged agreeably around the supper table with the other two couples: Bob and Cheryl and William and his date. William brought his next new guy, and one furtive glance when they arrived indicated to Ilana that she need not learn his name. William went through dates like a weed-eater because his expectations were high, and his tolerance was low. Nevertheless, he tried to find someone now and then, although memories of his great love, David, obscured the possibility of any real connection.

The evening resembled many Manhattan nights of red wine and professional conversation. It had a contented replete quality, which Ilana, in her distracted state, appreciated because little was required of her, and she could float. She noticed how similar they all were: in their thirties, educated, in similar clothes, and patently civilized.

We have been expertly packaged.

It was a surprising thought for her to feel outside looking in.

The nouns, adverbs, prepositions, sentences, and everything that formed conversation floated around her without purposeful cohesion. She had heard it all before. Adam was not slow to engage. He loved to engage, and he was always an interesting dinner conversationalist. She shimmied back into the conversation and forced herself to pay attention, if not to participate.

"Adam," Bob said, "you aren't considering the social consequences of what you're saying."

"Because social consequences are irrelevant."

"That's always untrue."

"Bob, you can't decide something isn't true because you don't like the ramifications. This is science, not politics. It's a fact that at any moment, we're only aware of a tiny fraction of what our brains and bodies are doing."

"Well," said Cheryl with smirky petulance, "I can't speak for you, Adam, but I'm fully conscious all the time."

"Are you? Of your memory storage? What about your gallbladder and liver functions? It's all neural activity that goes on without your consent or awareness, and your thoughts are no different. Decisions and choices are made by material biological activity in the nonconscious brain, and then those decisions are sent to the conscious mind, where we create the reasoning that works for us."

"Oh, uh-huh, let me see. I know, bullshit," Cheryl said.

"Elegantly put, Cheryl," William said and then grinned at Ilana, who caught his eye and tilted her head at him.

Adam explained, "You don't decide what you'll think next. Thought appears."

"Abracadabra." William toasts.

"Consider that you're born with your genes, and then you're subjected to years of your environment as well as your personal experiences, which affect the expression of those genes: what turns on, what turns off. Your brain is a fusion of all of that. There's research indicating that your brain is a step ahead of your consciousness with regularity, if not all the time. Are you living the controlled and conscious life you think you're living?"

Unconvinced, Bob said, "You think I'm not consciously choosing?"

"I believe that you are not deliberating the way you're convinced you are, and you're making fewer deliberative choices every year that passes, over time."

"How?" Bob asked.

"Some things don't take time, like fear or pain signals. If you touch that hot stove, your unconscious moves you instantly. It doesn't send a message to your mind: oh, that's hot, so I should pull away my hand. It doesn't do that because the conscious mind is slow, so if it's important, well, our brain bypasses attention."

"That's a reflex," Cheryl said.

"Reflex is only a label. There are innate unconscious decisions like that one, but there are also learned ones."

"Learned unconsciousness? Now you have my attention," said William.

"Driving is a good example of learned unconscious behavior. When you first start driving, you're aware of every car, every turn, and every stop sign, but a few years later, you realize you drove eleven miles to work and have no recollection of doing it."

Bob added, "I've got to admit that's happened to me."

"So, who did that? Who stopped? Who made the correct turns? Who followed the road signs? And what about when that car went over the line, and you swerved before you even realized it?"

"And one better," Bob said, "I had a dentist appointment. I left my apartment, got on the E train, and then, I kind of woke up in front of my office, but the dentist was in the opposite direction."

"Yes. Did you think about how that happened?"

"Nope. I got pissed off. There was no high-level brain function going on, just a lot of four-letter words."

"So, Adam, this is not truly a free will conversation," William said.

"No. Free will is a religious, philosophical, and judicial construct. I'm talking about the biology, about how your brain actually functions, what your neurons do, contrary to what our egos tell us."

"You know, Adam," Cheryl began, "when science tells me things that I know to be contrary to my life experience, I use my brain as a filter to consciously discard results that are not logic-based."

"You rely on your experience as evidence of what's true?"

"I do."

"I guess, then, you are experiencing, right now, the fact that you are on a globe spinning at over one thousand miles per hour? Because if you're not experiencing it, then it can't be true, right?"

Cheryl took a sip of wine. "I make all my own choices. I see no evidence otherwise."

"But, Cheryl, there's evidence in the way you're talking at this very moment."

"How?"

"Are you choosing your words, or are sentences arriving because your unconscious, which has stored vocabulary, the rules of grammar, social situations, and relationships, is choosing your words? You open your mouth, and out it comes. So, if you're not consciously choosing, and you're not, how's that happening? What's that mechanism?"

William admonished, "Mechanism? We are not machines, Adam."

"We are biological machines. Have you never said, I can't stop thinking about it, I can't get this song out of my head, I can't help the way I feel, I shouldn't have laughed, or I wish I could stop thinking and fall asleep? How could any of those expressions be common if we're in conscious control? Why can't you stop that song in your head? Why can't you fall asleep, or not love that person, or not laugh at that joke? And *mechanism* isn't bad, William. As AI develops, we will soon be transhuman: part cellular, part chip."

"Transhuman? C'mon," Cheryl chides.

"You're already inextricably connected to a computer, Cheryl. It's stuck to your hand. Leave your phone home for a week, I dare you."

"Interesting, Adam." Bob smiled. "But doesn't feel right somehow."

"I'd bet it doesn't." Adam smiled good-naturedly as he said, "So, Cheryl, does your mind wander?"

"Of course."

"Where does it go without you?"

William laughed. "Hopefully, somewhere with a swimming pool and cocktails. You're always persuasive, Adam, but this whole line of research and all this tech is a ways away."

"It's a bullet train, William."

William said, "Okay, with that, then, I will *choose* to ask you, and then you can *choose* whether you want to pour us all more wine."

Adam shot back with a glint in his eye. "Do you prefer red wine? Why? Did you decide to prefer red, or did you notice you preferred it?"

Ilana cut in, "Adam, now you're getting annoying."

"Right, right, sorry. I get carried away, I know. So, okay, I'll pour both red and white, and you can choose. Ha, ha! Pay no attention to the man behind the curtain! Right?"

The dinner conversation fell back into a more usual pattern. They talked about films they'd liked or restaurants to go to and covered some local news. Ilana continued to swim along in the shallows, not really in, not really out.

Ilana realized that she had very little of consequence to say to either Bob or Cheryl. All they had shared was what they did together. Their friendship was purely experiential, and so when things shut down, it turned off the light between them. They were couple friends. They enjoyed many of the same things; they shared time with a regularity that was acceptable to all their work schedules, but the strength of the net between them was deceptive. If one should stumble, it would not hold their weight, or if one should move away, it would unravel. No sustaining arteries underneath the skin side. Once they couldn't get together for dinners, concerts, or events, then she had little to say to them. The pandemic had wreaked havoc on superficial friendships. The time spent with friends became so treasured that fillers were unflatteringly spotlit. She no longer cared to fritter away an evening with Bob and Cheryl. Time had been revealed as the only precious thing.

Bob and William discussed the pros and cons of a change in the tax law while Ilana's thoughts wandered away. Tomorrow afternoon, she would take the train to Albany and sneak a peek at her past, at the life she was born to live, at her genetic history, about which she knew nothing. What would she feel? Her mind flowed around space like liquid. Her foot began to shimmy under the table. She wished they would all leave. Maybe even Adam could spend the night back at his own apartment. Could she ask him to? She looked at the clock again. William noticed, sought out her gaze, and held it. She sent him a small private smile. He told her once that at some point during his schooling, he realized he had crossed the line, learned more about people than he should have, and found he didn't like them. The resulting dilemma left him seemingly contemptuous and a great fan of cats. But she knew. She knew who he was, what he was made of, what he would do for a friend, what he would do for a stranger. They had the kind of friendship only possible between an ex-lover, out-of-the-closet man and his last woman. It was an animated, teasing, thorough intimacy, safe in the deep of each other.

Adam was having a great time, and his sharp blue eyes were glassy from the wine. He surveyed the dinner table and grinned genially at the two other couples. On the wall across from where he sat, he noted the two 11 x 14 inch watercolors, one of the Almafi coastline, and the other of Lake Como. He bought them from a sidewalk artist for Ilana because he knew she wanted to travel there. He decided right then that they would go together soon. The watercolors blended beautifully with his dinner. The apartment was scented with the garlic and oregano from his cooking. He enjoyed cooking. He appreciated the chemistry of it and the ta-da moment at the end as it all came together. He noted the mostly empty plates confirming that the meal had been tasty. Satisfied, he stretched his legs out under the table.

The conversation about his work had left him feeling contented. He enjoyed animated discussions with substance. He knew that sometimes Ilana thought he sounded too forceful, but he believed that was more a comment on her style than his. She touched everything with a subtlety that belied her own intensity. He glanced over at her now, sitting relaxed to his right, and perceived right then, surprisingly, how much she resembled Esther Ann Holiday. How could he not have noticed that before?

Esther Ann was the girl next door when he was in elementary school. She was class president and ran the secondhand book fair. She spun so fast, she had her own gravity, haphazardly sucking the other kids toward her, and the big-eyed, smudge-nose little boy Adam was in the kind of painful love that made him offer her his lunch box every day, even though he was really hungry. Once, in fifth grade, when he felt acutely vulnerable, Esther Ann scribbled a complete list of her friends and circulated the list for comments. He would never forget searching desperately, his eyes wide and wet, for his missing name. The humiliation was more than a ten-year-old could bear. He promised himself, sitting in the woods behind his home that lonely day, that he would never love again. Girls were too dangerous, with their giggling, their whispering, and their careless hearts. As he reached for Ilana's hand, he knew that he hadn't kept that promise. And in that moment, Adam understood; he understood Ilana's recent distraction. He saw with revelatory lucidity where they were in their lives, and he wondered what he'd been waiting for. It was all so damned obvious.

Adam shot up from his seat! The tax planning discussion stopped abruptly. He had unbalanced the room's rhythm. William and his no-name date looked. Bob and Cheryl paused their fork and glass, respectively, and Ilana eyed him, startled.

"I wanted to say something about financial portfolios."

"Okay, as a CPA, now you really are in my area. Adam, bring it on," Cheryl said.

"I think that Ilana and I would have a more dynamic situation if we merged our personal interests into a single portfolio."

Cheryl responded, "As your accountant, I'd have to recommend against that." She flinched as Bob elbowed her with that don't-be-an-idiot move perfected between long-term couples.

"What I mean is, here in the company of our very best friends"—Adam dropped to one knee—"Ilana, will you marry me?"

A suffocating pause.

What's happening?

Ilana went numb, the half-chewed remains of her distracted thoughts suspended. She had been focused on whether she should take a window or aisle seat on the train tomorrow. Her jaw dropped slightly, parting her lips. It was like being awakened from REM sleep with a slap in the face. All eyes turned from Adam to Ilana, and she tried desperately to recall the last few moments so she could figure out how the hell it came to this.

On his knee?

She felt her friends' heightened attention, like hands all over her body, some around her throat. Ilana's fingers and toes crunched. Her tongue was thick, and her skin dampened. It was an alarm so sudden and so pure in its physicality that it propelled her up and out of her chair, where she then stood stymied in the airless room. The anticipation around the table was tangible. She couldn't think. She couldn't think.

"Adam!" She blurted, "Very funny. Ha. He knows how much I hate surprises, so he's joking. So, then, cappuccinos?" She looked around.

The room sucked in on itself. Two shy hands went up for cappuccinos. Ilana grabbed a couple of plates and walked briskly from the room. A shivering silence settled on those remaining. Adam rose awkwardly from his knee and slid into his chair. He looked ten years old.

William cracked the heavy hush. "Jesus, Adam, you've got balls." He handed Adam the bottle of cabernet. "Here, finish this."

Adam's mind scrambled. He took the bottle.

William leaned in and whispered to him kindly, "Give me a few minutes to talk to her. I'll see what's up." He rose, politely excused himself, and followed Ilana to the kitchen.

Adam and William had a cordial détente formed of circumstance. They had different lives, and while they were only one Manhattan-mile apart, they lived in very different cities. These were two men whose paths would never have crossed if not for Ilana. They certainly would never have been friends. Frankly, Adam didn't feel that friendly toward William. As a psychiatrist, William spent his days analyzing people, and he knew that Adam's latent antagonism was territorial and all about Ilana. Adam knew how close they were, and it bred emotional insecurity. Discomfort had paralyzed and muted Bob and Cheryl. Bob pushed the other bottle of wine toward Adam.

WILLIAM AND ILANA met in the East Village ten years earlier. They shared the same Sunday morning ritual. They snatched up the *Times*, left their apartments in old sweats, cut down Greenwich Avenue, skirted Washington Square Park, and took a right onto MacDougal. There, at Café Reggio, they settled in. It was the best cappuccino in Manhattan. Real artwork hung in the tiny café, which was unevenly lit, with gimpy wooden tables that teetered mocking years of matchbooks and napkin shreds jammed under one leg. The espresso beans were pungent and rich with a suggestion of cocoa. The classical guitar music of Andres Segovia played on a loop.

On Sundays, William showed up with hangover eyes and bedhead. Ilana cozied into a corner table, makeup-less, with her hair heaped in a chaotic bun. She felt at ease there. It was the few hours in her week when she was not part of the rushing stream. This was her moment to sit in solitary calm on the banks of her life.

After a time, they recognized each other and nodded. It progressed to *hi*. Then, they would pass a few morning words. After several months, they were sharing a table. William believed that people revealed themselves by which section of the paper they pulled out first. He could tell things about strangers this way.

He commented, "You take out the Travel Section first."

"I do." She looked at him questioningly. "You going to shrink-wrap me now into a personality category?"

"The rapping shrink. Gee, I'd love to rap, but I am hopelessly rhythm-challenged."

"That is a disadvantage. I enjoy the Travel Section."

"Because you feel restless?" he asked playfully.

She arched her left eyebrow. "Because I like the pictures."

"Oh, sure, that's it." He turned his attention back to the Sunday Review. He was not deceived by Ilana's cosmopolitan trimmings, or by the nonchalant diffidence she displayed effortlessly. He was drawn instead by the gulf of isolation expertly camouflaged by her composed exterior. What seemed so perfectly assembled on the surface was exactly that: on the surface. He found her beguiling.

William had started his practice. Ilana had completed her MBA. They fell in love and began a sweet intimacy. Ilana had been with enough men to know how men who were physically attracted to her behaved. It was not something William could fake long-term. When all was finally understood and accepted by him, and between them, they decided that just because they weren't meant to be lovers did not mean they could not be in love, and they had remained sheltered in a friendship rare and profound.

Inside the kitchen, Ilana crammed food-laden plates into the dishwasher. William entered. She felt him standing there. She was aware that she was spinning. Her discomfort of being exposed or conspicuous usually kept her sufficiently gripped. Not now. And not with William.

She heard the tease in his voice as he said, "You always plan such interesting dinner entertainment."

"I'm raising the cover charge."

William removed the dishes she had shoved in, rinsed them, and returned them to the dishwasher. "It was a genuine proposal, although somewhat lacking in the traditional romance."

"Romance is for teen magazines. And don't misunderstand. Adam is the guy. He's brilliant, he's interesting, he's reliable—"

"Perfect. He can double as your Range Rover when you move to the suburbs." William took the teetering plate from her hand.

"Gee, William, that was almost funny." She clinked two glasses, carelessly breaking one in the sink. "Damn."

"And *what about* funny and exciting and sexy?" He took the broken glass from her hand.

"You know, for a therapist, you are perilously removed from reality."

"And you have been distracted for weeks, and I, as your best friend, do have some rights of disclosure, so cough it up, girl. What the hell is going on?"

Ilana's eyes lit up from the inside, a bloom of radiance, mischief, and the satisfying relief of a secret about to be revealed.

She took a breath and said, "I've found my mom."

"The cemetery lost her? God damn clumsy."

"You're evil."

"Mostly."

"My biological mom."

"Holy shit," he said sarcastically, "this night just keeps getting better."

"Your amusement is my sole goal in life."

"Oh, come on, Ilana. In all the years I've known you, this adoption thing has never been an issue."

"I know. But somehow, I started thinking about it. And then, I couldn't stop thinking about it."

"And this was, oh, let me guess, right after your mom died?"

"Forever the analyst."

"You had great parents, Ilana."

"I did. This has nothing to do with them. But recently, I've been feeling like, oh, I don't know, it's like being a little hungry all the time. And, William, you know, if I wait to ask these questions, I may lose the opportunity of ever knowing. It can all disappear in a day. I think we've seen that. Shutdown. Lockdown. Isolation. Wall-to-wall in funeral homes. The entire world has painfully seen how quickly people and normal can disappear."

He said carefully, "Ilana, you have not yet worked through your feelings of loss for your mother. You started running faster, working harder, and hoping it wouldn't catch up with you, which, by the way, it will."

Sitting down on the delicate hand-painted kitchen chair, she pulled her knees to her chest, wrapped her arms around them, and looked as vulnerable as any soft living thing that had lost its shell. Here, now, was the heart of Ilana peeking out from under the competent professional, the heart few people saw. William pulled the other chair close and sat opposite her. In the clear light of their friendship, her sophistication crumbled, revealing a childlike openness.

He spoke softly. "Have you considered that this whole search may only be an elaborate distraction to avoid facing the loss of your mom?"

Ilana paused. She knew better than to dismiss anything William said to her. All the flippancy of the evening disappeared. They sank into an earnest whisper. They spoke to each other like kids sharing mysteries while perched in a tree house and rapt in the quiet woods.

"It's not true that I haven't faced the loss of my mom."

"No?"

"I face it every minute of every day. Every time something good happens, and I can't tell her. Every time something horrible happens, and I can't tell her. I never realized how much I told her until she was gone, and I kept grabbing for the phone. I miss talking to her the same way I'd miss something as natural as eating." Ilana rubbed her eyes. "And I will miss the absurd new hat she bought every Easter, inedible bread pudding she made on Thanksgiving, and . . ."

Her thoughts were loud and they drowned out her words. She stopped. William took her hand. She understood that he knew loss too. For all his showy derision, he listened with a truly intuitive gift.

"But that's not it, or not all of it. William, it is something else. It's like a constant background static that, after Mom died, got louder. You know how when you're on the airplane and the pilot decides to give you an update over the intercom, and no one can understand a damn word they're saying over the static, but you feel like it's really important?"

"Yeah."

"They could be saying take crash positions or free drinks for everyone."

"B."

A small grin. "Well, it's like that. But I want to hear what's being said underneath the static in my head. Adam taught me that thoughts are material, so what material am I? Wouldn't what I'm actually made of have an influence on me?"

"Okay. Okay, so, what have you found out?"

"My mother was an unwed teen named Fiona Shannon. She's married to a guy named O'Holleran. No father was listed. They own a pub in Albany." And with a luminous smile, she said, "Evidently, I'm Irish."

"You know, there *is* something Irish about you."

Even this simple statement filled her up. Suddenly, she felt connected to something, and it felt glorious. She wanted to be connected. She wanted to have a history older than herself.

William continued, "What are you hoping to learn?"

"I'm curious. You know how people say you have your father's eyes or your mother's hair?"

"Yeah."

"Your uncle's sense of humor."

"Your point?"

Ilana repeated it slowly to make an impression, "Your uncle's sense of humor? Isn't that sort of an intangible thing to inherit? What if we are a compilation of all these intangible things: fears, impatience, kindness? What's pulling my strings? Which choices about my life did I freely make, you know, deliberately make? Am I really thinking things through? Am I intentionally deciding anything? Do I really have any choices at all?"

"Ilana, you are you, both your conscious and your unconscious, both you. Your brain is custom-made. It's an amalgam of your social world, your experiences, your unique sensory bubble, all of which influence the genetic hand you were dealt, but all Ilana Barrett."

"My unique sensory bubble?"

"What the zoologist Jakob von Uexkull called umwelt. Your personal world. The world that you see, hear, taste, and smell is not the same as mine. It's not the same as anyone's. We both eat the same dinner, and I like the taste of cilantro, but to you, it tastes like . . ."

"Soap."

"Exactly. You are a distinct package of you. Ilana, look forward, not back."

Ilana's shoulders hunched as her eyes drifted down and then around her kitchen. She noted the four plums ripening on the counter, the crock pot she had never used, the electric can opener, and the fancy butter plate, all of which looked like someone else's stuff. Did she ever wonder if she wanted these things, or did she get them because she was supposed to have them?

"I want to know more." She turned her eyes back to William. "You know who your parents are."

"Unfortunately."

"We can't pretend that it doesn't matter anymore. We are desperate to believe we are who we make ourselves, that we have some agency in our lives. William, did you know I've been afraid of the ocean my entire life? Since I was born. It used to mystify my parents when I refused to go in the water. Why is that?"

"Most likely a forgotten incident in the bathtub when you were a toddler."

"Maybe. But. What if my grandfather saw his son drown, and that trauma released a certain fear chemical response to water in his brain, and then that has been passed along down the line encoded? What if our genes do chemically transmit information like that, so you have red hair and a fear of water? Isn't that how epigenetics works? Genes get turned on and turned off due to your experiences? How can I really not know something as fundamental as *who* I'm made of?" Ilana put her legs back down and realized she was tugging on her hair, a habit she had never been able to control. The wondering had reached a fevered pitch. "Who knows why I am drawn to do this? But I am. I'm going to Albany tomorrow afternoon. I already bought the ticket."

He said, "Tomorrow! They want to meet you?"

"They don't know."

"Oh, Ilana, this is perilous. I don't know."

"Now, *you* sound like Adam."

"Birthday gifts, graduation presents, *these* are the kinds of things that people like to be surprises, but unexpected offspring? Generally, no."

"I'm not going to talk to them. I'm going to a public bar for a drink, that's all. I'm going to sit in the corner. I want to see what I'm made of. Can you blame me?"

"I suppose not. I would probably feel the same. But why go alone?"

"I want to," she said. With her tone soft and tremulous, William could see that this was the absolute core of her. "I wonder. And I'm not wondering so much if my birth mom regretted giving me up. I know she was a teenager. I get that. I do." Ilana sighed. "Oh, I don't know. Maybe I want answers to questions I can't even form."

"Maybe."

"Something in me needs this journey, and it is not about the past; it is about looking ahead, moving ahead—somehow."

"Okay," he whispered.

She whispered in his ear, "Why couldn't you have been straight? Everything would have been much simpler."

"But simple is so very common." He pulled back and looked into her eyes with palpable affection. "And neither one of us is common."

Ilana saw Adam peek in. He slowly entered, laden with dinner plates. She jumped up to help him. She recognized the expression of betrayal on Adam's face when he saw her huddled with William in the thick of each other. She knew it upset him further, alienated him further. She had no idea how to fix that. William took the plates from Adam and gave him a reassuring glance. Adam turned away. No one spoke.

After the company had gone, after the crumbs had been Dust Bustered, after the little red ring of Cabernet had been sponged from the well of the large wine glass, Ilana joined Adam in the bedroom. By that time, the silence between them had gained mass. With each passing minute, it had become harder to be the first one to speak because to be the first one felt like an admission of some kind, a giving in, and they both felt wronged. Block after block of ice stacked up between them. Someone had to speak.

Ilana used math to organize the path forward because numbers never failed to calm and focus her. *It isn't fifty-fifty*, she thought. *It is not fair.* Yes, he had made her conspicuous, and yes, it was insensitive to spring such a private moment publicly on her, but he must feel humiliated; that was worse.

Worse for him. Ugh. I have to say something. Say something.

Adam waited. He could see her moving around with his periphery, but he couldn't look directly at her. Ilana powered around the apartment, pushing in the chairs and stacking the placemats. *Nothing could be left out of place*, he thought, *nothing but him.* He waited with his lips drawn into a thin line. The surprise proposal was one of the few purely impulsive things he had ever done. It taught him a stinging lesson.

Ilana washed and brushed and flossed and lotioned and eventually ran out of things to do. Finally, she slipped in between the white sheets, which was typically her favorite moment at the end of her day. She savored the crisp, flat softness against her bare skin, but not this time, not tonight. Adam put down the book he wasn't reading and turned to her.

Say something.

She took a tiny chip off the ice between them. "I'm sorry about the way things went tonight."

"No, problem. It was such a fun night."

"Asking me like that was so sudden and public."

"Oh, now the pragmatist wants a gondola and roses?"

"Of course not." Ilana regretted embarrassing him. Their unspoken understanding was always that marriage was inevitable, but recently, too many things in her life were being revealed as inevitable, and Adam had been telling her that even her thoughts were not her own but were delivered as the result of some hidden inaccessible mechanism. She could easily have said yes to him tonight. It would have been a nice moment, full of surprise, happy friends, another bottle of wine, and warm wishes, but she hadn't. She hadn't. Did she decide not to? Did she deliberate in that seminal moment and make a decision? No. No, she reacted. She might have said she reacted thoughtlessly. And now she was trying to make it make sense.

"Adam, some things are private moments. You know that. You know me."

"Yeah, believe me, I got that."

"You surprised me with something I saw as privileged between us."

"You've been distant and remote. I figured that was why. And frankly, it never occurred to me that you would say no."

"I didn't say no."

"Felt like no."

Looking at him now, she regretted the entire night. She should not have hosted anyone. This whole evening was a mistake. Gently, she reached out and touched his arm.

"I am sorry. Truly." Her regret was genuine. The angry ice that had settled in between them cracked. "You could not have picked a worse moment. I wasn't paying attention. I've been consumed by this Albany trip. I can't stop thinking about it."

"That, I believe."

"Albany is blasting in my head. It has drowned out everything else. If there was anyone in the world who might understand that, it's you."

"I don't think you should go. I think you could get hurt there. I don't want that."

"I can't get hurt because I have no expectations. And you also know, better than anyone, that I am a practical and cautious woman, who is not prone to impulse. You can trust I will be careful. I only want to get a look at that world. I'm not talking to anyone. I'm stopping in a pub for a glass of wine. That's it."

"What about us? What about our plans?" he asked.

"Can we please let it wait until I get back, and then I promise we'll figure it all out?"

"All right."

"All right." She smiled warmly at him.

When Adam turned on his side to switch off the light, he became aware of one of those furtive, annoying, tiny black dots that sometimes appear before your eyes, and when you try to focus on them, they dart around, you can't catch up, and then, they're gone. It was a premonition he was too educated to recognize. He flipped off the light. His hands fell quietly onto her body. He kissed each of her lips tenderly. They would make up now. Their lovemaking had always been warm and soft. She relaxed into the calm of the connection they shared. He rolled on top of her and sank in. While Adam played her, with familiarity and practice, the door to her mind slammed shut, and inside, she was alone with one thought: *Tomorrow.*

❖ ❖ ❖

THE MORNING was already toasty when Ilana quietly closed the door to her apartment and took the steps down to Perry Street. It was earlier than usual. She hadn't slept well, but she felt good about sticking to her commitment to walk to the office. Unfortunately, she had decided against the sneakers, which was a mistake. By the time she approached Thirty-First Street, her toes felt tight inside her bone-colored sensible pumps. Everyone's feet swelled when walking around in the sticky city summer. Her soles slapped the pavement, which was heating up. She had the day's plan. Her train for Albany left from the Moynihan Train Hall across from Penn Station that afternoon. It was a two-and-a-half-hour ride. She would catch the late train back. Easy. Ilana turned the corner and bought an orange spice muffin from the ornery street vendor under a green and white umbrella. Unwrapping the muffin, she stopped and realized that she wasn't the least bit hungry. She handed the muffin to the pale man haunting the alcove of the Chase bank entrance, and in return, he yelled vile things at her. He cursed her face, her clothes, her childhood, her bed linen, and her kneecaps. She preferred this. It made it easier to keep walking. The shadows who lived on cardboard and who squatted in recesses were unpredictable. It could be anger, accusation, negotiation, raving, or any number of various god blessings, but it was the quiet ones that hurt her, the quiet ones with the fathomless eyes and dogs by their side. They were swept out each morning from restaurant entrances and office niches all over the city, and each night, they returned as surely as the darkness. When it hurt, she felt an impotence so raw that she bit her tongue as she kept walking. Better to keep moving. It was easier when they chased her and called her nasty things.

Tonight, she would be in the company of her birth family. Of course, they wouldn't know that. The prospect was exhilarating. How lucky it was for her that Fiona O'Holleran owned a public bar, where she could slip in and slip out on her own terms. This was the most exotic thing she had ever done. She checked her watch for the first of fifty times that morning.

Gripping the metal door handle that led into the offices for the Lyric Opera House, she hesitated. She knew once she opened that door that she would need to focus. With the immutable deadlines and the dramatis personae, a storm was always raging behind these doors, and she was expected to be the composed cool hand. When it came to her job, Ilana used all her resources: her Manhattan private school upbringing, her MBA, her industriousness, and her ability to swear effortlessly in five languages. Every time the general director asked if there was anything else she needed, she replied, "a stun gun." And that always made him laugh. He gave her significant latitude because he approved of her pedigree and because she delivered. She had settled with ease into the punishing hours and relentless demands because her father had been a Lutheran doctor where long days and longer nights were the models she had watched as a child. He was a quiet, thoughtful man with patients who sincerely cared for him. He read medical journals voraciously and had a gift for diagnosis that was respected by his peers. If someone was ill or in pain, he was always nearby, and that had kept him away from home most nights. As a teen, Ilana hardly noticed when he died because nothing changed. Ilana and her mother were used to it being only the two of them. Theirs was a bond without boundaries.

Ilana swung open the door and headed for her office. "Good morning. Kris, don't forget I'm gone early today."

Kris looked up from her desk as Ilana passed. "Yup, got it. Vincent wants to know if our health plan covers Prozac."

"I put Prozac in the water cooler last year." Then, she winked at her.

"Not the worst idea."

Vincent yelled out from his office. "Caterer for our Gala Tribute Performance wants to make a statement and go totally vegan."

Ilana stopped walking and looked into Vincent's office. "Opera audiences are meat eaters."

"There's an understatement," he responded. "What do you want to do about wine?"

"Drink it all the time."

She turned, entered her office, sat down at her desk, and buried herself in the budget.

Without any detailed consideration, Ilana had begun researching her adoption. She made inquiries, called in a favor from an old classmate, and located the documents. She found that now it was easy to slice open and cannibalize the unrefined confidentialities of others. A vast amount of information was being collected and stored; computers were fat with identifiable facts, becoming centralized, and talking to each other. Google sent out its spiders every night, and AI engines were capacious gluttons, for good and for bad. Privacy was eaten alive byte-by-byte. She felt the blush of personal exposure, and it all troubled her. She knew that control of your personal narrative was vital. Control was what being civilized was all about. The singular qualities that she presented were curated over time so that the garments that clothed her personality looked good on her. It was this artifice that kept the social world greased and running. Lies, rehearsed excuses, massaged résumés, edited histories, and unreliable memories were all part of a constructed identity. Chillingly, now, our clothes were coming off. Now, with a modicum of digging, even the oldest, most vulnerable skeletons could be exhumed. Lives could be picked over and licked to smooth bone. And even knowing all of this, even though she despised the death of privacy, she couldn't stop herself from looking.

With her newly acquired information, she made her plans as though it was something she had always intended to do when it most certainly was not. Now, her mind was relentlessly chewing. It was thrilling but like a horror film. She asked herself why she was going down the dark basement stairs. She laughed derisively at the ingénue who heard a noise in the basement and went down in the middle of the night to check it out, and here she was, poised at the top of the murky staircase.

As cool as Ilana appeared, sitting behind her desk, her toes were gripped, and her jaw was clenched. She crossed her legs and sat back from the edge of the chair. She dropped her hands into her lap. She checked the office clock. Again.

Still early. Work.

She picked up the costume inventory and scanned it. All the operas they performed captivated her, but what she told no one was that it was not the music that drew her in. She was certainly never going to tell this crowd that when it came to music, what she truly loved were songs she could sing along to; one doesn't get a lot of encouragement for that in an opera house. What appealed to her about the operas were the stories—the tragic, insane, bloody, explosive, epic tales. *Really*, she scolded herself, *who on earth could like the flawed libretti of the operas and be lukewarm on the music?* Furtively, her heart broke for Isolde, for Tosca, and it had nothing whatsoever to do with the music. She knew that made her a philistine. It was a flaw, a chink in her sophistication. She told absolutely no one. Not even Adam.

"Ilana?" She looked up. Vincent stood in her doorway.

"Yes?"

"The orchestra."

Leery, she asked, "What?"

"Wires."

"Not taped down?"

"Second violinist tripped and knocked over the music stand, which scratched the first violinist's arm."

"Is there blood?"

Vincent smirked. "Not yet."

"Wait. Aren't they married?"

"Not currently."

"Give it to the chorus master."

"He's online trying to help the tenor get a flight for tomorrow's performance. Flight was canceled. And I'm more afraid of violinists than vampires."

"That's your survival instinct." Ilana rose from her chair.

"Hey," Vincent asked, "are you all right?"

"Of course. Why?"

"I don't know. There's something—"

"I've got this." She headed for the door,

She concluded years ago that orchestral musicians were thin-skinned. In their minds, they were all soloists and certainly not pieces of her puzzle, forced to wear black and stuck in a dark pit. As individuals, they each had personalities, and so did each section of the orchestra: the brass, the strings, the percussion, and then, the orchestra as a whole had a personality; clearly, from Ilana's perspective, there was way too much personality in that pit for any hope of harmony.

She checked her watch on the way down to the stage. (She had required that everyone in the company wear watches and leave their phones at home. Several hundred workers with cell phones in their pockets during rehearsals and live performances was too much risk for her comfort.)

She arrived on stage to an awkward quiet. Every ten seconds, the quiet was broken by a single long ominous note blown by the mischievous tuba player, and then, again, quiet. He was Ilana's favorite. She exchanged a look with him.

The assistant conductor, Armando, sat with his arms folded and eyes squinting. His accent was always worse when he was agitated, which he clearly was. She approached and sat down in the chair next to him. She stretched her neck and then glanced slowly around.

"*Soooooo*," she said, "pretty quiet in here for rehearsal."

Armando seethed with unfocused irritation. "Maestro stormed out. Wiolinist cry." His arms shot upward. "Is too much drama! Is too much drama for good work."

"But Armando, how could there be too much drama at the opera?"

"I tell you secret. Right now, I tell you a secret you don't forget.

You ready for secret?"

"I am."

"I hate them all." He nodded approval at his own remark. "Every one. I hate the flute because is too peppy, and the trumpet because it play reveille, and why, why wake up people? I hate the percussion. It pounds my head. I hate the keyboard, too many teeth." He slapped the arm of his chair for emphasis. "Too many teeth!"

"Armando, I have an important question for you."

"Fine. Fine. Question."

"Are you sure you're in the right profession?"

"No."

The tuba player blew another long, low note. Ilana cocked her head and gave him a look. The roguish humor played in his eyes. She really liked him.

She crossed her legs, brushed a hair from her eye, and then asked casually, "So, where is our maestro?" Her calm was both airy and contagious. Armando began to cool off.

"Take a walk," he quipped and folded his arms again. "He walk and leave me with them." He spat out the word "them" like it was poison.

"Okay." She stood. "Everybody, ten minutes. I'll find him."

Half an hour later, with numerous things left undone and numerous questions hanging in midair, Ilana stunned everyone by walking out. She admitted to herself that it felt a little bit liberating and a little bit evil. She'd been told once that, in the end, when people consider their lives, they don't regret what they did, but rather what they didn't do. She was doing this, and she felt exhilarated! She grabbed a cab for the train station.

Moynihan Train Hall was a relief from Penn Station. Brand new, this would be her first time inside. Whenever she had been in Penn Station, she felt bullied by the loud noise and heavy-fisted surroundings. It was an extreme place of snaking industrial corridors cluttered with commuters, chair sleepers, walkway runners, people waving goodbye, and people crowding toward the exits. Moynihan would be a big improvement.

Ilana jogged to the platform at her normally fast pace, arriving at the last moment, not one second wasted, ever. Obediently, she lined up with all the other passengers. Directly in front of her was a toddler with one hand holding tightly to his mom and the other holding tightly to a toy. It was a blue stuffed egg. A little blue stuffed egg. Ilana's mind wandered away.

One spring morning, after training wheels and before braces, Ilana dug her tiny fingernails between the brittle twigs of a conscientiously constructed bird's nest and lifted out a perfect tiny light blue egg. Such an unimaginable treasure. She held it with a tenderness that awakened a new endearing feeling inside her little girl body, a feeling of needing to care for someone else, a sweet responsibility for this vulnerable life, which was frail in the cup of her palm. Her mother cautioned her against touching it, but she couldn't help herself; the fragility was too inviting. The tiny egg cracked, revealing an almost fully formed baby bird inside. Little Ilana watched, with her eyes tearing, as the tiny life struggled and died in her hand. She looked up at her mother's compassionate face and then dropped her head, so sorry, so desperately sorry for what she had caused. Her body shook as she sobbed.

"I wanted to see. I only wanted to see. I had to know."

Her mother sighed and hugged her sympathetically. "Not everything is meant to know, Ilana. Some things need their mystery to survive. You should remember that."

Ilana wondered what it meant that she remembered those words as she boarded the train destined to take her back in time. She made a note to talk to Adam about this recovered egg memory that her brain served up out of seemingly nowhere. It appeared suddenly in her thoughts, which did smack of a process behind the scenes. And how curious, in light of it, that Ilana had never eaten eggs. As far back as she could recall, she was repulsed by the thought of them. Adam could confirm for her that this was a circumstance where a conscious event, the death of the baby bird in her hands, encoded some kind of unconscious revulsion that she had obliviously and mechanically obeyed all her life. Is her revulsion of eggs a chemically created response to emotional guilt?

Three hours later, the train pulled into the Albany station with a screech, and Ilana jumped, startled. She had been awake, and yet, she had absolutely no recollection of the ride. She had not been aware in any real sense. She didn't remember leaving Manhattan or any of the scenery along the way, whether she had eaten a snack or gone to the restroom. Her eyes had been open, and her body sitting upright, but the last couple of hours were a total blank. Where had she been all this time? It was reminiscent of that time she drove by herself to Hampton Bays. She left, and then she was there. It was creepy to be on autopilot, to function cleanly while absent.

She exited the station and raised her arm to call a taxi. She got in, gave the cabbie the address, and made a conscious decision to watch the landscape pass by. It was hard to manage her meandering thoughts for even one minute. She concentrated.

Be more present.

He drove. This was the cranky Irish section of town, old Albany with blistered blacktop, dome-covered lampposts, and pint-sized row houses. Contrary to the city of strangers Ilana lived in, community was these people's lives, people who knew far too much about each other, people who shared a primitive intimacy; generations of knowing could be peeled from them like sunburned skin, layer after layer, down to pulp. Ilana watched the modest neighborhood pass by the cab window; her mouth became dry, her throat was so parched that it stuck to itself, and she had to swallow hard and consciously. It was not the kind of neighborhood she had pictured. She imagined straight picket fences around modest cottage houses, with blue shutters, welcome mats, and kids playing in the front yard. What she saw was a broken-down car on the lawn of a side yard, a screen door off its hinges, and two kids' tricycles upended in the street. There were several rusted portable charcoal barbecues on porches, and one porch had an awning where a long rip had been repaired with gray duct tape. Nothing in Ilana's life had ever been repaired with duct tape. In what way could she be like the people who lived here? Did she carry any of this inside of her? Did her genetic recipe inform anything about who she was?

Ilana clearly recalled the night she first thought about it all. It was an opera fundraiser three years earlier. She was introduced to a young man named Adam. He was a neuroscientist, and they fell into a relaxed conversation. She asked him about his work, and the subject turned to consciousness. She became increasingly captivated as he spoke, as though he were telling her things she had always longed to know. She knew she was adopted, and she knew she was surely shaped by the world she grew up in, so how could she not be curious about how her genes, her world, and her choices interact? He told her that there were approximately 25,000 genes in human DNA, and the bulk of what they do and how they interact is undiscovered, the ultimate mystery of self.

She asked, "Could we discover that every single thing we are, or say, or do really starts in the unconscious?"

"Yes." Adam shrugged and offered her a glass of wine that he snatched off a passing tray. She took it.

Ilana pressed, "What will happen to our concept of self if science proves that none of us are really thinking our choices through?"

"What if autonomy and decision-making are illusions?" he asked.

"Yes."

"I don't know if science should tell people that sort of truth. We are a treacherous species known to torture and kill to protect our myths."

"What do you think would be the consequences?" Ilana watched him sink into his own thoughts.

"Well," he answered carefully, "initially, of course, no one will believe us. We don't have a history of responding kindly to changes that alter our bloated self-concept. Ask Galileo, Giordano Bruno, or

Darwin."

"Okay."

"But with time, they will have to accept it because that's the fundamental trouble with a fact: It doesn't go away. I expect the religions will start yelling first, followed closely by the sociologists and the criminologists. Most likely, scientists in some parts of the world will be ostracized, maybe even executed." His voice took on a secretive quality, his eyes flashed, and he leaned in closely. "And then, who knows, maybe chaos?"

"Chaos?"

"It would be worse than discovering that Earth isn't the center of the universe, or that we weren't plopped here fully formed at the whim of some supernatural deity, and that instead, we are a small biological blip in a larger natural order. Not in charge of anything, not even ourselves."

"Chaos? Oh, I don't know about that. Sounds extreme."

"To accept that we are organisms driven by our material biology and by the physics of the universe and not by some mystifying superior essence?" Ilana was mesmerized, watching his mind work. She listened. "We would have to face that we're the highest functioning and most manipulative biological organisms on this mediocre planet, perhaps not the smartest, because we're currently destroying our own habitat, and certainly, very certainly, not the nicest." She heard a disturbingly prophetic quality enter his tone, and it seemed he was talking to himself. "And it will be *that* realization, the realization of our inconsequentiality, the awareness of our utter irrelevance, that will undo us. It will fundamentally alter what we believe it means to be human."

They stood silently for a moment. Then, on the left side of the room, a chamber quartet began Debussy. Adam asked her cheerfully, "So, more wine?"

"Um . . . sure."

He walked to the bar. Ilana stood glued to the lush carpet. There was a rushing in her ears. She loved that he had given her so much to think about. She hated small talk, really hated it. This was a more interesting conversation than she'd expected to have that night. She observed the room: the silk gowns, the socially required (and not quite genuine) laughter, the white tablecloths, the starched tux shirts, the painted fingernails, and the mirrors of each in the eyes of the other. That was when she noted that the evening appeared different to her. She was seeing plainly, seeing bare, without the euphemisms she'd absorbed. She stood an arm's length from the caterer's exquisite carving station, and for the first time, she saw the rare roast beef for exactly what it was: a chunk of cow muscle bleeding onto the platter. Next to that was a plate stacked with a baby pig's charred rib cage. There were lamb chops with individual blue paper footies, with elegant curlicues, where an eater could hold on, without dirtying their fingertips, while gnawing at the cooked loin. Her stomach revolted. She took a long, deep breath. Adam rejoined her with two glasses of wine. He gave a large donation to the Opera Guild that night and then took her phone number.

Later, Ilana wondered if the drive for information about her biology and this trip to Albany were somehow sparked by that night, by that specific conversation. Did Adam unknowingly light this fuse, or was William right, and it was her mother's death at the core of it? Or was it both?

"Lady?" The cabbie raised his voice. "Here, lady." The cab had stopped. Ilana looked. She stared at the sign hanging in front of O'Hollerans Pub. It showed a leprechaun trading his pot of gold for a quart of Irish whiskey.

Piano music and loud voices could be heard there in the street, even with the pub doors shut. Ilana felt heavy and sunk into the back seat of the cab. What was she doing? Even though the waves of the pandemic had crested and flattened, it had left behind an uneasiness for small, closed spaces. Claustrophobia was widespread, and although she fought it, still the pub looked awfully small and cramped. She could tell the cab to turn around and go directly back to the train station. Had she come all this way to turn around?

"Lady!" The cab driver prodded her, annoyed.

"Oh, yes." She shoved the credit card into the reader, added a good tip, and hit enter. She brushed a spec of black lint from her bone linen pantsuit, and she firmly grasped the metal of the door handle. She counseled herself.

In. Out. One drink. Call cab. In control.

She shoved the cab door, and it swung open with an embarrassingly long squeal, calling attention to her, which was her last desire. Her head swiveled quickly from side to side—no one. She emerged from the taxi instantly out of place on this worn road. She slammed the cab door shut. It pulled away quickly, too quickly, and she realized she should have paid him to wait. She turned and faced O'Hollerans and wondered if it were true that she had no expectations. Ilana stood, unsure whether she was going in or not.

O'HOLLERANS PUB is the local joint a short walk from the river. Pubs like this are the Irish equivalent of the piazza after dinner in Tuscany, or the New England churchyard on Sunday morning. It's a gathering place. And inside, O'Hollerans was alive. It was a life form with body heat and connective tissue; so much hung in the air here: cigar smoke, yeast, hops, decades of words spoken in haste, in anger, in affection. The place was scrubbed but hadn't looked clean in years. It looked used. It was used. Neon beer signs colored the bar area, and every conceivable libation stood on stacked shelves in front of a large mirror. The O'Doul nonalcoholic beer sign was crooked, cracked, and being used for some kind of french fry target practice. The wooden barstools were discolored, and the seats were ass-rubbed smooth. A regulation dartboard and pool table crowded into the back. The television had a baseball game on, which locals were watching without sound because the bar was filled with music. A pair of arthritic hands, age-spotted and gnarled, pounded out folk tunes on the yellowed upright piano keys.

Eighty-four-year-old Nellie taught herself to play the piano in her uncle's pub back in County Cork. This bawdy, big-boned woman taught herself most things. Her chunky legs straddled the piano bench, her teeth were in a highball glass on the wood, and her silver hair ran wild. There was something inherently joyful about her. When she banged out the last note, the mustached man in plumber overalls slapped the top of the piano.

"Damn. If you don't know every song they is, Nellie."

With a toothless grin, she said, "I've been around." She still had the wisp of a brogue. She raised her shot glass and yelled. "Shoot 'em!"

From someone in the crowd, she heard, "Amen."

Nellie downed her shot, and a few others followed her lead.

Over at the dartboard, Maggie aimed. She stretched out her right arm that came to a point at the tip of her ringed fingers. She was a worn woman with threadbare moral fibers that were only as permanent as a throw rug when brand new. Her arm recoiled. She shot. She hit it. Yelling, slapping, money changed hands. Cafferty grinned and left the group to head for the bar. Maggie stepped in his way, swinging her hips with exaggerated seduction.

"So, Cafferty, when are you giving in to yer better instincts and marryin' me?"

"Maggie, you know I won't marry anyone who can beat me at arm wrestling."

"But I'm a pussy in the bedroom."

"I'm a dog person."

Maggie threw back her head and laughed. It was a full-throated free sound. It was the kind of laugh that fed sincere envy deep in the soul of even the most disapproving.

Over at the bar, two male voices rose from gruff to a growl and then aggression. Shea O'Holleran, a fleshy, sixty-year-old man with a puffy face and a full head of curly hair, was scalding. He was a hard-drinking, opinionated, personality bellows, and there was one subject those in the know knew to avoid when talking to Shea.

Nose to nose, he provoked the unknowing younger man on the barstool. Shea recited with full-throated passion right into the man's face, "*Time held me green and dying though I sang in my chains like the sea.*"

The younger man looked squarely at Shea and said, "Fancy talkin' that don't even rhyme is all I got to say. And I have a right to my opinion."

"And I got a right to refuse service. Out!"

"I'm not done my drink."

"The hell you're not."

Several locals shook their heads, knowing exactly where this was going. With startling agility for a portly man, Shea scrambled over the bar top, scattering glasses and spilling booze everywhere. He grabbed the shocked young man by his blue collar and ran him toward the door. The doors blasted open. Shea chucked the man out onto the sidewalk, knocking Ilana to the pavement. She had been standing on the other side of the door, trying to decide what to do. Now, sloppily splayed on the ground with her legs spread, down on one elbow, dirty and stunned, Ilana looked up at Shea standing over her.

"Jesus, Mary, and Joe!" Shea exclaimed. "Missy, you okay?"

"Um." She wondered the same.

Shea bent down, jammed his stubby fingers invasively into her armpits, and hoisted her back up to her feet.

"Ah . . ." She shook free. "Um, yes. I think."

The young man looked at her sheepishly. Shea used his big flat hand to brush her off vigorously, nearly knocking her down again and touching her in all the wrong places. Jostled, Ilana raised her hand to stop him.

"Fine. Really. No, I'm good. Please stop. Please."

"Sorry, Missy, and now your snazzy outfit's all fucked up."

"I'm okay. Really, please stop brushing me."

"It's his fault." Shea pointed at the young man. "This idiot thinks that second-rate, sniveling excuse for a writer, Eugene Field, is better than Dylan Thomas." When Shea spoke, his face got red, his veins bulged, and his heart fell out in his words.

"I gotta right to my opinion," the young man insisted.

While straightening her jacket, she added offhandedly, "Even if it's misguided."

"See. From a perfect stranger." Shea studied Ilana, and she saw something fierce in his eyes, which alarmed her. "Do I know you?" he asked.

"No."

Shea turned to the young man. "From a perfect stranger, you're misguided."

"Come on in, Missy, a drink on the house."

Shea spun around and yanked open the door. He held it for her with an impatient insistence. She paused on the edge of it all. She looked through the doorway. Dark. It was those stairs to the basement from the horror films.

Shea hastily motioned her to go. "C'mon. Drinks ain't gonna pour themself."

In later years, when Ilana looked back, she would wonder what drove her to step in that day. It was the step that changed everything.

The barflies sensed the ambient shift when Ilana stepped into their world. It was a gentle surface displacement. Not a single person broke with their conversation, no one lifted their eyes, no one shifted in their seats to look, but everyone noticed. Strangers were rare here, unknown women even rarer. Elegant female strangers in fancy pantsuits? Never, not ever, not even once.

She carried herself gently and still felt like a naked bulb in a dark room. Shea indicated for her to sit, and she took the barstool closest to the door. The place was suffocating, and she had a creeping (and, she was certain, ridiculous) sensation that everyone was noticing her. She felt like her slip was showing, or she was trailing toilet paper from the bottom of her shoe. Ilana had always had an intransigent resoluteness to blend, and she was mortified to be conspicuous. She wore the right thing, she used the right fork, and she waited patiently in line for her turn. She was someone who thrived backstage, where she felt confident and in control. She was not blending now, and it made her mildly nauseated. She liked familiar territory, and nothing at this moment was familiar. The control that was so admired and accessible to her at work had vanished. She shifted on the barstool, wishing she had worn something else, something dark, something less expensive. This was a sweatpants kind of place. How could she not have figured that? What was she thinking? Wearing the wrong thing made her skin crawl. She sat straight-backed on the stool, crossed her legs, and tried to look insouciant.

When Ilana was eleven years old, she misunderstood the invitation to a friend's birthday party. She thought it was a costume party. She arrived in an elaborate banana outfit. She walked inside and froze, mouth open, little girl mortified. All the other children stared openly. A few of the boys began to laugh out loud. Ilana's mother, seeing the situation, announced loudly, "Ilana, do not forget. I'll pick you up thirty minutes early so we can get to that awesome costume party we're going to. Don't ruin your costume. See you then."

One of the little kids blurted out, impressed, "You have two parties?"

"Uh-huh."

Ilana's drowning eyes reached back to her mom, and she didn't think she could ever love her mother more than she did at that very moment, except perhaps when her refined and tasteful mother picked her up from the party thirty minutes early, dressed like a huge orange.

On the barstool, Ilana kept her eyes down.

What am I doing here?

"So, Missy." Shea slapped the bar top. Ilana flinched. "What'll it be?"

She thought quickly, something easy, something to keep her wits about her, something common. What? "A Diet Coke, please," she said, having no clue how uncommon an order that was here. She noted uncomfortably that the man sitting on the barstool next to her turned and stared. She felt her face flush.

"Diet?" Shea replied, "Christ, you're barely there as it is. Here, I got a smooth McCallan's for you; it'll help your appetite." He poured her the whiskey shot. Ilana didn't want to encourage conversation with this bartender. She needed a chance to get her bearings and recapture her calm. She decided against insisting on the soda or ordering the white wine she actually wanted, and so hoped to cut off communication.

"Thank you." She gently pulled the shot glass toward her and then glanced away, indicating their conversation was over.

"So." Shea leaned onto his elbows on the bar top directly in front of her. "You read poetry, huh?"

She looked back, surprised he was still talking to her. "Only a little, years ago, in school." She gave him her ending smile, a slight nod, shifted in her chair, and looked away. *It's a clear signal*, she thought, *really very clear*. It was not possible to misunderstand this message.

Shea continued, "Oh, so what do you read now?"

Much too well bred to ignore him, she responded, "Unfortunately, I don't have time for much pleasure reading now." She took a good look at him for the first time and said the absolute wrong thing. "You know, you look a bit like Dylan Thomas."

Shea enthusiastically slapped her on the arm, practically knocking her off the chair. "I love this girl." She hadn't yet gotten over the man's fingers in her armpits. "You lookin' for a job, Missy? I could make room for a gal like you. Classy-up the joint. Minimum wage, but free booze."

"Thank you, but I already have a job."

"Yeah? What job?"

"I work for the Lyric Opera Company in Manhattan."

There was a beat of considering silence. Shea cocked his head for a split second as he processed this. "Yeah? You sing?"

"No."

He yelled over to the piano, "Ey, Nellie?" The elderly wire-haired woman at the piano looked over. "The lady here sings."

"No." Ilana tried politely but firmly to correct him.

"Yeah? Wha d'ya sing, hon?" Nellie yelled back.

"I don't sing!" Her voice shot out atypically loud, but she was committed to making this point extremely clear. She quickly recoiled, feeling too conspicuous. She lowered her voice. "I'm the production manager. Schedules, budgets, things like that."

"Oh." Shea yelled loudly back over to Nellie, "Never mind. She don't sing."

"Naw, I didn't think so. No chest." Nellie's eyes twinkled.

Inside Ilana, the desire to get the hell out was increasing along with her blood pressure. Her face felt hot, and she was considering a rude flat-out dart for the door.

"So, what, you're like a numbers person?" Shea asked, interested.

"Sort of."

He turned to the man next to her. "How 'bout that, Cafferty? Pretty lady here's a numbers person."

"Not surprised," Cafferty responded plainly.

Ilana turned her attention to the earthy man on the stool to her left, hoping to find a way out of the conversation with Shea. Cafferty looked at her with a kind of hostility. No, it was like ridicule. It was not calming. Not at all.

"What do you do?" she asked, not caring but trying to move the conversation away from her so she could slip into the background and get the hell out of there. She could call a cab from the street and wait outside. It wasn't dark yet, so it should be safe enough. What was she thinking, coming here?

"I work with wood." He opened his hands. They were chunky, callused, dry, and painful. She looked at his face, and like everything in this environment, she thought it was harsh.

Shea added, "Cafferty's the best goddamn carpenter in Albany, probably the world. Turns down more jobs than he takes. Made a set of cabinets for my den that would make your eyes water."

"Yeah, well, my eyes water every time I think what you owe me on them."

She was relieved because they were talking to each other. She lifted her eyes, scanned the room, and cautiously prepared for her exit.

"If I didn't owe you money, we wouldn't be so close," Shea quipped.

"Well, I sure wouldn't wanna risk our friendship."

"See?" Shea slapped the bar top in front of Ilana, and she jumped again. "He's a hell of a guy. So, Missy, you remember Dylan Thomas all the way from school?"

Aw, shit.

Cafferty said, "It's his favorite subject. You'll never get outta here now."

Yes, I will.

She brushed some dirt off her pant leg and searched for composure.

Shea leaned in too close to her. "What was your favorite?"

"My favorite?"

"Poem."

"Oh." Ilana shoveled into the snowbanks of her cold memory and thought back to high school. "It was about Christmas."

"*A Child's Christmas in Wales.* A masterpiece!" Shea broke into a loud and spirited recitation of the first few lines.

Ilana's entire plan to slip in unnoticed was blown when her linen pantsuit and her dignity hit the sidewalk. She had not had time to fully prepare. She was emotionally teetering, which was not her nature. This was a mistake. She knew that now. Adam and William had been right.

Stubborn. Stupid.

She needed a graceful exit because being polite was as much a part of her as her bone structure. Shifting in her chair, about to step down, Cafferty said to her, "Shea's a poet."

"I've been a man of verse all my life," he boomed.

A voice from behind him butt in, "Aw, horseshit," the forty-six-year-old flame of a woman, ladled generously into a polka-dot tank top and latex pedal pushers, said as she entered from the back room. Shea goosed her as she passed him, and she gave off a little yelp.

Shea winked at Cafferty. "Behind every great man, there's a woman yellin' horseshit."

"You can't call yourself a poet if you never write anything," she replied.

Ilana swung her legs around and reached into her purse for cash.

"I write plenty. I just don't show you, Fiona."

Fiona?

"Yeah, heard it all before, Shea." She wiped the bar near Ilana.

Ilana's body shuddered involuntarily. Her lips parted.

Fiona?

The emotion and adrenaline burst simultaneously from every single cell in her body. It was an internal upheaval of organs and an involuntary contraction of muscles. Her heart and stomach seemed to swell into her throat, cutting off her breathing. Her pores gasped open, her pupils spread, and her skin dampened. This was drama in its most primal, most physical, most operatic form, and the always-poised Ilana felt a fainting abandon that barely allowed her to stay in her seat. She knew she would not be moving for several minutes because she was uncertain of her legs. Her view of the room tunneled down to one person, her knees trembled, and she had to press them together to stop it. Suddenly, she wondered, mortified, if she might actually throw up in public.

"You're no poet," Fiona continued. "You own a pub, and you drink too much."

"All self-respecting writers embrace the fluids," he replied.

Even as Ilana demanded her body compose itself, it openly defied her. If there was ever a doubt that she was not in conscious control of her thoughts, of her body, it could not be more obvious than now. Inside, she was screaming at herself to relax. She couldn't slow her heart rate, she couldn't unwind her muscles, and she couldn't take her eyes off Fiona. She almost wished Adam were there so he could study this. Her body was doing exactly what it chose with no concern at all for the begging of her conscious mind to calm the hell down.

She's so young. My mother is so young. Polka-dots . . . my mother wears latex and polka-dots?

Cafferty turned to Shea. "Why don't you read us somethin' you wrote?"

Fiona responded smartly, "Because it don't exist."

"No, because all the good ones wait until they're dead to publish."

"Fine. I'll kill you in your sleep tonight, and we won't have to wait any longer."

"Oh, you can't do that."

"And why not?" Fiona baited him.

"Cause I'm the only man who can keep you satisfied, you wild armful!"

Shea grabbed her. He bent her over his arm, and they kissed with more sloppy, deep tongue passion than Ilana had ever seen in real life. She looked away, feeling personally ashamed. She studied the little round wet circles her glass made on the bar top. This was what one expected between two cinema heartthrobs, from a respectable distance, like a movie screen, but here, now, two midlife, fleshy, pub denizens? This over-the-top public display increased her panic. If her legs had been working, she would've bolted, but they weren't working, and breathing was all she could manage.

Fiona pushed him away. "Aw, you're a pain in the ass."

Again and again in Ilana's mind—*My mother.*

The piano keys banged out a final loud rousing chord. Nellie leaped up from the piano stool and, with a raucous, toothless, full-throated cheer, said, "Slainte!"

The same guy in the crowd yelled, "Amen."

Ilana grabbed the shot glass in front of her and threw back the whiskey in one gulp, damn glad to have it. Its warmth slid down her throat—smooth and foreign. She didn't cringe from the straight shot of whiskey, something she had never had before; it felt homey.

Her eyes stumbled over Fiona, studying the unapologetic cleavage and latex-lacquered thighs. Ilana gawked at the playful seduction in Fiona's every move: demonstrative, flirty, campy. They could not possibly be related. How could they possibly be related? Genetics?

Bullshit. There's nothing here.

A mitigating calm, which had to be chemical, spread over her. It was a satisfied feeling, like during the credits after a film when she stayed in her seat, a little sad to know it was over but sweetly sated nonetheless because somewhere inside, she knew the ending all along. There was not now, and there had never been, even one recognizable similarity between Ilana Barrett and Fiona O'Holleran. Not one thing; they shared nothing. Nothing in Ilana's world had anything to do with Fiona—not her choices, her future, or her life. She was the daughter of another woman. She knew who her mom was. Her mom was her mom.

Fiona whispered something to Shea, and when she walked away, Shea slapped her hard on the ass. She yelped, turned back, and arched one eyebrow. *Her left eyebrow.* And that was it; that was when Ilana froze, watching her signature gesture on another woman's face. With a sudden flash of insight, she saw the resemblance: same height, same weight, same body frame, same eye color—their bodies were nearly identical. *She even has that little crinkle in her right ear.* Her hair was a darker auburn, but still like Ilana's. Ilana stared openly at Fiona, seeing her with new eyes. *How could she not have seen it? They're practically copies. How can no one else see it? It's embarrassingly evident.*

Fiona yelled at Nellie. "Hey! Ma! Put your teeth in."

"I like 'em where I can see 'em, Fi."

Ilana whipped her head around to the ribald, borderless woman at the piano.

Grandma?

Fiona answered, "Come on, we paid a fortune for those choppers."

"You were taken like a virgin on the docks."

Oh, god.

She felt the man on the barstool next to her shift toward her. She felt his eyes on her like thin unwanted bug legs up and down her arms. She turned to him, frustrated, and lost her usual composure.

"What?" Ilana asked, more annoyed than she'd intended.

"Your car breakdown?" he asked.

"Car? No." She held his eyes confrontationally, and he did not look away, "What?"

"I was trying to think of what a fancy lady like you would be doing in a place like this. Short of a car wreck."

"No car wreck."

Stop talking to me!

Cafferty leaned toward her. She leaned quickly back. "So, you okay, opera lady who doesn't sing?"

"Certainly. Of course."

"'Cause you don't look okay."

"Well, I am." She did not need this man talking to her right now, or ever.

"What are you doing here?" he asked.

With as much polish as she could muster, she said, "Having a drink."

"Right. Well, normally, you'd blend in with all the other Manhattan upper crusts crusin' in for a shot of whiskey, but I read something different on your face."

"I'll thank you not to read my face at all."

"No problem."

Fiona called out to them, "Willow called. Dinner."

Ilana had seen enough and felt enough. She was exhausted by the pitch of the last fifteen minutes. She reached for her cell phone to call a cab. She pressed. Nothing. She pressed harder. Battery dead.

Perfect.

She had to plug it in. She had to find an outlet. Her head was down as she searched for the charger in her purse, so she didn't see Shea bound up behind her. He grabbed her arm with such force that she nearly fell off the barstool. He had come around the bar, moved toward the backdoor, and gathered up Ilana like an extra glass.

"Come on, Missy. Eat with us. I need someone new!"

Frantic, she said, "Oh, no, really. No!"

"Only an hour."

"Thank you. I can't." She insisted. He did not let go. She couldn't believe he was touching her *again*. It was so physical and impolite. She could actually hear her private school teacher ranting about personal boundaries.

Shea hustled Ilana toward the door. "C'mon."

A thin skin of danger hung around Shea like it does with people who laugh too loud. It wasn't the kind of danger that would make you avoid him in a dark alley, but rather the awareness of a certain unevenness to the ground when you walked near him. He was a man used to getting his way, and his grip on her arm said that clearly.

"Only down the block, Missy, and Jesus knows you need the meal." They were already at the back door.

Fiona smiled at Ilana warmly and waved her hand dismissively. "Don't fight it, hon. Shea brings home every stray customer he fancies. Happens all the time. Do the whole family a favor and give him someone else to jaw at tonight."

The whole family?

Ilana was strung between curiosity and apprehension.

"You too, Cafferty." Fiona yelled, "Ma, bring your goddamn teeth."

Shea kept a strong grip on Ilana's arm as he walked and said intensely, "I've gotta tell you right from the start that I don't like Yeats, Pound, or Larkin. Pompous bunch of bastards."

She was pulled along with the human tide right out the back door.

They walked along, passing small homes, close and neatly cropped, with all of their backyards the same: a screened plank porch, three steps, and then a thin grassy green stripe that led down to the river. It was a neighborhood where no one bought bottled water, and folks cut their own hair even before the pandemic. Shea tugged good-humoredly at Ilana as they traversed the yards leading to the

O'Holleran home.

Enthusiastically, he jabbered on, "And that's when I knew. It wasn't only words but their sound too. The sounds of the vowels, right, Missy? That's what Thomas did. You know that."

Ilana strained to follow his words as she walked along and wished he would let go of her arm, and although she had tugged a few times, it felt rude to say something or insist.

Shea continued, "Anyone can stumble into sentimentality. And some of those stuck-up bastards make poetry like brainteasers that a guy can't figure out without some kind of brainy education. They're only writing for each other; it's mutual masturbation is what it is! Right?"

"Ummm."

Masturbation? I need to calm down.

Shea continued, "But when you read Thomas out loud or listen to his recordings, you hear it's about the sound as much as the meaning, you know? You know what I mean? The sound is inside the word."

"Oh, opera is like that."

"Yeah? How's that?"

"It is the long vowel sound that opera singers make such good use of in their arias. It's why some aficionados insist that Italian opera cannot be matched because the language is inherently rife with long vowel sounds, especially at the end of words. It affords the singer unrivaled opportunities."

Shea pointed his finger at her and said with stark intensity, "I like you."

It did not make her relax in any way. This statement was scary somehow. Shea had serrated edges. Was he dangerous or only different? She couldn't tell. There was something treacherous about his passion.

She tried to catch some of the conversation going on ahead of her. It was a mixed chorus of several voices. She saw that Fiona's spiked heels aerated the ground as she moved. *More proof of our dissimilarity*, Ilana thought. Fiona walked with ease along the morphing grassy surface, while Ilana stumbled clumsily along in her sensible wide-heeled pumps. At the top of her list of things she wished for was the desire to be physically graceful. She knew her posture was a little stiff. She was not one of the little girls who did well in ballet class, and her mother quickly moved her to music instead. She had assumed that her inflexibility had been solely a characteristic of her body and not a reflection of her mind, but at this very moment, she was reassessing that assumption because her same body was walking smoothly directly in front of her.

As the sky darkened, the group ascended the three cement steps that led to the well-lit screened porch. They filed in. The screen door spanked. And there she was, miraculously inside the home she should have grown up in, inside the world she was born to, and surrounded by people who shared her blood, were baked with some of the same raw ingredients, and shared her code. Her fingers and toes prickled as though they had been asleep and were now waking. Her skin felt sensitive. All these physiological signs of her discomfort would've interested Adam. She grabbed a quick, short breath, and then, with pure lucidity, her hungry eyes consumed the little home. This was as unexpected a moment in her life as possible. This was her heritage, her lineage, her origins; these were her roots, and they were . . . *Plastic?*

There seemed to be a lot of plastic: knickknacks, plastic doilies, plastic flowerpots, and a plastic swan by the door. The home was a vintage thrift store and cluttered beyond all reason. There wasn't a smooth surface or a straight line in sight. She sensed there existed a careless order of some kind but couldn't imagine a template for it. She noticed a scent she couldn't place. Subtle scents came from everywhere. They clung to the drapery fibers, lay along the floor moldings, and mixed in with the wallpaper paste. It was the wraith of decades of home-cooked meals, of pets, of Christmas trees, and of stale cologne. It was what life actually smelled like, and there was something comforting about it. Her goal had always been for her apartment to smell fresh, crisp, and new, whereas this place smelled used and lived-in; as she stood there thinking about it, she suddenly didn't know which was preferable.

Shea and Cafferty kicked off their shoes and walked into the main room. Ilana was left on the porch with Nellie and Fiona. She tried not to stare.

My mother. My grandmother. Oh, my god.

This was all so exotic and overwhelming. She was spilling out of her boundaries, seeping over the brim, a full cup and someone keeps on pouring. There was so much new information from her senses that it was difficult to categorize comfortably. Her mind was collecting information and storing it for review. Later, she would put all the pieces of this puzzle together and into a picture that she could step back from and consider. She smiled because if Adam were there, he would explain how that was the storytelling part of her left hemisphere; one of its functions is to make sense of it all.

Nellie and Fiona slipped off their shoes. Following them, Ilana slipped off her sensible pumps, exposing an embarrassing hole in her expensive silk sock. She tried quickly to turn it under her foot.

"Got a hole there, honey," Fiona pointed out to be helpful.

"Yes. I work late, so I haven't had time to get to the store."

"The store? Only take a stitch or two to fix it," Fiona said.

"Oh."

"People throw away stuff too easily now—socks, food, husbands. Damn crime."

Ilana heard this and realized it never occurred to her to fix it. In the realm of possible endings for a flawed sock, repair was not considered. She had never owned a sewing kit. This was the first time she recognized that as a discreet declaration of who she was not, and a judgment, yes, that too. Did she believe she was too busy, too successful, or too educated to fix anything? Somewhere inside, she did not want to be the woman who sewed. Is value intrinsic or earned? Standing there, in a common space with these people, her behavior seemed profligate. And an internal whisper asked if maybe she wasn't the good person she thought she was. After all, doesn't everyone think well of themselves? Balancing on one foot in this home with all its smells, chatter, and plastic, a new clarity peeked in. *Buy sewing kit.*

Fiona walked into the dining area, leaving Ilana alone with Nellie. Ilana stole a long look at her. She had vague memories of her grandmother. She remembered when she was young, they would go to high tea together at The Plaza. The sweet cream was thick on fresh berries, and her grandmother taught her how to fold her napkin exactly right.

"Holy Saint Francis, does he got a tight ass," Nellie said. Ilana's eyes darted to the fleshy woman's eyes and then followed her gaze out of the porch room and into the main room to where Cafferty stood with his back to them. "Look at the sweet yams on that sucker." Nellie leaned in close to Ilana and whispered with her toothless grin under flashing and mischievous eyes, "You know, it's true what they say about men with big hands."

Ilana knew her mouth had dropped open, and her eyes widened. Again, she wracked her brain for some appropriate response and came up with nothing.

Nellie said, "You look hungry, girl."

"I guess, I am."

"Aw, that's too bad. Willow cooked. Should've eaten first. We all did."

Nellie wobbled out, leaving Ilana standing alone with the plastic swan companion and holding her shoe. She considered her options. She could leave. Now would be the moment. She could slip surreptitiously back out the door and find her way to a main street or to anywhere she could charge her phone, unsure where or how far that may be. That was risky. If she stayed, she might have to participate, and she didn't know if that was possible. She tried to remember that calming breath methodology from that yoga class. Was it in through the nose, out through the mouth, or the other way around?

"Looks like you wanna run away." Cafferty broke into her thoughts.

"No," she lied.

"Oh." He opened out his arm and indicated for her to precede him into the main room. "Willow gets hotheaded if we're not at the table in time. She takes the timing to heart."

It's only dinner.

She smiled coolly and walked past him, noting that she was shoeless. She felt ridiculous. Ladies always wore shoes. *That's a rule, isn't it?* She stepped into the main room awkwardly, aware that her big toe was inching its way toward the hole in her sock. She didn't want to bend down and call attention to it, but it made her feel like a cartoon character.

It mattered to Ilana to dress with style. She learned early in her career that in the business world, professional women needed the added signal of a very expensive suit. She wondered if that would change now that so many people had learned to work remotely, many of them half-dressed or in stretch pants, and they still rocked their jobs. The right suit, a fine silk shirt, and appropriate shoes were requirements as women chipped away at the icy glass ceiling. She relied on the image it created to say things about her before she opened her mouth; consequently, now, her soiled, wilted linen pantsuit, her cheeky shoelessness, and the upsetting hole in her sock made her feel the same over-her-head feeling she struggled with since she got out of the cab.

Inside the O'Holleran's living room, every inch of wall space was covered with captured family moments in dime-store frames, every thread of carpet had been well toe-kneaded, and many lives over many years had been a witness to its hospitality. Ilana saw dozens of furniture pieces, thousands of curios, something on top of everything, but everything with a place, and each thing was clean. It reminded Ilana of the corner drawer in her mom's kitchen. It was the most tantalizing cubby in the house. Inside, odd things lay together: the Automobile Club card under the nail polish remover pads, which were next to the broken meat thermometer, to the left of the five drone ballpoint pens held together by a rubber band. That drawer was like this home—a mishmash mystery. The bedlam hid things. It was a place that, even when opened and fully lit, still had shadowy corners. She could sense that. These were people with secrets. She was one of them.

The dining room table was set with plastic plates, and no two glasses were the same. It resembled a Moroccan street bazaar. Ilana's flawless breeding nudged her. "You have such a lovely home, Mrs. O'Holleran."

"Yeah? Thanks, hon. It sorta has its way with us."

Willow O'Holleran's stick legs carried her out of the kitchen holding a ceramic water pitcher. She was twenty-three years old, thin, and splattered with freckles the size and color of the eraser on the end of a #2 pencil. She halted abruptly at the jumbled dining table, and then, with reverence, she placed the pitcher down. She scrutinized the table.

"Willow," her mother began, "We got an extra . . ."

"Wait!" Willow interrupted. She spun on her heels, and she was gone.

Fiona yelled after her daughter, "Ey, Willow, we have new company."

Willow barreled back in with a salad bowl. "I see, Mom. But I need a moment to organize my thoughts."

Nellie leaned into Ilana. "A lifetime ain't long enough to organize her thoughts." Nellie sank down between the fat arms of the bulging orange armchair. It hugged her snugly.

Suddenly, Ilana realized what a gift this was. How could this have even happened? All she needed to do was relax, calm down, and have dinner. She has a sister, at least a half-sister. Even with all the craziness and embarrassment, this made her gleeful. She was connected to someone else, connected on the inside.

Willow paused to regard the table. She seemed pleased. She turned to Ilana. "Well, hello." Willow's voice felt like a gentle warm hand on Ilana's shoulder, and for the first time since she arrived, Ilana's smile was genuine in return.

"Hi."

Shea butt in, "Willow, this is Missy. She reads."

"Actually, it's Ilana. I hope it's not an imposition adding another for dinner."

"Oh, not at all. I love to cook. I always set an extra place or two. Never know who Pop's gonna drag home from the pub. Hi, Cafferty."

"Hey."

She turned to Shea. "And I read too, Pop." Willow fluttered off again for the kitchen. "Six minutes. Six 'til dinner."

Ilana turned to Shea. "Would it be all right if I used your phone briefly? My cell battery died on the train and—"

"You bet, Missy, use my library. Landline in there." He pointed to a closed door across the room.

"Thank you." She turned and carried herself with the confident nonchalance that had shaped her upbringing. Ilana knew that her mom could never have imagined the confusion that had simmered to life after her death. Her mom could never have imagined where she was having dinner this evening.

As she walked toward the library door, Cafferty's eyes followed her. She specifically felt them crawl down her neck, between the shoulder blades, past the waist, and into the sensitive small of her back. She yanked open the library door, stepped in, and quickly shut the door behind her. She sighed and leaned up against it. She breathed in, fully appreciating her first moment out of view.

In the room all around her, from floor to ceiling, foot-by-foot were rows of hardbacks, ripped bindings, and yellowed pages; she was standing in a literary cave. Her feet stepped gingerly around the paper stalagmites reaching up from the floor—eight, nine, ten editions high. She scanned a few titles. There were classics and contemporary books, hundreds of them. She cautiously leaned over, stretching her arm as she reached for the phone on the end table. She was thankful to be wedged into this one moment of gratifying privacy.

She dialed.

At the same time, back in Manhattan, William directed group therapy. His nurse, Carol, popped her head in.

"Doctor?"

Surprised to be interrupted during the session, he said, "Yes?"

Carol crossed to him and whispered into his ear, "It's Ilana Barrett. On line one. She says it's an emergency, and you can't call her back."

In the ten years that William had known Ilana, this had never happened. He turned to the group. "I apologize. An emergency, and if any of you were in an emergency situation, I would take your call too. Please continue with each other. And Mr. Gluck, no spitting." He left the room, entered another office, and quickly grabbed the phone.

"Ilana?"

"Oh, William, I'm so sorry."

Calming his voice when he heard the tension in hers, he said, "It's okay."

"I know I shouldn't interrupt. Tell me no one is suicidal."

"I've got three on the ledge and one holding pills. It's all right, Ilana. What's wrong? What's going on?"

"I'm here. I'm in here in their house. For dinner."

"Wow. I guess they took that well."

"They don't know."

"What?"

And it gushed out. "First, I was knocked down onto the pavement by two men outside the bar, and then he shoved his fingers into my armpits and lifted me, and then she showed up in latex and polka dots, and next, there was the whiskey. That helped, actually. But I wasn't really prepared to take off my shoes, and now I'm feeling nervous, and my toe is coming through my sock, and there's this gruff man here who looks at me with this rude kind of, oh, I don't know, and I don't know whether I should sneak away or sit down to dinner and—"

"Ilana," William interrupted. "Ilana, do you know *anything* about these people? Should you even be in their home?"

She rambled, "I've had this kind of standing-on-a-cliff feeling from the second I got out of the cab. I've been completely out of control, and you know I don't *do* out of control. William, I don't do it at all. I'm confused, and I—"

Bang bang!

She gasped and froze.

"Ilana?"

"Oh, god."

"What?" William's voice was fraught with concern.

Bang!

"A gun."

"A gun?"

"Someone's shooting!"

"Get out! Now, Ilana."

Bang!

"Shit. Is it inside?"

"Are you alone?" he asked quickly.

"Yes. Alone. Yes."

"First floor? Can you sneak out a window?"

She looked. No windows were visible. There were only books in front of the windows.

"All the windows are blocked."

"Blocked? Ilana, listen, I want you . . ."

The library door swung open abruptly, and Ilana spun, slamming down the receiver.

Shea said lightly, "Don't worry, Missy. Just Boney. Good, you're off the phone. Come on for dinner."

Frightened, she stepped back. "Unfortunately, I have to go. That call was, um, that I have to go."

"No one escapes." He winked at her. "Not without dinner." He took her arm.

Stop touching me!

Bang!

She flinched, vulnerable, terrified, and at the mercy of strangers, strangers with weapons. Adrenaline coursed through her limbs. She shuddered as they approached the library door. What to do, what to do? She searched for options. She had no hope of protecting herself. There'd been no self-defense classes, hidden six-pack, or years of kickboxing. Her body was thin and weak. She had flimsy bird arms. She knew she had flimsy bird arms. And no shoes. She had no shoes!

No way out.

Shea indicated for her to go through the opened door first. She prepared for mayhem and primed to make a shoeless run for the porch. She stepped through and into the living room, trembling. This was the first time in her life that she'd ever been truly frightened.

Her eyes darted around frantically to assess the situation. Was someone bleeding? Was someone dead? Who had the gun? She saw Nellie lounging comfortably and unfazed. Cafferty and Fiona were staring blithely out the window. All was calm. Complete calm. Ilana followed their gaze out the window and toward the river. And then, through the windowpane, she saw a man. He was a stringy man of uncertain age. He aimed his handgun at the sky.

"Shooter!" Ilana crouched, panicked.

She was the only one. The others looked at her like she was nuts.

Fiona commented to Cafferty, "Jumpy."

He answered, "Manhattan."

"Oh." That explained it. "Well, you'd better go get Boney before Old Man Leary next door gets his cranky balls in an uproar."

Cafferty responded, bored, "Yup." He turned and headed for the back door.

Willow yelled from the kitchen, "Two. Two minutes 'til dinner."

Fiona saw Ilana crouched down, looking wide-eyed, and spoke to her like she was a three-year-old. "Uh, hon?" Ilana looked up. "It's okay. Boney's harmless."

Checking the room, Ilana slowly stood. "He's shooting. Who is he shooting at?"

"God," Fiona answered.

"God?"

"Yeah."

"At god?" Ilana confirmed.

"Yeah. Years ago, his wife and daughter were killed in an accident. Every once in a while, he gets royally pissed off and tries to waste him."

"God."

"Yup." Fiona shrugged. "What are you gonna do?"

"Well, he's sick. He needs help." They watched through the window as Cafferty approached Boney, who took aim again at the sky.

"Naw. He gets over it. Then, he's fine."

"He could hurt someone."

"Boney? Naw. All heart, that man."

Ilana watched Cafferty through the windowpane. He easily disarmed the man. Boney stomped around in a tiny circle. Then, he threw his arms out beseechingly. Cafferty listened with his head down, nodding. He said a few words. Boney dropped his arms, and instantly all the life drained out of him.

Ilana's blood was still up. "I'm sure it's illegal to discharge a firearm in this neighborhood."

Fiona smiled. "Yeah, well, honey, we don't arrest our neighbors around here."

Nellie piped in, "Around here, we make 'em eat Willow's food."

Outside, she watched as Cafferty put his arm kindly around Boney and led him back to the house.

Fiona yelled to the kitchen, "Willow, adding on Boney."

"One minute," was the reply.

A moment later, when the phone rang at the O'Holleran home, Patrick, a lanky, young man of eighteen, was on his way down the stairs and grabbed it in the hallway.

"Hello? Ilana? Nope, there's no Ilana. You've got the wrong number." Patrick hung up. He entered the main room.

Shea introduced, "Missy, this is our son, Patrick. Patrick, Missy." Patrick had a healthy, energetic air.

"Hi." Patrick held out his hand, which was the first normal gesture Ilana had seen since she arrived in Albany. She shook it.

"Hello."

I have a brother. Oh! I have a brother.

Her eyes filled embarrassingly. She wished to hide the teary flash of emotion, which she couldn't have hidden in a coal-dark cellar. Ilana threw her gaze out the window and studied the falling evening. Very little direct radiation remained of the day, and still, the ground steeped. It had broiled. Throughout the neighborhood, windows gaped futilely for a breeze. She knew it wasn't cooler out there, but still, the memory of an errant breeze was enough to make her lean out wishfully. She took this moment to gain control.

Fine. You're good.

"Now!" Willow yelled.

Ilana jumped and hit her head on the window sash. Willow blasted through the swinging kitchen door carrying a tray. They all hustled to their seats. Cafferty pulled the chair out for Ilana with a sarcastic flourish. She nodded with the same exaggerated motion and disingenuous smile and sat down. She surveyed the family, her family, as the raucous passing of plates began. They poured beer and whiskey, and all talked at the same time. It would have been so much easier if Ilana could have had time to reflect in private, to get some perspective. Everything had happened too fast, too chaotically. She served herself from the passing platters.

Boney sat across the table from her. When he was outside, she couldn't see how elderly he was. She couldn't appreciate the paucity of his white hair or the translucence of his thin aged skin. Time had played roughly with him, his cheeks were veined, and his chest was sunken from carrying too much weight in his heart for too long. She saw how very frail his fingers were as he passed the serving platters. It was impossible to imagine how he could have held the gun at all. His neck was bent forward in submission. He had not spoken one word to anyone. No one spoke directly to him. This was clearly what he wanted. This was their way. They had a tacit understanding that his grief could not be overcome. Ilana felt ashamed for how quickly she had judged this fragile, broken man. He took one small potato. He lifted his eyes to her as he handed her the serving plate, and she got a glimpse of a profoundly grieving soul. She felt his ache like a sharp slap. She swallowed with difficulty. He looked back down at his meager meal, but she couldn't take her eyes away. And then, a tiny drop hit the rim of his plate, and she saw that he wept soundlessly. She wanted to reach out to him, to touch his pale hand with kindness. She wanted to let him know that she understood, that she, too, knew grief, that she, too, knew what it felt like to have no family left. She was an only child whose father was long gone and who had recently buried her mother—her one, her only true mother. She wanted to gather up the scraps of Boney and soothe him. At this instant, this broken, feeble man claimed a little piece of her. The hurt buried inside of her called silently to him, and he heard it. He looked up suddenly. He saw it in her eyes. He would not smile—because he did not smile—but he knew, and what little that was, it was for them both.

And then, Ilana saw that the laws of her world, laws that she'd been taught were absolute, did not apply. If a man was in your backyard firing a handgun, you didn't call SWAT—you passed him the potatoes. She would need to study the new tenuousness of the rules that had guided her life, rules that gave her solace, rules that she believed were immutable. Were there too many rules that existed on a groundless plane? She wondered if the regularity of those rules in her every day created an echo of behavior so loud that she came to believe it was reality.

"Missy?"

She looked up quickly, interrupted in the depth of her thoughts.

Shea continued, "Our Patrick starts college near you this fall."

"Really? Where?"

Patrick answered shyly, "NYU."

"That's terrific. Congratulations. It's a great school."

"Got a scholarship." Fiona flushed with pride. "Patrick is the only one in our family ever to go to college."

Not completely true.

Fiona noticed Nellie and pleaded, "Ma, put your teeth in."

"Don't need 'em." Nellie stabbed a slice of pot roast. "Willow, did you boil this?"

"Naturally, Grandma, two hours for safety from E. coli."

Nellie slapped the dry, shriveled meat onto her plate. "Well, it's dead, all right."

Ilana held her smile. She wasn't quite sure what it was about Grandma that made her want to laugh. Perhaps it was because the entire time the old, wrinkled, wired-haired terrier was complaining, mischievousness hung in the pauses.

Ilana questioned Patrick, "What are you majoring in?"

"Computer science. I wanted to computerize the inventory for the pub this summer, but Dad won't let me."

"I don't need a computer inventory. I run out of whiskey, I buy more."

"What's this?" Nellie looked at Willow and held up her napkin accusingly. It was as thin as onionskin.

Willow said defensively, "It is a napkin, Grandma."

Fiona turned to Willow. "Have you been separating the napkins again?"

"They're two-ply. I separated them all, and now we have twice as many. And even though I don't expect a thank-you from this group, I will not waste."

Ilana listened with curiosity. She remembered the hole in her sock. She wastes. She wastes terribly without ever giving it a thought.

Buy sewing kit.

Patrick said, "Yeah, and so no one's surprised, she separated the toilet paper too."

Ilana blurted out, "You did?"

Willow responded proudly, "I keep the old rolls and reroll them. It's very time-consuming but saves a bundle. You know there are some people out there with nothing."

Nellie barked bluntly to Ilana, "Aw, she's cheap as a limey's word."

"I am not cheap, Grandma. I'm frugal, and I'm socially conscious, and you should stop saying limey."

Patrick slyly prompted Ilana, "Ask her where she got the sweater."

Ilana looked at the sweater. It was a blend of unusual black and white threads.

"It's lovely," Ilana said. "I've never seen one quite like it."

"It's an original." Willow winked at her. "I work at Pet Island Groomers. I couldn't stand to see all that waste. So, at the end of the day, I collect all the long hair, and voilà, canine couture!"

Nellie, deadpan to Ilana, said, "She knits dog hair."

"Oh." Ilana was at a loss.

Willow rubbed the sweater. "I'm terribly fond of this one. Sheepdog and Lhasa, very sweet dogs, both of them."

"Enough dog hair talk at dinner." Fiona grumbled.

Shea perked up and addressed Ilana. "Missy, did you know that the poet John Berryman committed suicide believing that the blue sky was the blue eyeball of God watching him?"

"A rather creepy image."

"God is watching us all," Willow added sweetly.

Fiona reprimanded, "Oh, Willow."

"Oh, okay, Mother, he's watching everyone except you."

Cafferty, under his breath, said, "Uh-oh."

Fiona replied pointedly, "We don't all believe that stuff."

Shea said, "Yeah, well, of all the people who say they believe in the Bible, nine out of ten of them haven't actually read it. Not all the way through. It is one screwed-up user's manual, I can tell you."

Cafferty leaned in toward Ilana and whispered, "Buckle your seatbelt."

"Oh, and they won't admit it either," Shea continued. "They'll tell you they know their Bible, swear they know it. But they cherry-pick and ignore the down-and-dirty of it. And they'll get real unchristian-like if you tell 'em that."

"Oh, Pop." Willow glared at him.

Ilana's heart quickened uncomfortably. In her life, she had never gotten into a heated discussion about religion. It wasn't done in polite company. The temperature in the room climbed. Alarmed, she decided to attend assiduously to her plate. She would cut her pot roast into little pieces. This was the most exotic night of her life, and now that, thankfully, the focus was off her, she was spellbound to take it all in. She would sit, eat, quietly observe, and never see any of these people again.

Shea said, "People created all the gods. They wanted answers. They needed rules. Yours is no more real than the gods of Olympus. Any open-minded person can see that. Why do you think they start religion with kids? Cause you got to get 'em before they can think, bury that stuff deep in the brain of a kid before they can look at you and say, 'What the fuck,' talking bushes, walking on water, a prophet riding a flying horse. Ha!"

Patrick offered shyly, "Pop, religion has also done a lot of good in the world."

"Aw, c'mon, full of disgusting stories about incest, murder, dismemberment, rape. It's worse than the local news. If it were written today, it'd be banned from the schools."

Ilana looked up and saw Willow's very pale skin.

She admonished her father softly, as was her nature. "Oh, Pop, the religious texts are an inspiration. You never tried to understand them."

"Well, I'm glad you do, Willow, because I've decided to sell you into slavery, which, according to your Bible, I can." He winked at Cafferty. "I'm hoping for a good price."

Nellie piped up, "Then, don't sell her as a cook."

Ilana bit her grin. She was starting to love this old woman.

Fiona reprimanded him. "Shea, we've got nice company."

Shea turned suddenly to Ilana. "Yeah? And what do you think, Missy?"

Oh, shit.

Ilana stopped cutting her food. She stalled. "About?"

"About gods. Any god."

She cleared her throat and said, "Actually, I think it's impractical *not* to believe."

"Impractical? How's that?"

"Well, if it turns out there's no god, then there's no downside to believing. If it turns out there is some god, and you don't believe, the downside could be pretty substantial." This purely analytical response brought a moment of silence to the table. "Believing in god is really like buying afterlife insurance. Maybe you won't need it, but if you do, you'll be glad you have it."

Shea smacked the table, delighted. "Afterlife insurance."

Nellie chuckled and nodded at Ilana. Now they were friends.

Shea added, "Didn't I tell you? I like this girl. I think the worst religion—"

"Settle down, Seamus." Fiona said this softly. Ilana noticed the abrupt surfacing of this quiet power in a woman most likely to be taken for frivolous. The hinge between Fiona and Shea moaned and then gave way. He turned back to his food.

Fiona met Ilana's gaze. She held it. They regarded each other as though alone in the room. Ilana felt something shift. It was a sort of merging of thought. She suddenly suspected that Fiona could read her.

She knows. Oh, she recognizes me!

There was a stinging sensation on her skin as her body blew up, and blood flooded Ilana's face. Fiona tilted her head. Ilana could see her on the verge of asking something profound.

"Peas?"

At first, Ilana didn't recognize the word.

Please?

Then, she saw the proffered bowl of green peas.

"Oh. Thank you. Thanks." Ilana accepted it and attempted to coax herself back from the cliff.

"See?" Shea added wisely, "Nothing gets up the appetite like a good row. What's so funny, Willow?"

Willow was giggling. "Sorry, nothing."

"What nothing? Who laughs at nothing?" Shea wanted an answer.

"I got the giggles, Pop. Isn't that funny the way that happens? Can't seem to stop giggling. Hasn't that ever happened to you?" she asked.

Shea replied too quickly, "Of course not. Men don't giggle."

"Shea." Fiona's voice was crisp, biting, and final. An uncomfortable pause settled around the table.

Ilana couldn't stand it and started talking. "I remember one time in an economics lecture, which is a far cry from funny, when I got the giggles, and I had to leave the classroom because I couldn't stop." Willow looked at her gratefully, so she continued, "It's a mechanism in the unconscious mind; we know so little about how our mind works. It's a perfect example of the fact that our conscious mind is not the seat of control, not like we think it is. If it were, we could tell it to stop giggling, and that would be that."

"What do you mean?" Shea asked, interested.

They were all looking at her, and she continued parroting Adam. "You know, researchers are discovering more about how we think. What we think we decide might actually be prompted below our awareness level."

Willow looked to Patrick for a translation. "What do you think, Pat? You're the smart one."

But Patrick was looking at Nellie. "Grandma?" he asked. The old woman's face had gone ashen.

"Ma?" Fiona asked. Nellie's mouth gaped. Her eyes bulged. She was not breathing.

Ilana dropped her fork in a terrified panic. "She's choking!"

Willow turned with inconceivable calm to Patrick. "It's your turn."

Oh, shit.

"Is it?"

Oh, shit.

"Yes."

Do something!

Patrick put down his fork, got up, and walked (with no apparent haste) behind Nellie's chair. Ilana could not stand by idly. She sprang to action, bolted over, flooded with adrenaline, and primed to assist.

"What should I do?" she asked, rife with panic.

"I got it." Patrick put his arms around the chair and his fist over Nellie's abdomen and yanked hard, administering the Heimlich. Nothing. Patrick yanked again with considerable force. Nellie coughed. The blockage was dislodged. It shot out of her mouth and landed on the table. The old woman gasped, wiped her mouth, grunted satisfactorily, and turned back to her food. Unruffled, Patrick returned to his seat.

Oh, god. Oh, god.

Ilana was severely shaken. "Mrs. Shannon, are you all right?"

Cafferty's head shot up, and he looked at Ilana suspiciously.

Nellie answered, "Okay, providin' the food don't kill me."

Ilana noted the languid faces around her. They looked back blankly.

"That's what your fuckin' teeth are for, Mom."

Ilana sank back down into her chair, holding back tears, and reached for her beer glass, which she drained while thinking, *Who the hell are these people?* And suddenly, she wanted to be home, to be in her own apartment. This was insane. Perhaps none of this would have ever happened had her mother's death been easier. Perhaps all those months grasping for an understanding that didn't exist led her on this path. Perhaps there was more to discover about herself, but it was unlikely to be found around this dining table.

"Nellie, if you don't wear your teeth to dinner," Shea admonished, "from now on, you get oatmeal. That's it . . . oatmeal."

"A rabid dog doesn't salivate enough to wash down this meat." Nellie croaked.

Home.

Willow said, "There's nothing wrong with the pot roast, Grandma."

Home.

Fiona broke Ilana's thoughts. "So, Missy, are you married?"

"What?"

"Married. Are you married?" Fiona repeated.

"No," she answered.

Nellie regarded her skeptically. "You're a little ripe, aren't ya?"

"Grandma, you're so rude." Willow smiled sympathetically at Ilana. "Don't mind her. Sometimes, she leaves her manners at the bar."

"I'm in a serious relationship."

"Well"—Fiona reached over and patted Ilana's hand with patronizing encouragement—"then there's still hope, isn't there?"

And that was the exact moment when something released inside of Ilana. She grabbed urgently at her impulse to laugh out loud, managing to mold it into a cough-like hiccup. She looked quickly away from Fiona and found Cafferty staring at her with the slightest of grins. While there was something unsettling about this man, there was certainly something soothing about him. He held her eyes, and she realized that he was seeing her. Really seeing her.

Under his breath, Cafferty teased, "There's still hope."

Ilana responded in a sarcastic whisper, "Thank god."

"Please don't bring up god again."

"Not a chance."

"There's more pot roast," Willow said with an eagerness to serve.

"Thank you, Willow," Fiona said, although no one reached for the platter.

The doorbell rang, and when Shea left the table to answer it, Ilana sat back, crossed her legs, and took a long, slow breath.

Lieutenant Costello, a stout, spongy uniformed police officer, entered the front foyer like he lived there.

"What do you want, Costello?"

"Want you to stop watering down your whiskey, Spud."

"Them's fightin' words, Wop."

"Don't start with me." They smacked each other good-naturedly on the arm. Costello continued, "Hey, got a report about some woman in trouble here."

"Trouble? Nah. But any woman here is in trouble, right, Costello?"

"I'd say. I surely say that."

"Ha! Well, we got an opera lady here for dinner."

"No shit?" Costello looked into the room and yelled to the only face he did not know. "Hey, lady, you Ilana Barrett?"

Startled, she rose to her feet. "Yes?"

For someone whose entire intention had been to slip in and slip out unnoticed, whose whole plan was predicated on the importance of being the fly on the wall, Ilana had managed to be the center of attention every second since she had gotten out of the cab. The intensity of it all was beginning to make her feel physically weak—and now . . . the police.

Costello yelled from the foyer. "Your shrink called the police." Eyes widened around the table as they turned to look at her. "Said you're in danger of somethin' or another. You in danger?"

Nellie interrupted, "Well, she's eating Willow's food."

Brutally embarrassed, Ilana replied, "No. Of course not."

Willow turned to Patrick. "So, she's crazy?"

"No, no, he's my best friend." Ilana quickly corrected her.

Nellie winked. "Sure."

"Something about a gun?" Costello asked.

Fiona answered, "It was Boney."

"Oh." Costello nodded knowingly. "You shootin' at God again, Boney?"

Patrick realized. "You know, someone called earlier for an Ilana, but I thought your name was Missy."

Ilana crossed to Costello with enviable control, veiling her awkwardness. "Thank you, Officer. Everything is fine. I'll call my friend right now and reassure him."

"Yeah, I'd do that. He was a bit wired up by the time he got to me."

"I'm sure." How could she have forgotten about hanging up on William? "If I could plug in my cell . . ."

Shea pointed to the hall phone. "Right there, Missy."

She saw another landline and wondered if they were common around here.

"Thank you." She picked up the receiver.

The O'Hollerans shifted in their dinner chairs and exchanged questioning eyes. She could see their confusion, and it made her playfully glad to be the cause. She liked that she could be anyone here, tonight, right now. She could act any way she wanted, say anything she wanted, and be gone in an instant with no remedy left behind. No one in this house had any real notion of who she was. She was entirely out of her life: no past, no connections, no tomorrow, and no one watching. In one fully realized instant, she felt wholly and unequivocally free. Free. Even, from her own actuality. The lifelong meticulous construction of Ilana Emily Barrett, if it were laid in pieces here, could not be reassembled by a single person in this room. She was Missy, the opera lady from Manhattan, and that was the extent of it. This luscious anonymity felt like a full indispensable breath of air, the sort of breath that stayed snowy all the way down her throat. Serenity spread out from the core of her. At this moment in time, in this peculiar place, no one had any expectations for her. This was the opposite of what she had anticipated. She had never seen how obsessively expectation and circumstance held her identity hostage. Maybe she wasn't looking to understand the choices made by her, or for her, but to escape them? Does freedom exist only when nothing is known? All those decisions—little ones, big ones, and all the influences in school, at home, every interaction she has had, every action she has taken—put her in a box, a box papered with labels. Each action, each step, had been a brushstroke on the sign that defined her. Right now, in this home, she was no one; she was released, if not from her own conscious and unconscious machinations, at least from the outward construction and expectations of who she was. She was free to examine who that self had turned out to be and to pretend to be a new self who could be like or unlike her old self. She was free from her *self.*

William yelled into the phone, "I called the police!"

Ilana whispered, "You're such a good friend."

"I had to use my medical license to get the number and address! My medical license, Ilana!"

"I'm sorry. The gunfire was from some sad old guy. Harmless, really."

"Harmless gunfire is an oxymoron."

"I understand why you say that, and I know it is hard to understand what I'm saying from where you are right now, but—"

"Okay, you can't talk, I get it. You're in trouble. Say coffee so I'll know."

"William."

"If you say coffee right now, I'll know and—"

"Really, I'm okay."

There was a pause as William thought it over. "Look," he said, "I am not exactly cavalry material because I look shitty in blue, but I can put a call into Adam, and he'd run up there barefoot after you."

"It's unnecessary. I admit things got uncomfortably heated during the family holy war, and even worse when Grandma nearly choked to death, but after we all agreed that my ripeness was not yet fatal, well, it completely broke the tension."

A pause.

"Ilana, don't screw with me. I'm an expert on crazy."

She lowered her voice. "I want to say something to Fiona. I need to find the right moment. Although they don't seem to be overly concerned about the right moment for anything here. It's a bit of a free-for-all. I'll call you as soon as I get home. I'll take the late train tonight."

"I'm not happy with this, Ilana."

"William, trust me. You know me." This last comment hung in the air.

Clearing dinner in the O'Holleran home was a communal affair. The family stepped all over each other, piling, carrying, and rinsing. It was an orderly bedlam warm from the energy of its movement. Ilana had maintained an airy conversation about college with Patrick. She drifted through the well-acquainted subject matter with the poise of regained control, and the composure that others had long admired in her had opened up like an awning above her, and she stood effortlessly under the eave of it. Patrick was easy to talk to one-on-one. She liked him immediately and kept reminding herself he was her little brother. Joy. She wanted to throw her arms around him. It had been one of her fondest dreams.

"What'll be hard for me," Patrick continued, "is giving up baseball. I don't think a day has gone by since I was seven that I didn't hit and throw baseballs."

"That's no joke," said Willow as she handed him a plate to rinse. "Every morning, he's been out there hitting balls over and over at the break of day."

"Gotta be some kind of robot to hit as many balls as Patrick," Shea added.

Interesting, Ilana thought, *the repetition in sports training*. People called it muscle memory, but of course, she knew there was no such thing; a muscle can't have memory. This must be an instance where the body controlled the brain, instead of the other way around. The routine repetitive movement creates a neural pathway in the brain, moving the movement from conscious to unconscious activity over time. This was the goal of sports training. Stellar athletes perform unconsciously.

Patrick said, "There are so many general ed requirements. I wasn't sure, you know?" He handed Ilana another dish, and she realized she had not been listening to him, but she had kept drying and stacking.

"Once you get settled in the city, you'll be amazed at how much easier it is to know what you want." She smiled and hoped the comment made sense.

Into the placid calm of her familiar mind and the routine movements of cleaning up stepped Cafferty. He moved right up behind her. She felt him inches away. She shifted her feet, indicating he should back up. He didn't.

Personal space! Why don't these people get it?

Then, without her consent, her body reacted to his nearness on its own: her heart sped up, and her skin got clammy. He leaned in to reach for a hand towel, and his breath felt hot and damp on the nape of her neck.

Too close.

She stepped purposefully back on his foot. "Oh, sorry." She wasn't.

Patrick said, "I knew some kind of housing near the campus would be really hard to find."

Now, she had to struggle to listen. Cafferty's arm brushed the small of her back, causing a sudden and involuntary contraction, which she hoped no one saw. He did.

"Housing is always the issue in Manhattan." Her voice was breathier. This physical reaction had something to do with scent and skin, and it angered her as it circumvented her disapproval. She realized with intimidating alarm that she needed to fight her body's crippling urge to lie down naked on the goddamn Formica. Ilana stepped to the other side of the sink, enforcing space between them.

Fiona ran in. "Gotta dash to the pub!"

"Mrs. O'Holleran, I was hoping to have a private word with you," Ilana said.

"Not now, hon. The Butler brothers are dwarf-tossing. Finish up in here, will you?" And she was gone.

Patrick dried his hands and followed his mother. "I'd better help. They can be ornery, and Pop's kinda hot-blooded."

Kinda?

Instantly, Cafferty and Ilana were left alone in the kitchen. A prickly silence. He went to move and stopped. She went to move and stopped. They stood. Then, they turned back to the sink and continued with the dishes: scrape, scrub, rinse, pass, dry, stack; scrape, scrub, rinse, pass, dry, stack.

After a minute, "Dwarf tossing?" she asked as she stacked the plates and searched for a conversation to cut the thick air.

"Yeah. You take turns hurling a dwarf onto a mattress. Everybody bets. Whoever hurls the dwarf the farthest wins. Don't think it's legal anymore."

She put down the dish, stunned. "You're not serious."

Cafferty picked up the plate and put it in the cabinet. "Shea doesn't allow it in his pub. I hear it's real popular in Australia."

"I think they prefer little person. And it's cruel."

"Dwarf takes twenty percent."

More to herself, she said, "I don't believe it."

"Not surprising."

And there it was, the challenge she had felt from him all evening.

"Oh?" She met it. She had been off her guard and overwhelmed, more so than at any time in her life, but the calm of the after-dinner clean-up, coupled with the everyday exchange with Patrick, had allowed her usual composure to resurface. She felt on top of her legs.

"Got a feeling you come from a pretty whitewashed world, opera lady."

"Not only have I traveled all over this world, but I live in the most sophisticated and colorful city on Earth. My life is not parochial in the least."

"Yeah? I bet when you traveled 'all over the world,' you went from one Hilton to another."

She hated that he looked at her as though he knew her. She handed him the dish towel.

"Excuse me. You don't know me. And I've something to take care of." She went for the door. He tossed the towel on the counter and followed. They entered the screened porch and reached for their shoes.

He baited her. "Something about Nellie?"

There was no response as she put on her shoes.

Cafferty continued, "Sure was odd you knowin' her last name like that." He slipped into his work boots.

With one shoe on and one off, she looked at him. "What?"

"You called her Mrs. Shannon when she was choking."

"Where I come from, that's polite."

"Maybe. But, hell, I've known Nellie my entire life, and no one's ever called her Mrs. Shannon. It's Nellie. You could line ten regulars up in the pub, and they won't even know it's Shannon."

Trapped. She knew Nellie's last name because it was on her own birth certificate: Fiona Shannon. She said nothing and pretended to have trouble getting on her shoe.

He pressed. "I was sittin' there wondering how an opera lady from Manhattan, you know, stoppin' in, spur of the moment, like, for a shot a whiskey, would know something like that." He cocked his head.

"Well, wondering is good for the plasticity of your brain." She finished putting on her shoes, turned for the door, and said, "Nice meeting you."

"Hang on. I'll walk with you. I'm going there." Cafferty swung open the screen door and stepped out with her.

In the cooling summer night, they walked along the riverbank toward the pub. Unusually peaceful, the river sighed with small movements. She liked it when night laid its palm over the day and erased color. The gray shadows made her feel snug, safe, and unexposed. Never a child afraid of the dark, Ilana found night more soothing than day. Day made demands.

Two enormous mutts rumbled out of the obscurity and ran at them. She stepped quickly behind Cafferty as they jumped on him with the kind of irrepressible glee only a dog in love can marshal.

"Guys, down."

"Yours?"

"Adopted me last year. Turned up outta nowhere. Eat more than a family of eight." The dogs loped along playfully. "You got a pet?"

"I had a plant."

His short laugh surprised her. It wasn't cynical but genuine. He threw a stick, and the dogs took off in a heavenly frenzy.

"Not much affection from a plant."

"Even less from a dead plant." She thought about the tall, shriveled, brown ficus still standing in her living room.

"You killed it?"

"Committed suicide."

"You that hard to live with?"

"The horticulturist seemed to think it was lonely."

"Lonely?"

"Evidently."

"Guess you have to go to some really expensive college to come up with that." He shook his head. "So, that's it, then, for pets? One suicidal plant?"

"Last year, we installed an aquarium in our office. They said fish were proven to reduce stress, and there's a lot of stress in live theatre."

"And did it?" The two ecstatic dogs returned, and Cafferty threw the stick again.

"Not really," she remembered. "Made things worse, actually. Every morning for two weeks, I came in and tossed another dead fish into the trash until there were none. Each time the office manager cried, said a prayer, and quite oddly, had tuna for lunch."

Cafferty's laugh was low and pleasant. It reminded her of the tuba player, and this relatable connection warmed and built a tenuous bridge of familiarity.

"So, your plant died of loneliness, and you're a serial fish killer. Sounds like you're a dangerous woman."

"Hardly."

Here was something she hadn't been called before. She liked it. She was weary of being predictable. Perhaps if that was all she learned from this adventure, that would be enough. She considered how many times she went to the same restaurant and ordered the exact same meal. She remembered that whenever she went to the movies, she attempted to sit in the same seat on the aisle. Her life was replete with unspoken rules and rigid patterns. She thought about how many times the Lyric Opera's general director had complimented her on her reliability. *Not*, she consoled herself, *that reliability is a bad thing*, but it made her life, in some ways, redundant. Her days echoed. Does that repetitive behavior stem from practicality, laziness, or programming? Adam always told her, "The brain loves a pattern." Next time, she committed that she would go to a new restaurant, and she would order something exotic. Next time, she would sit in the middle of the damn theatre.

Fewer rules.

They walked in silence, and the soothing river washed on by. She felt settled. Water had this effect on her. All kinds of water. When she was home, she would walk along the Hudson River whenever she could. Looking out now at the Hudson here, about 150 miles north of Manhattan, she liked that this same water would wash past her apartment downstream sometime later. There was an appeasing continuity to that. When she couldn't sleep, which happened frequently after her mother died, she would click on YouTube and play the sound of rainfall all night. Nothing was more consoling than the sounds of a distant thunderstorm.

Cafferty's dogs returned again and again. He never tired of throwing the stick.

The dogs ran ecstatically with their legs fully stretched.

"Wow, those dogs are happy," she said.

"They know the meaning of life."

"Oh? Share."

"They won't tell me."

"I don't know why," she added with amusement, "they certainly seem to like you." She enjoyed the two dogs jumping over each other blissfully.

"They like me because we understand each other and have stuff in common."

"Like what?"

"We like watching basketball. We like jumping in the river. They like cookies. I like cookies."

One of the dogs returned, careened up to Ilana, and shoved the stick at her leg. Startled, she looked to Cafferty.

"Throw it. It's all they want. They're simple."

She did, and they darted full sprint after it.

"They only want to run and eat and lay on the rug." He looked at her. "Most people think too much. Too much thinking convinces folks that things matter. That *they* matter."

"You don't think you matter?"

"We'll all be the exact same amount of dead. Nothing matters but a waterproof roof and tasty cookies."

"This is the Cookie Philosophy of Life."

"Life stripped of bullshit."

They walked on in an agreeable silence. The dogs dodged about in the dark. The river passed, and no street noise competed with the water lap. Her mind stretched like the muscles in her limbs, grateful for the cool, open space. The sharp emotions of the day, which began when Shea shoved his stubby fingers into her armpits, through the revelation of her mother, the gunfire, the choking, and the police, had all left her with an extraordinary relief to be walking quietly. The breeze was welcome, brushing along her forearms. She wanted to walk all night long. She breathed in fully, and she was about to analyze every single thing that had happened when the dogs dropped the stick right at her feet. She smiled at them because the look of ecstatic focused anticipation in their eyes was idyllic. Maybe this was the meaning of life—pure, uncomplicated desire. She bent down and threw the stick as far as she could. They walked on.

For Cafferty, walking beside her, he realized he was unusually attentive to this stranger's movements. He asked himself if it was only because she was new. He wondered why he was attracted. She was not gorgeous. *Hell, Delores D'Agostino at the deli brought more to the party.* But she was pretty in a direct way, in a way that wouldn't wash off in the shower or speak out boldly in a crowd. Her thin legs strolled in sync with her hips like a perfectly aligned hinge. He could almost make out the curve of her ass through the beige linen pantsuit. She was someone who shouldn't be here, and he liked puzzles. He always had a puzzle going on the coffee table. They were images of the natural world, of lakes, forests, and the night sky. He had no investment at all on how long it might take him to finish. Some days, he'd only put in one piece.

He reveled in his dinners with the O'Hollerans, and tonight had been especially fun. He liked life in the extremes: solitude or commotion. When he was home alone, he was lazy in the silence; when he decided to go out, he liked life at a howl. The O'Hollerans lived at a roar. Nine nights out of ten, Cafferty ate by himself, surrounded by what mattered to him: his dogs, his woodwork, and frozen pot pies. On that tenth night, he shared in the O'Holleran's high-strung chorus. He had known these people all his life. Few who lived here strayed far from the neighborhood. Some of them stayed from lethargy, some from convenience, but most because they lacked imagination. Cafferty stayed because he understood that life was in the core of the fruit. Cafferty was surrounded when all alone, countersunk into his world. He liked his *ownliness*. He exerted power over his life as formed and solid as a marble fist. He recalled, as an adolescent, watching quizzically while siblings and friends struggled to "find" themselves. He was born himself and raised by an exhausted woman.

He knew his mother, knew her better than any of the others, because he was quiet, and so she confided in him, her eighth child, her youngest son. He knew that she believed he wasn't listening, but he was. His mother was defeated long before he came along. She was a frail woman, married at sixteen, a mother by seventeen, and a grandmother by thirty-five. She never gave a thought to what she might have wanted out of life. Life was something that happened *to* her. She revered the church because she was desperate to believe there was a purpose that she could not ascertain, some kind of reward that gave sense to it all; otherwise, it was unbearable that after every day, there was the next day. By afternoon, her muscles were jelly. Eight children, the laundry by hand, the market on foot, the constant cleaning and cooking, only to wake up and cook and clean again, most of the time pregnant. Her arches fell, her breasts sagged, and the earth tugged on her. On a good day, she'd find a few lost coins in the sofa cushions. On a bad day, one of her sons would come home with something spilled carelessly on the shirt that she had just washed. She would smile at them, and then, she would close the bathroom door, sit down on the toilet seat, the only private spot, and secretly weep. At night, she sank into the white-sheeted cool mattress, and each time, she fought (if only for a few seconds) the thick door of sleep. It was the only moment she had all to herself. She tried not to think of what she had to do the next day, or how all her days were the same. She tried only to notice, in that one blessed moment of peace, while her legs throbbed, while her back ached, while the skin on her hands shriveled and her heels cracked, that she was—in that singular moment—still. It was her paradise to be still in the darkness that asked for nothing. She was not a morbid woman, but she thought of death as a relief, a nice, long stillness in the dark.

Cafferty witnessed the toll her life took on her. When she cried in the bathroom, he alone heard. He made promises to himself about his own life then. Even as a young boy, he made his own choices with impunity. He didn't remember himself as the third-grade boy who was desperate for his mother's attention and disappointed when she missed his school events. He remembered only that growing up required a substantial amount of self-reliance. His home was a boiling stew of love, of drink, and of yelling. It was impossible to achieve peace with ten people living in the same small home, half of them going through puberty at any one time. Life was already out of control when he came along; he was only expected to observe and stay out of trouble. He was certain his parents never knew his grades, the names of his teachers, or any of his friends. The disregard might have made him angry had not the reasons been so clear. It was all too damn hard. It had turned him away from the traditional lifestyle and toward the tranquility of being alone. He was a man truly happy with his life. He recognized that every night when he walked his dogs along the river, and he felt that this night too.

Cafferty stopped walking and turned up the path leading to a small home. Looking up, Ilana recognized nothing. She'd been carried along the stroll breezily and contented, and she had no idea how long they'd been walking.

"Where are we?"

"My house," he responded, pointing to the house in front of them.

"I'm not going to your house. I'm going to the pub."

"Oh, so you're not only a fish killer; you got a bad sense of direction."

"I've got an awesome sense of direction. I have always had a sense of direction. People comment on my terrific sense of direction."

"Guess something's off tonight."

She stood, perplexed. "I'll find the pub myself."

"Wait two minutes, and I'll walk with you," Cafferty said.

"I don't need to be walked. I'm not a poodle."

"Good thing, or Willow'd make a sweater out of you."

She didn't want to smile, but she did. This night was the first time she noticed each time her body took the reins without her permission, at times against her conscious permission.

Cafferty continued, "Okay, one minute. I've got to get this shirt off."

"Oh? And why is that?"

"Got pot roast in it." He showed her where he had stashed pot roast in the breast pocket.

Sheepishly, she replied, "I ate mine."

"Rookie."

"So, that's why those dogs like you. You smell like pot roast."

"It's their favorite. Hey, you can wait out here if you're nervous."

She rose to the challenge. "I'm not nervous."

"Up to you because I need a shirt."

He turned and walked inside. Ilana stood. Truly, she wasn't

nervous. She was unusually at ease, but also curious, very curious. She walked to the door, peeked inside, and then stepped into the house of wood: dark, large plank wood floors, mahogany paneled walls, dramatic rosewood cabinetry, Brazilian cumaru end tables, and intricately hand-carved bookcases. She was charmed by the birds with their wings carved into the windowsills. It was architecturally enthralling. So much detail. Cafferty was in the other room, and she was free to study his home. She felt pulled around the living room, compelled to run her fingers along all the different types of wood: pine, oak, maple, birch, and some she didn't recognize. All the different trees together, it was like a forest, or she thought, a lot like the different instruments in her orchestra, all complimenting elements blending to an artistic whole. Stuffed honey-colored armchairs created a fully masculine atmosphere of well-being. There was a puzzle on top of the coffee table. She bent to look at the legs and recognized the Green Man carved into the footing. The lighting was soft from floor lamps with creamy shades. She would not have chosen a single thing in this room, and yet it was perfect.

She was drawn to the massive mantle, which framed Cafferty's fireplace. She touched the molding. The uneven grain had taken the stain differently, and she studied its natural inconsistencies, finding depth in what she might have seen before as flaws. The molding was a thick bullnose that fit perfectly in the cup of her palm, and she ran her hand along the buttery wood. The earlier whiskey at the pub and then again at dinner had mingled with the beer, and that, added to the walk along the river, had left her in a sweet and airy state. In this home dwelled a remarkable tranquility. She had to admit, here, where she was absolutely unknown, she reveled in the release provided by anonymity.

Right next to her *RING!*

Startled, she jumped. She yanked her hand away from the mantle as though she'd been caught doing something naughty.

Cafferty strode in from the other room, crossed quickly, and grabbed the phone.

"Hello?" He had only one arm in his T-shirt, so the shirt fell off his shoulder. She stepped back into the corner. He smelled like the woods, like earth, like fresh green moss. She breathed in. His chest was smooth and hairless, and his Irish skin was burnt brown from working bare-chested outside in the summer sun.

He spoke into the receiver. "Okay." His body blocked her from moving. Her shoulder blades, hips, and the small of her back were flat against the wall. She attempted to slide her body a respectable distance away, but the bookcase was on one side, and he was on the other. She assumed he'd move, but he didn't.

"No, I'm not workin' tomorrow. Maybe Monday, maybe not." He listened for a second, and then replied calmly, "Well, if I'm there, then I'll be working. Have a good night." He hung up.

Ilana couldn't focus. Something was wrong inside of her, very wrong, and control was unachievable. Her body had been calling the shots all night long, and it was doing so now. She struggled to find something to say to camouflage the groaning urge of her body, which was so thunderous, she feared it was actually audible. Her mind scolded, *Step away, step back.* But she didn't. She didn't step away. She didn't try. She stayed.

"Don't you. Don't you usually take off Sundays?" she asked weakly.

He did not cede one centimeter of space. What was going on between them was obvious—it was screaming.

"Don't follow a schedule." His breath was on her. "Take off when I want."

"Um. That's lucky."

"Not luck. I decide."

"You decide."

"I decide," he said.

"You decide everything?"

"Not everything. Some things decide for you."

Ilana's body had always obeyed, but even as she commanded it to get a grip, she felt that slippery feeling in her underpants. Her heart pounded in her ears. Not one cell of her flesh waited for conscious permission. It felt like a torrid, rushing ache. She tried to squeeze out words, but no words came. In her life, no moment had ever felt as inevitable as this. Who was making her choices now?

Cafferty watched her. He could sense her confusion. He had no clue why. Why? It was plain enough. He needed to lick her. He saw her flush. He recognized the quick little breaths she was taking. He knew what her body wanted. Didn't she know? He ran his palms all the way down the sides of her arms and over her hands. He spread her fingers and slid his own in between them. It was the most invasive and erotic feeling she'd ever had. She experienced the textured coarseness of his workingman's fingers with a convulsive pleasure that she tried to control. The struggle raged inside, her mind trying to wrench back control from her body, as though they were two separate organisms. Cafferty's hands were wide, autonomous, and accustomed to reshaping what they touched. It was this communion of roughness and his utter confidence that seized her. Her legs wavered. He caught her. She stated the truth with supplicating nakedness.

"I don't know you."

"But do you know what you want right now?"

"Um."

"Say no. A simple no. It's up to you." Then he whispered, "I know what I want."

Yes, it is no. No, it is yes. Had she ever craved anything this fiercely in her well-planned, exceedingly polite life? No. Had she ever felt a physical pull like this? No. Her body was roaring at her.

He pressed his whole body in on her, and still, he wasn't close enough. His desire was greedy. She was, in fact, completely out of her mind.

"Yes or no?" he asked again. "You say."

"Yes." She didn't believe any other answer was actually possible.

Slowly, as he leaned into her mouth, he whispered, "Don't think."

❖ ❖ ❖

SKINNY DAYLIGHT entered through the cracked shutters and fanned out along the floorboards in the morning bedroom. Sheets and pillows were strewn. A chair by the dresser was askew. A bandana hung tied to the bedpost. Ilana lay nude in an uninhibited sprawl on Cafferty, who slept on the one remaining sheet. Slowly, her eyes opened. Without moving one single sated muscle, her eyes roamed the room, straining for context.

Where?

She felt sunken in, floating warm, like her limbs were liquid. It was the most pleasant sensation. There was no border between her body and the surfaces it touched. The temperature in the room was amniotic. No tension existed in any muscle of her body. She was fluid. She was a placid, glassy lake dreamily still and infinitely deep. She was in a perfect physical state until recognition. Her brain fog cleared. Memory triggered.

She bolted upright. "Oh, shit."

Cafferty grabbed her with one arm and pulled her back down, reluctantly opening his eyes.

"Oh, shit." She sprang back up again. "Oh, no."

"Ilana?"

"No. Oh, Adam."

"Adam?"

She leaped out of bed and began to search rabidly for her underpants. Cafferty watched, slowly waking, as she scurried around, propelled by reality, propelled by self-reproach.

"I'm such a shit. Shit. Shit. He's so decent, and so honest and so..."

"Lacking?" he offered.

"Don't you say that." She looked under the bed.

"Adam makes love to you without messing your hair."

"Why do you say that?" She rummaged through the sheet. "You

can't know that. How could you know that?" She looked under the dresser.

"Cause your body was starved. You really oughta treat it better."

She whirled around and demanded an answer, stomping her foot like a little girl. "Underpants?"

"Shower curtain."

"Oh, god." She whined and ran into the bathroom. "This was not the plan."

"You always got a plan?"

"Yes," she yelled from the bathroom. She reentered with her panties on backward and continued her search. He said nothing.

Petulantly, she said, "Bra?"

"Oh, that was early on. Bookcase." And that was when she unraveled right there in the middle of his bedroom, like someone pulled a small hanging thread, and it all came apart. Shaking like a child, wet eyes. Cafferty got out of bed, perplexed. "Here," he said, grabbing his bulky cotton shirt. He fit it around her like a robe. Kindly, he said, "There. Ah. Okay? Ah. Is that okay?"

"I have to talk to Fiona and get the hell out of Albany."

"Do you always panic like this after? Is this, you know, normal for you?"

"Normal?" She stood taller and tugged on the bottom of the huge cotton shirt, trying to resurrect her self-respect. "No, it's not normal. Nothing is normal. Nothing has been normal since the moment I got out of the cab." She ran her fingers through her hair and took a breath. "And I never panic."

"Good, because it is six-thirty on Sunday mornin', and it's too early to go calling on Fiona. I'll make breakfast."

"Breakfast?" It didn't even sound like English to her raging mind.

"Yeah, you know, food? Or don't you feed that part of your body either?"

"Oh, I don't know." It was more a comment on her entire state of mind than a response to his breakfast offer.

"It's okay. I make a good, filling oatmeal." He headed for the kitchen.

He left her behind in his bedroom. She could see that he was baffled, but so was she. She opened the shirt and looked at her body. She turned to the mirror over his dresser and touched her breasts. Why had they never responded that way before?

What's happening to me?

She studied the room. Disorder had been her lifelong enemy, and this room was disheveled. She was unequivocally a stranger here.

In the kitchen, Cafferty pulled out the pot, poured in the oatmeal, and added the milk, brown sugar, and raisins. He woke up with the taste of her still in his mouth. He threw two pieces of bread into the toaster. Perhaps it was all the biblical talk at the dinner table the night before, but it occurred to him that the Bible had the right verb when it said, "he *knew* her" to describe sex. They had done things that he'd not done with any other woman, and it felt completely natural. More salt. Little butter. Cinnamon. He had known every inch of her skin. They fit like two teaspoons lying right up against each other. He couldn't get far enough inside of her. He thought of nothing else as he cooked. He knew she'd relax, come around. It was all too obvious. Of course, this Adam guy would have to go.

The breakfast room was tiny and irregularly shaped. The small walnut table and two chairs sat under a curved bay window. The day was already laying its warm palm on the panes. They sat close and shared the hearty breakfast. Cafferty talked on casually. As they ate, the blow of her waking up there softened. Coming from a long line of Irish storytellers, Cafferty spoke with leisure about his walk up the Appalachian Trail. Ilana listened and took in with silent pleasure the room, his voice, the oatmeal, the toast, and the hot, smooth coffee. His story was pacifying. He had a gift for details. She could see that by looking around his home and by reviewing the breakfast that he'd made, with the lightly browned toast precisely cut in half and expertly buttered to the very edges.

Cafferty described many of the characters he'd met along the trail and then one particular couple. "They were strange, the both of them. City professionals. Moved like a coupla ATVs, careless and loud, stepping on everything along the way. And in camp, at night, they'd figure out to the inch how far they had left to go."

"Keeping track of their goal? That's not a bad thing."

"Missed everything. Saw the dirt trail under their feet and nothing else. More interested in saying they'd done it than in doing it. They started to piss me off. We'd been walking together, loosely, for about three days, that happens on the trail, and then we got to the last day."

"You summited?"

"No."

She cocked her head and waited for the explanation. He took a big bite of toast, chewed, then continued, "We were about one hundred yards from the top after about twenty-one hundred miles. I don't know exactly 'cause I wasn't keeping track of every inch. And these two were charging up this mountain like their asses were on fire, leaping over stones and stuff, not even looking around, and that's when I quit walkin'."

"You quit?"

"Yup."

"Right before the end?" she asked.

"Yup."

"Why?"

"Felt like it."

"Come on." She looked at him oddly. He was completely foreign to her.

"When I stopped, the two of them turned and called back to me. Was I hurt, or sick, or having a heart attack? They tried to talk me into finishing. I was almost there, they kept saying. You can do it, they yelled at me. I know, I said."

"But you didn't go."

"After six months, after the blisters, sunburn, bugs, and annoying people, it would take a lot more will to walk away minutes from the top. That was the bigger challenge. To come that far and then stop."

"And you thought *they* were strange?"

He looked at her plate. It was clean. She noticed.

"I guess I was hungry. I usually don't have time for breakfast. My alarm blasts, I grab a muffin, and I keep moving."

"Yeah? You seem like someone who does everything you're told."

"I like being busy."

"I like having time."

"I wouldn't mind a couple of extra hours in the day to do more of the things I enjoy."

He raised his eyes from the last bite on his plate. "Those things come last?"

"My job requires a lot of my time."

Ilana looked out the bay window. Her body was full and warm. She didn't feel like she needed to jump up and get on to the next thing. In this rare moment, she didn't hear her life drumming its fingers or feel that incessant momentum. The current that drove her urgently through her every waking hour had been switched off.

Cafferty said, "Yeah, well, guess it's all a matter of what you're willing to sell." He put down his fork.

"What does that mean?"

He wiped his chin. "You're born. You get so many minutes. You die. That's kinda it. How you spend your minutes is the only thing."

"Professional success allows you to spend your minutes doing something intellectually challenging, living in comfort and safety, enjoying your time."

"You said you don't have much time for enjoying."

"Oh. I did. I suppose we make trade-offs."

"Well, I work the days I want. I've got two rules: I don't set my alarm for anyone, and I don't eat with people I don't like."

"Not looking to save the world, Cafferty?"

"Nope."

"Don't want to make some kind of difference or accomplish something meaningful?"

"Nope." Cafferty tilted his head. "Only want my freedom."

"Freedom can mean different things."

"Nothing simpler than freedom. Am I deciding what I'm doing today, or is someone else?"

"Living day by day is not the most thoughtful way to plan for your future."

"I'm not trading today for tomorrow. Don't ever expect tomorrow. Happy to see it, and to know, if it comes, I can do whatever I damn please."

"Okay, well, I like the community, the challenge, and the responsibility of a big enterprise." She took her last sip of coffee. "I like the security that comes from a professional career, even though the daily responsibilities can be restricting."

"You know, you remind me exactly of the bird they got living inside Harrows Drug store."

"Really?" She lifted her left eyebrow. "A bird?"

"Yeah, got the best cage in the city, but still trapped." Cafferty got up and poured some more coffee.

Ilana felt a sudden driving urge to defend herself. "I've got a great life, a coveted job, a great—"

Guy. oh, Adam, oh, oh.

Her heart fell, her spirit fell, her blood pressure fell, and she felt faint. Last night was an inexcusable breach of trust. She remembered wondering if she was a good person. Well, here was her answer.

How can he forgive me? How can I forgive me? This is the worst thing I've ever done.

As though he could read her, Cafferty asked, "You in love with that Adam guy?"

She paused. "Well."

"That's a no."

She corrected him defiantly, "I didn't say no."

"Aren't pauses for that answer."

She studied him for the first time. He had an ordinary face, gruff and sunburned, with some flakes of dryness around the nose. His eyes were dark and had a hint of coolness to them. Who was this?

She spoke with relaxed frankness. "I'll bet you can be a very aggravating man."

He let the judgment sit a moment as he considered it. "I think that's right." Then, he moved his chair closer. "I believe I've been told that more than once." He leaned in, collapsing the space between them. "And you, you've got a lot of knots and splinters, flaws and rough edges, but I think I can fix you with a real good sanding." He placed his palms solidly on her bare knees and spread them. They opened to his touch as if they were not hers at all.

"I shouldn't be here," she said with a mixture of desire and sadness.

"Yeah, but you are, and you've already blown it all to hell, and it's only you and me here, so, for right now . . ." With deliberate slowness, he lowered his mouth to the inside of her thigh.

FIONA SHANNON O'HOLLERAN used up her childhood only blocks from her current house. Being a child disagreed with her. She had always felt older than her mother. Her mother, Nellie Shannon, was ravenous when it came to a good time. Nellie ran away from home and lived every day fully after reveling in that escape, which was a story she told, retold, and told again.

One foggy night, when Nellie was fifteen years old, she escaped out of her bedroom window and slipped secretly on board a ship that had docked for the night in Cobh Harbor on the Irish coast. It was only a few days before her wedding. Without a word to her miserably poor family, she left behind forever the penetrating dampness, slimy bait, and marriages arranged by necessity. She didn't know what living would be like on the other side of the Atlantic, but she knew that she would not go willingly into a life of cracked laundry hands, fish soup, and caring for a husband three times her age. Nellie was a pioneer. She was in that very first generation of women who looked at what life had planned for them and had the courage to walk into the unknown. She struck out into a world unaccustomed to independent women. She had exactly the right spirit for it. Her irascible charm and piano playing carried her all the way to Albany, New York, USA. It was what she wanted, and it was worlds away from home.

Nellie married for love. Her husband had been what they called "a good man"—not particularly smart, nor successful, nor talented, but "a good man." They all said it about him. It was gouged out on his headstone. "Patrick Shannon. A good man." He did not provide well. Their lives were a struggle of secondhand clothes and food baskets from the church, but they had laughter, and they had music, and no fish soup, not ever. Her home was the favorite meeting place for the neighbors. Nellie was always aware of what her life could have been, and so she kept the promise that freedom gave her. She lived where she chose, and she married whom she chose at a time when poor women chose nothing, when poor women learned to cook, to scrub, and to duck. Nellie appreciated her freedom in ways the ensuing generations never could. Consequently, she lived uncensored. She knew that regrets were for fools, so she kept her one regret wrapped up in an old towel and shoved it way back under her bed. It was a book, a tattered paperback novel. She could pick out a few words here and there. Her family home was so rural that she never went to school. Now, she told people that her eyes were bad, so she didn't read much, but when she was a younger woman, and she rode the bus, she carried this book. She would open it and turn the page at regular intervals. It gave her a thrill to be seen as someone who could read. It never occurred to her that no one noticed.

Nellie's daughter, Fiona, also had secrets. Late on Saturday afternoons, she would climb in through the basement window of the neighborhood church (where the latch had been forever broken) and make her way up the back shaky stairs. Something about the deserted solemnity of the empty church soothed her; the open-armed saints embraced her kindly, the pews were an inviting place to stretch out, and the altar was a witness that kept quiet about mysterious things. So, while her father's brothers debated (at the very top of their lungs) the day's politics and prices and her mother's friends debated (in a delicious whisper) the local scandals, little Fi would rush to the solace of the church. The walls were generous, and once inside, the disharmony of her relatives and the din of the street ceased. She sat peacefully in the warm palm of the church. She took deeper breaths in this stillness. She spent many late Saturdays there. And even back in those days, when her innocence was as fresh as her soap-scrubbed face, when her life was new and her heart too roomy, even then, the pews were old. They had been transported from some older church destroyed in some foreign place. Lying on her back, she ran her pinky finger through the little gouges made by the fingernails of other children, other children from far away who were bored by the homily, and she felt a kinship with them.

Now, occasionally, when Saturday afternoon came, she tried to recapture that feeling of solace, but the theft of it slapped her hard, and her thoughts moved quickly on, denied in her adulthood even the recollection of such blessed serenity. Fiona was not a woman who could afford to look back. She was only one step ahead of the crack in the earth that followed right up to her last footfall. She had secrets and would protect them at any cost. She loved her gregarious, wild-mouthed husband, and those times when she wondered why she picked a loud man, she remembered it was because the quiet was so very dangerous.

Sixteen-year-old Fiona was silent about her pregnancy. Only her mother knew. They didn't even tell her father. The disappointment on his face would've scalded her, and she was already aching. This was an old-fashioned Catholic neighborhood, so it was best to keep secrets about certain things. Fiona gained weight slowly and all over, so it wasn't until the seventh month that Nellie sent her to Saint Bernadette's Catholic Home for a rest; there, she was to deliver the baby. Nellie told everyone that Fiona had gone to a fat farm. The locals noted how successful the farm had been when Fiona returned home three months later much thinner, although slightly pale and lacking her usual piquancy.

Saint Bernadette's was a dismal boarding house in the center of the city. The nuns performed their earthly penance by running it. They were brittle women, sexless, and looking longingly toward death. Fiona had known musical nuns, cheerful nuns, and even mischievous nuns, but there were none of these at Saint Bernadette's. When a particularly stern Sister Mary Margaret asked Fiona if she wanted to unburden herself, relieve her soul, and discuss her sin, Fiona felt the little life inside of her kick hard. She knew that was a sign to keep quiet, so she did.

The young sinners housed at Saint Bernadette's shared little in common, not economic stature, education, or society; the only thing they shared was "their troubles," as it was called. They had come to "their troubles" in different ways: some had fallen in love and paid a price; some were victims of the unspeakable; some had dated casually before their defenses were built; too many were nice, romantic girls, insecure, without the benefit of sex education, with soft hearts and bad luck and timing.

Fiona's roommate, Emily, had a life to her eyes and a curve to her body that sucked in teenage boys and their fathers alike. She told Fiona that she frequently fought off both the same evening. Even friends of her own father could not keep their hands off her. She felt hunted when she walked down the street, when she sat down to eat, when her teachers met with her, when she went to the doctor, and even when she visited a cousin. In naïve defiance, she dressed as she pleased, comfortably in tight jeans and soft braless shirts. Some nights, Fiona and Emily would stay up late, and Emily would muse about the power this kind of attraction gave her. Fiona saw through this. Beneath her compelling charisma, Emily was a timid girl, acutely sensitive, and Fiona felt sorry for her. She knew she'd be back. She was prey in a spotlight.

Saint Bernadette's was durable, orderly, and quiet as a crypt. Evidently, God was especially sensitive to noise because the sisters rarely spoke. One particular night, when Fiona stepped barefoot out of bed for her third trip to the toilet, the cold, unforgiving wood floorboards met her bare soles, and she knew her life must be lived in a home filled with pulsing voices and plush carpet. She promised herself this. There must be forgiveness under your feet, a little give; everyone deserves a little give. And later, when Shea installed the wall-to-wall carpet into their little home, Fiona dug her toes into it with relief. It was forgiving. She made everyone take off their shoes. They think it's to keep the carpet clean; it's so they feel the forgiveness.

Fiona's days passed working in St. Bernadette's kitchen, an ascetic, bland place, where salt was considered a rare spice and not a staple. Most of her nights were one long game of solitaire during which she generally cheated. Fiona was grateful to have a place to go, but she was not at ease, and she did not feel safe. She felt judged. Many of the girls prayed with the nuns. Fiona did not. God had clearly forsaken her.

After the initial sharing of the humiliating news, Nellie and Fiona did not talk about it; when Fiona arrived home after it all, Nellie asked, "All right, then?" The response was "Fine." That was the end of it between them. Nellie never asked her daughter about her time at Saint Bernadette's, if the birth was painful, or whether it had been a boy or girl. The best she could do was move on. It was all Nellie was capable of. Even as a teenager, Fiona understood her mother's limitations. This situation was too much for her to navigate. Nellie was a woman who had fixed everything by moving on, and it became her motto, her philosophy, and her religion. But Nellie had moved on from everything she hated. Fiona was asked to move on from something she loved.

Before Fiona went away, she had a tight friendship with two neighborhood girls, but it didn't survive; her experience had created a gulf between them. She no longer shared with eager candidness because her secret made her cautious. This holding back turned their friendship into a shallow pool. She dropped out, never finishing high school, because to go back and pretend she was the same seemed absurd. She wasn't the same, not even close. When her class graduated, she was already working. It was clear to her that her entire life's trajectory had been altered. It was a harsh time.

A few weeks after Fiona returned from Saint Bernadette's, the storm that she had waited for blew in. She crept out of the house and walked alone in the daylight dark to the cemetery, getting soaked by the weeping sky. She carried a small stone, the size of her fist. It came from Saint Bernadette's tiny garden. Ceremoniously, she laid it next to the tombstone of her deceased little brother, Joey, who'd died in childbirth. She left it there as a marker for only her eyes to know, not because her baby girl had died, but because she was as good as dead to her. Fiona's time at "the farm" was in a box, tied up, double-knotted with strong string, and shoved way back on the shelf of her memory. It had been vigilantly webbed by spiders and purposely undisturbed for three decades, and that was exactly where she needed it. Two years later, she met and married Shea.

Fiona and Shea O'Holleran hit the road. They were newly married and anxious to drive across the country. They speculated about the adventure of it, about flying like birds on the wind, loving no plan, having no timetable. Instead, they found themselves to be cranky travelers, loathing the hours in the cramped Toyota and the way the cinch of the seat belt put their asses to sleep. They were tired of the threats of the airwave evangelists and the sameness of the roadside food served up lukewarm to Muzak or Barry Manilow (they couldn't tell the difference). They lost patience for the plastic Big Gulps, the soulless motels, and the smutty gas station bathrooms.

Fiona and Shea learned they were not birds at all but trees, and their lives were sustained through their roots. They wanted to be home, home for good.

Fiona was especially nagged as they drove through California. She looked at the scenery with the squinted eyes of someone hearing what they believed to be a lie. She looked around because something wasn't right. Then it came to her, and she asked Shea in a whisper, "Where's death?" There was no winter. The world didn't die, turn white, and begin again. And even more disturbing, she realized that they had driven for hundreds of miles and not passed a single cemetery. She looked at Shea eerily. "Are things kept alive here?" They set off to solve the mystery of death in California. It took three sets of directions from three vastly different Americans for them to locate it. Fiona's mouth dropped open, and her eyes widened. The cemeteries were not part of the community. They were away, out of sight, in massive, flowery places with death in neat, even rows. One was called Forest Lawn. Fiona thought it should be named Endless Lawn because there was no forest, and in her life, she'd never seen so much vivid green grass. It was too massive, too manicured, and artificial, resembling another California theme park. In the old, eastern towns, the cemeteries were at the center of it all, right next to the church. They had cracked stones, shiny stones, big angels, and little squares. They had cockeyed stones, broken stones, and vine-smothered stones, stones as dissimilar as the people beneath them. You passed your dead every day on your way to the market. You swore at them. You laughed at them. You blamed them. They remained within the community. The past was present. In California, death was locked away unnaturally, garishly made up, and staged to find the most flattering light. She missed the cemeteries of her home. They were real to her.

Traveling the coarse, grayish bedding of forgettable motels had not been enough to cool off the newlyweds. Fiona came home pregnant with Willow. Sometimes, she wondered if this had some effect on how she turned out. Willow was not as grounded as the rest of the family.

Life challenged her. She moved around like a June bug. Fiona did not understand this, but she accepted it because she loved her daughter very, very deeply, enough for two. Leaving on this trip was the second happiest day of Shea and Fiona's life together, and returning home was the first.

❖ ❖ ❖

AFTER BREAKFAST, Ilana and Cafferty climbed into his pickup truck. Her dirty, wrinkled linen pantsuit resembled her state of mind.

She tried to smooth her pants. "I can't believe you don't own an iron."

"Why would I have an iron?"

"What about your guests?"

"Don't have guests."

"What am I?"

"Hell if I know." It was what they both felt. Usually, Cafferty wanted his women to get out early, even before breakfast, but he hadn't minded having her there.

A Sunday morning drive. She liked it. It reminded her of the walk along the river in the dark the night before. They didn't need to talk, and it didn't feel awkward. She watched the world go by. She had no desire to analyze the opera budget, review the donor situation, or speculate on the orchestra's upcoming contract. The silence suited her. The crooked streets fell behind, the cityscape faded, huge maple trees took over the side of the road, and half an hour passed. She was looking but not seeing, deeply hypnotized by the passing trees and comforted by the soft morning sun that reached through the windshield and warmed her arms.

He turned to her. "Aren't you going to ask where we're going?"

"Evidently not to the O'Hollerans."

"Your sense of direction is back. Still, too early for the O'Hollerans. They're night folk. I've gotta stop by a lady who's been calling me too much about a job. Thought you'd like to see outside the city. We'll go to the O'Hollerans on the way back." They drove in silence. Ilana tried to keep her mind on the scenery and live in the warmth of the moment because the future was chilling. Every time her mind wandered that way, she forced a U-turn. Managing her thoughts took constant concentration.

On both sides of the street stood rich Victorian homes with semicircular paved arms that embraced the grassy yards between them and enormous trees with platter-sized leaves and one-hundred-year-old roots that marked time. These homes had been here for several generations.

Cafferty pulled up and stopped in front of the Peterson home. He jumped out, walked around the front of the truck, and swung open her door.

"Should I wait here?"

"You're with me." He offered her his hand.

"All right."

She slid out of the old pickup truck looking decidedly disheveled and slipped her hand in his. She hadn't held hands since high school. She had never held hands with Adam. Funny that it felt so natural. She attempted to fix her hair and straighten her clothes. He stopped her.

"You're good," he said.

"Liar."

The Peterson's marble foyer had a museum quality. It was massive, sterile, and cold. When the renovations began, the grand old home fought back with irreparable pipes, hidden doorways, electrical gridlock, and dry rot, but finally, it acquiesced to the stripped indignity of total restoration. The Petersons spared no expense in restoring the life out of it; decades of character had been torn away. Everything was new. They had money and time, but Cafferty could see they had no respect. They did not preserve the living soul of this stately family home. It was a clean kill. He liked the original house. In his own home, every single piece of furniture had a home before him. If he hadn't made it himself, then it came from someone else's bedroom or library. Furniture pieces had lives. He valued that. His mother had a wooden table in her kitchen. Every mark and scratch told a story of a moment in their lives.

Cafferty and Ilana waited in the Peterson's foyer. She studied the woodwork on the elegant banister to the second floor. She recognized it. "This is you." A statement. She walked up to it and ran her hand along the wood. "Nice."

"Cafferty." Mrs. Peterson rushed down the stairs garishly overdressed for a Sunday morning. "Wonderful. You're here. What a surprise. I've been calling you for days." A grin barely camouflaged her annoyance. "You are so hard to reach."

"Yeah. I've heard that."

Cafferty turned to introduce Ilana. "This is Ilana—" He hesitated. Ilana and Cafferty traded a look. Yes, he could sketch the little freckle on the inside flesh of her upper right thigh, and yes, he knew if he licked the underside of her arm, her stomach muscles contracted involuntarily, but no, he did not know her full name.

"Right." Mrs. Peterson summarily dismissed her and turned to him. "So, Cafferty, about the railing . . ."

Ilana stopped listening and stepped back. She had never been so dismissed—without a nod, without a brushing of the eyes, without even that disingenuous social half-smile. This patronizing disregard was a new experience. Ilana had never been a victim of these social class distinctions. She had always been on the other side. If she ran into Mrs. Peterson in the lobby of the opera house, Ilana would have been accorded a kindly deference, which, until this moment, she thought was simple common courtesy. Here and now, it became clear to her that all the members of the highly valued privileged class probably assumed that their value was intrinsic. It was disconcerting to face that her value did not come from who she was, but rather from what she was, and right now, she was the chick who came with the carpenter.

Mrs. Peterson continued, "And so I want to make a change."

Cafferty said flatly, "Yeah?"

"Don't misunderstand. It's magnificent. Everyone says so. But I was over at a friend's house, and she had fleurs-de-lis on her mantle that looked so lovely. I want to add them along the side of the railing all the way down."

"No."

She was startled by his directness. Mr. Peterson entered from the back.

She continued, "Of course, I'll pay whatever your hourly rate is."

"I don't sell myself by the hour. It's by the job, and this job is done."

Mrs. Peterson looked for help from her husband, who stepped confidently forward, clearly the businessman, to make the deal.

"What's the issue here?" Mr. Peterson asked with authority.

"No issue. I looked at the space. I made the sketch. You approved it. It didn't include fleurs-de-lis 'cause fleurs-de-lis doesn't belong here."

Ilana leaned back as he spoke. Cafferty had not raised his voice. He had not moved a muscle. Nevertheless, a warning pulse reached out from him and unbalanced the room.

Mr. Peterson's eyes flashed as his back went up. He explained slowly, "Mrs. Peterson has changed her mind."

"Yeah, I get that."

Mr. Peterson said, "Surely it can't be that complicated to add a few fleurs-de-lis to make the customer happy."

"Not complicated. Easy as hell, but I won't do it."

Mr. Peterson felt provoked. "Why not?"

"Because it's right as it is."

"It's not right until I like it. After all, it is my railing, my money."

Cafferty grabbed Ilana's hand and headed for the door. "Yes, it is."

Mr. Peterson responded with anger and disbelief. "We'll hire another carpenter."

"A good carpenter won't touch it. If you hire a bad one, well, like you said, it's your railing."

Mr. Peterson made a last snappish attempt to enforce the rules of the free market by adding, "We won't give you a good reference."

"Okay." He held the front door open for Ilana, and they left.

They walked toward the pickup truck. She dropped her head, laughing.

"What's so funny?"

"The stupefied look on his face."

"Yeah, lots of these people think I work for 'em."

"Don't you?"

"No. I work for the job. The materials and the space are my boss."

"You're an interesting man, Cafferty."

"Not really. Simple, just like my dogs. Don't tell me what to do, and every once in a while, give me a cookie." He opened the door for her, and she got into the truck.

The drive back was not remotely like the pleasant drive there. Stacks of unspoken words piled up between them. This was so different from the casual silence they shared earlier. This silence was the monster under the bed. She considered her actions of the last twenty-four hours and wondered if she was in some kind of shock. Perhaps she struck her head on the pavement outside O'Hollerans when Shea knocked her over. How could she have behaved like this? Betrayed like this? She found the possibility of a severe concussion consoling. Forty-five minutes later, the pickup truck stopped in front of the O'Holleran home, and still, not one word had passed between them. Finally, she turned to him.

"It's Barrett."

He looked over, confused. "What?"

"My last name. It's Barrett, Ilana Barrett."

"Oh. Okay." He nodded. Another long silence. "I'll come back to get you."

"I'm going straight home. I'm very late getting back."

"Busy, huh?"

"Yeah." A pause. Her words were oddly strained. "I heard you say you're not working today, so what will you do?"

"Sunday afternoons in the summer, I drive north up Miller Road 'til it dead-ends at the old Morris property. If you're not shy about the trespassing signs, the five-foot fence, and the rock climb, you can spend the whole afternoon swimming naked at Miller Pond."

"Skinny-dipping?" Her face lit up. "I did that once at camp. We had to sneak out of origami class to do it."

He had no idea what she'd said. "Come. Big bakin' rocks, cool water."

He leaned toward her. Her flesh responded. The ingredients of who she was and who she should have been, between how she'd been raised and what she was made of, between what she believed and what she'd learned, were bewildering. Her body wanted the feel of his hands, and her mind screamed to get out, get out, get out. And beyond it all, she stood on the emotional cliff of revealing herself to her mother.

"I've got to get back. I'm negotiating a deal for a new production of *Les Troyans*." She looked away. Neither of them knew how to end this. It felt unnatural. "When I finish here, I'll get an Uber to the train."

"Oh. I get it." He looked straight ahead. Another long silence, then sharply, he said, "I'm not opening your car door."

"Right."

She opened her own door. She turned and swung out her legs. She shut the door gently and walked toward the house. Anxiety was a solid fist in her stomach. She walked. Step. Step. She tossed her hair, feigning a casual movement. She stretched her neck, attempting to soften the grip of his eyes on her back.

Inside the truck, Cafferty sat rigidly, watching her leave. He gave her time to change her mind. He waited for her to come to her senses, dash back to the truck, and tell him when to pick her up. He knew she would. Last night spoke for itself.

But Ilana didn't turn back, and the furious screech of his tires as he shot away traveled all the way up her spine as she approached the porch door.

Fiona glanced out her kitchen window and waved Ilana in. Once inside, she poured them both some coffee. Fiona wore a flamboyant, striped, skintight summer dress, vacuum-sealed over every curve. For Ilana, it sparked a pickle jar memory from long ago.

When she was nine years old, she twisted and pressed and tapped and pulled until her hand was red and hurting, but the cap to the glass pickle jar wouldn't budge. Her mother, who had been watching, crossed to the utensil drawer and said, "You know, Ilana, some things in life respond to finesse, not power." Her mom pulled out a teaspoon. She slipped the tiny tip of it under the lip of the lid and pressed down lightly, instantly releasing the seal, and the lid opened with magical ease. Ilana looked at her red hands and never forgot that lesson. She wondered if a spoon was needed to get Fiona out of that dress, and she smiled to herself.

Ilana couldn't articulate why she felt compelled to have this conversation with Fiona; she just did. She hadn't intended to, or she wasn't aware that she had, and for a moment, she wondered if this was something her unconscious had always intended and if it had tricked her into coming here. Had it clouded her awareness and lay in wait like an enemy inside her own brain to gain control? It was unnerving to think of her own mind that way, as something that might plot against her and *be her* at the same time. It was her, wasn't it? She had never consciously intended to have this conversation, but once she saw Fiona, something she couldn't name inexorably drove her toward it. The wondering inside of her was reaching a perilous pitch. For now, though, she had to focus and not ponder. How was it that she could put away things to think about later to focus on something else? Where do those things go? Was there a temporary holding tank in her mind?

Alone in the kitchen with Fiona, who was busily gabbing about the Butler brothers and the tossing incident, Ilana studied her. Away from the craziness of last night's dinner and its aftermath, she discerned a thread of commonality between them, a thread so thin and so tenuous that she was unsure whether it was genuine or imagined. She asked herself as they chatted if she felt some connection to this house, to this town, or to this woman.

Fiona handed her the sugar. "Missy, no offense, but I think that outfit's done for."

Ilana recoiled self-consciously. "Oh, yes. I missed my train last night, and I found myself sort of stranded."

Fiona left it at that, but her sly grin made it clear that she knew exactly where Ilana slept. Ilana guessed everyone knew where she slept and flushed red with embarrassment. She gathered up the leftover shards of her self-respect and spread them out around her like a broken shield. She straightened her posture. She crossed her ankles.

I am not screwing up today. In control. Yesterday was yesterday.

"Want to borrow something of mine?" Fiona asked hopefully. "I've got a ton of things that'll fit you. Our figures aren't that much different. You just can't see yours. You've got this one-tone, baggy, bland thing going on." Fiona, realizing how that sounded, said, "Not that it isn't great on you. It is. It's . . . ah . . . dull. To me, anyway. You know what I mean? I mean, why not show it?"

"Yes, you do have a great figure, Fiona."

"Exactly, and no need to leave anything to the imagination, right? Imagination should be saved for women with bad figures where it can do some good."

Ilana imagined herself returning home in one of Fiona's outfits. It might be worth doing to see the shock on Adam's face.

Adam! Oh. Oh, shit.

Ilana's heart sunk miserably. Unforgivable betrayal. Her blood pressure fell so low that she wished she could put her head down on the red Formica table. Actually, she'd like to put her head through the table. How will she ever deal with telling Adam the truth? She will tell the truth, of course; she will not lie—she hasn't sunk that low.

Fiona continued, "I have a lavender rayon two-piece with a mini-skirt that would look snappy on you. And sweetie, you might have better luck finding a full-time man if, you know, you advertised a little."

Just when Ilana couldn't have imagined smiling, Fiona made her grin. "Thank you, Fiona. I'll remember that next time I go shopping, but for now, I'm fine, really."

Fiona raised her *left* eyebrow as if to say some people can't be helped.

Ilana had not crafted the words that would come next. The plan had been to say nothing, but then nothing had gone as planned. Her undeniable yearning was more powerful than her common sense.

Fiona gabbed leisurely, "Shea always sleeps in on Sundays. It's because he writes all Saturday night. I give him shit, but he really does write. I don't know what it says 'cause he never shows anyone, but I can tell you he does it."

"I really know very little about poetry, but I'll bet he's good at it. There is something expressive and dramatic about him."

"Yeah. He's all that, all right. Willow isn't around either. She scours the garage sales on weekend mornings. Bit of a squirrel the way she collects things."

"Yes, but charming."

"You think?" Fiona asked happily.

"I do."

"Yeah, I guess. So, now that you got up my curiosity, what did you want to talk to me about?" Fiona looked at her expectantly. Ilana's stomach squirmed.

With a professional air, Ilana said, "Fiona, it is a sensitive matter, which is why I wanted us to be alone."

"I'll bet I know." Fiona's eyes flashed at Ilana.

Ilana cocked her head and looked into the woman before her. "You do?"

Do you know me?

She felt an assembling sensation. Ilana was suddenly sure that a poignant and physical reconciliation with her biological mother was going to fill her with sweetness. She relaxed into a flood of well-being.

"Yup." Fiona looked at her impishly. "I gotta pretty good guess. I'll bet old Cousin Neil, who lived in Manhattan, is chewin' dirt and left me rich in his will. That bastard always had a shine for me."

Ilana stared. Fiona had no clue. She had no idea. It's not obvious. Ilana took a long, staccato breath in. It was not too late to stop. The intensity of the last twenty-four hours was becoming unendurable, and exhaustion was setting in.

Do I do this?

"No, Fiona. It's not about Cousin Neil."

"Did anyone die and leave me rollin' in it?"

"Not that I am aware."

Do I do this?

"Damn. I already had that money spent. I saw a fantabulous light blue bodysuit." Fiona leaned back against the sink, readying for the tale. "Okay. So, out with it, then. What's your story?"

Ilana uncrossed her ankles and put both feet firmly on the floor. Part of her could not believe she was doing this, and another part was driving for truth, driving to open this chapter of her life, driving.

Ilana began. "My story is sort of your story."

"I suck at riddles, hon."

"Right." Ilana hesitated, knowing that her next words would exact a fundamental change in both of their lives and also knowing that words cannot be unsaid. She encouraged herself. *It'll be fine. After all, this is a woman who invited the gun-toting Boney to her dinner table, a woman who disapproves of throwing things away, a woman who lives in a cozy community of extended family.* She knew that this woman would open up her arms to her. When Ilana's mother was alive, this moment was not even a thought. Now, here, she was living it, starring in the climax of her own personal opera. Ilana would not have been surprised at all to hear the sudden rise of the string section from the other room.

"C'mon honey, out with it," Fiona said.

"Fiona, thirty years ago, you gave up your newborn girl for adoption."

Fiona froze as solid as the little rock she buried in the church cemetery.

"I am, or rather that was . . ." Ilana swallowed. She cleared her throat. She took a breath, and with warm eyes, she continued, "Me."

Alarm soaked Fiona, wrapping around her like a drenched and suffocating blanket. Her arms lay heavily by her sides. She remained very still, fearing one slight movement would knock down her whole life. Looking into the eyes of this grown woman before her, the memory of the one event Fiona had fought a vicious and bloody battle to suppress burst through. No words came to her. Nothing came to her. Fiona stood up and stepped back with terror in her eyes.

Ilana saw her alarm and quickly explained, "Fiona, I was adopted by a wonderful older couple who gave me all the love in the world. I have been very happy, loved, and well cared for."

Fiona whispered, "Sweet Jesus."

Panic began to build inside Ilana because she could not read Fiona's reaction except to note that it was extraordinarily severe and that her arms were definitely not open.

Ilana pressed, "I have found myself curious recently, after the death of my mother mostly, so I followed the paper trail to find you and . . ." Her words trailed off.

Fiona reached back for the countertop, needing something solid. The past struck her with blunt force. She could have been no more distressed if Ilana had risen from the dead and stood in front of her as a skeleton dripping dirt.

Ilana saw Fiona tremble and added, "I'm sorry you're upset. I know this is a surprise. I don't mean to upset you. I—"

Fiona interrupted, "Go." It came out like a choked plea.

Ilana stood and said quickly, "I don't want to disrupt your life in any way. I mean no harm. Please talk to me. I only want to know you so that you can know me."

"Quickly. Go."

They stood for a moment, staring at each other.

"Fiona, please, what were the circumstances of my birth?"

"Grief and pain were the circumstances. Go!"

Ilana felt slapped. The intensity escalated, and their voices dropped even lower. "What do you mean *grief*?"

Fiona trembled outwardly. And then, Ilana's trembling began.

"Is Shea my father?"

"Course not." A quiet wail escaped from her. "He can't know! Oh, Jesus . . ."

"Were you raped?" Ilana asked. "Is that why?" Her throat was closing.

Fiona shut her eyes tightly, looking like she wanted nothing more than to open them and find herself alone in her kitchen.

Ilana's voice cracked. "Fiona? Are you okay?"

Fiona spoke with near violence. "Before it's too late, please get out!"

"Too late?"

Shea bounded into the kitchen in his crumbled bathrobe with a lit cigar. Fiona spun away from them. She shook as she turned on the sink faucet and picked up a dish.

"Ah." Shea began, "The morning stew of kitchen voices. Missy, here for breakfast? Glutton for punishment, 'ey?" The room was charged. Shea searched Ilana's face and Fiona's back. "What?" Shea asked.

Ilana raised her eyes to Fiona, who threw her a beseeching glance rife with sheer desperation. Ilana summoned her strength, and with remarkable poise, she responded to Shea calmly. "Actually, I came to say goodbye, Shea, and thank you for dinner. I have a train to catch. I need to get back to my home."

"But we've hardly had time to beat our poetic gums."

"I wanted to leave my card in case either of you ever want to call, for any reason." She fell into formality, her familiar cloak.

"Wanna go to the opera, Fi? What do you think?"

Without turning from the sink, she responded, "Nope."

"If you change your mind, please, as my guests, any time." Ilana held herself firmly, although her voice was higher and tighter than usual. There was nothing normal about Ilana at this moment, and her self-control was awe-inspiring.

"We could bring Nellie," Shea said as he put the card in the kitchen drawer. "She's a musician."

"I'll look forward to it. It was very nice meeting you both." She sculpted the controlled smile to perfection. She turned smoothly. The porch screen door was a football field away. She crossed it. Swung it open. Stepped through. The door banged shut behind her with everything left unsaid.

Shea eyed Fiona. "Something wrong here?"

"Yeah, something's wrong," Fiona said with too much irritation. "Human beings aren't supposed to lie on their ass all day, Shea O'Holleran. Morning's half over."

He put up his feet. "God said it's a day of rest, and since he and I have had words lately, I figure it's the least I can do."

He picked up the newspaper, and she crossed with feigned detachment to the window. She stared out at the young woman, walking away quickly. She noticed the color of her hair, the shape of her body, and wondered how she could not have known immediately. How could she not have seen it the second she entered the pub? It was clear. There she was. Her daughter. Her baby. Fiona watched until Ilana was small in her view, she watched until she turned the corner, and she continued to watch for a very long time after she was gone.

On the street, Ilana stumbled away from the O'Holleran home, blinded by the flood on her face and thrashed by her raging thoughts. She was in pieces. In twenty-four hours, she had shattered her life. She cried with her face in her hands during the Uber ride to the train station. In her seat on the train, hunched over, she put her head on her knees and cried through each minute of the ride home. Her thoughts were punishing and unrelenting. Sobbing, she walked down Perry Street toward her apartment. She gasped as she lugged herself up the stone steps to her apartment building. She was still crying as she shoved her burden through her front door, heaving her body inside. Unable to lift her limbs, she leaned hard against the door; it slammed shut, and she threw the deadbolt. Her back slid down the door to the floor of her apartment. She cried for who she was at that moment, for the mother who was horrified by the sight of her, for succumbing to a passion with a complete stranger in a world that was not hers. She cried from guilt and from shame. She cried for Adam. She cried for the loss of her own mother, yes, mostly for the loss of her sweet mom. She cried so hard and so enduringly that the only possible end was blank limpness. Everything she had hoped to settle had been upset; now there were more questions than answers. Now that hungry, wondering thing inside of her that had struggled to be fed had achieved escape velocity. Something had been unleashed.

KNOCK! The hardwood flooring was cold and solid against her cheek. She lay in a fugue state inside her front door. The knock repeated a little louder. She pulled herself upright and wondered, *How long have I?* The knock was loud and aggressive.

"Ilana!"

Dazed, she jumped up, turned the deadbolt, and swung open the door. Adam stood on the other side. His mouth dropped open. He didn't know whether to reach in and hold her or to step the hell back. Ilana stood in observable chaos: her hair was knotted, one leg of her linen pantsuit was hiked up over her knee, her entire outfit was wrinkled and dirty, her eyes were bloodshot, and her cheek was red and dented from where it had been on the floor.

"Jesus Christ, Ilana." Adam stepped in, closed the door, and carefully reached out to her. "What happened?"

"I . . ."

"Were you mugged?"

"No."

"You should sit."

"No." She looked down.

"Did this happen in Albany?"

"I'm . . . ah . . ."

"Ilana, do you need a doctor?"

"No. Adam, I'm . . . I'm . . ."

Sorry!

"What can I do?"

"Nothing." And overcome by sadness, she said, "You can do nothing. You have done nothing."

"Are you hurt? You were supposed to be home last night. I called, but your cell phone was off. What happened to you?"

The last twenty-four hours ran through Ilana's mind with more throbbing clarity than she cared for. "I'm sorry you were worried. Forgive me, Adam, please. I need some time alone."

"I won't leave you like this," he said.

"It's all been overwhelming."

"Come over to the sofa. Come sit down."

"No."

Don't be nice.

She cringed at his kindness. "Let me get cleaned up and a good night's sleep."

Adam shuffled from foot to foot, subconsciously trying to throw off-balance the huge, unmanageable creature that had suddenly stood up between them. Something perilous lingered in her tone.

Ilana shuddered. She could not possibly have Adam there. She wasn't ready. She needed to think. Time. Time to think it through and to even know what she thought.

"I don't feel right leaving you, Ilana. You clearly need me."

"Please."

He'd never seen her eyes look like this, like molasses, syrupy and impenetrable. His course of action was unclear. He thought she looked too vulnerable to be left alone, but he also thought she was too vulnerable to argue with. He knew he should respect her wishes.

"Please," she entreated.

He leaned in gently and kissed her dented cheek. "All right. I will be on my cell all night. I can be here in nine minutes. Call." She managed a nod. "Are you sure?" She nodded again.

"But you don't look . . ."

"Thank you," she interrupted with finality.

They stood for a moment. He backed up to the door. She opened it. He stepped out. Gently, she closed it. He heard her throw the deadbolt. He waited, shifting uneasily from foot to foot. Then, he walked away, and he kept walking.

Initially, Adam walked with great speed as though he was trying to outrun something. He walked all the way to Midtown. He felt threatened. His body processed the menace, pumped cortisol, and released adrenaline. He stopped abruptly and stood on the bow of Times Square, looking out at the multicolored turmoil. The sidewalk beneath his feet felt uneven. The neon looked blurry. Was that from the day's heat? Or were his eyes wet? Air moved around him. It was the breeze from people moving on, all people with somewhere to go; he had nowhere to go. Bustling, angling, shifting, stepping, people everywhere. He was the only still thing in all of Times Square. He saw Ilana's distress. He had to calmly examine it. He never feared change. Change had been good to him. No one had changed as profoundly as he had. When he was an eighth grader, his milky blue eyes were hidden behind thick glasses; his teeth housed an entire Erector set of reconstructive metal; his complexion was ravaged, and he carried an extra thirty pounds. His appearance shook his confidence, and his grades were maddeningly average. Morphing into the dreamy homecoming king of five years later took effort and perseverance. Since then, he had always played life as though he was born to the privilege of his good looks and success, but it was a play, an act at which he excelled, but an act nonetheless. Whenever Adam looked into the mirror above his sink, that fat, ugly, average boy always looked back. He had wanted so desperately to be someone else that he became someone else. To him, it was a tribute to his capabilities and not the natural development of his body, and it was because he knew for certain that he was that ugly loser from middle school that he had been cautious about asking too much from the beautiful woman he loved. He thought he was the only imposter in the world. The only one who knew he was disguised. He didn't recognize the masks all around him.

His eyes skulked around Times Square. He didn't know what he was looking for or looking at. And then, he saw it. It was reflected in the glass of a deli window. The mirage came into focus. He saw a grand, grassy lawn. He saw Thanksgiving dinners, school performances, and pony rides with their kids. He saw clearly that Ilana was the woman he would grow old with, and he knew that it was settled, that at least this one thing was solid. This was his future, their future. In a rapturous instant of wholeness, he realized what he had not known before, and he saw clearly for the first time what Ilana had been missing from him. It was this, this sense of ultimate personal abduction. The realization of their inevitableness freed him. What an intense relief is such certainty. Joy. Blissful, he laughed out loud. He knew that he was not the only man to have found ecstasy unexpectedly in Times Square, but he was the most elated. He knew exactly what he had to do. It all made sense. When he stepped off the curb, he was committed and determined. He considered running back to her apartment to take her with seductive force into his arms and let her know it would all be right. He could tell her they were destined for a whole and romantic life together, to let her know that he fully understood that he'd been holding back. Now he understood the nature and the need for absolute surrender. He finally understood! He was so close to turning around, so close to running back to her—but he didn't. He would respect her wish for privacy because passion has its place and time. He did not know, he could not know, that this was the final evidence that he would never understand.

Ilana picked up the phone right after Adam left and called William. She needed his therapeutic friendship. Thirty minutes later, he rang the bell. She let herself back up off the floor and opened the door.

William, who spent the majority of his waking hours engrossed in the dramatic stories of others, listened to her with trained focus. He said nothing. She left out nothing. An hour and one bottle of cabernet later, she finished recounting every moment after arriving at the pub. William considered carefully his first response. He looked intently at her, and he gathered his wits. He needed to say the right thing. She was tremulous, edgy, and waiting for the punitive judgment. She knew what she deserved. She cupped the wine glass. Her hand shook.

"So," he said pointedly, "where to start."

"Yeah." She looked away and caught sight of the dead ficus.

"First," William began, "this Cafferty creature, the carpenter with the rough hands."

Weakly, she said, "Yeah?"

"Did he have a smooth ass, or was it hairy?"

"William!" It lifted the weight off her just a bit. It was exactly the right thing. She sighed with a sad grin.

"Hey, I'm trying to get the facts."

"You cannot minimize this. The betrayal."

"I'm not. But there is a lot to unpack here, and I want to stress that we will unpack it, and it is also not the end of your world."

"Of course it is."

Her fingers looked frail, and he took her hands in his. They sat in quiet companionship. Ilana knew for all the gifts that life had given her—her privileged education, her quiet good looks, her sense of practicality—it was the gift of this friendship that she most treasured.

"Okay. So, this attraction was magnetic and purely physical," he confirmed.

"My body was out for itself. It was like an independent thing."

"We're still animals, Ilana. We react viscerally to scent and touch the same as other mammals. Our only outstanding difference is our level of self-control—or even self-denial." He split what was left of the wine between their two glasses.

Ilana leaned back into the cushions of her sofa. The blinds were tightly shut, and one lamp shone. In the corner, the dead ficus dropped a dead leaf onto the floor, and she heard it. Everything looked new and unused. The room smelled of nothing at all.

Does anyone real live here?

Ilana did not have a casual relationship with ambiguity, for her ambiguity was a transient state that lasted for one second before total clarity, but total clarity always came. Knowing the right thing was only a matter of thinking it through. Why couldn't she think this through? She was either completely blank or bombarded with thought.

William asked, "What's your guess why Fiona became so upset?"

"I'm not her husband's child?"

"That may be why."

"Shea has quite a short fuse. He was a little scary. But I feel like it's more than that. It has got to be. Here is a woman who doesn't blink when her mother stops breathing, who has no trouble dealing with dwarf-tossing or a man shooting at the Messiah, but one look at me, and she's unglued?"

"Unglued. Huh. I admit that I've always found you deeply disturbing." He toasted her and finished his wine. Ilana thought of how many nights they had spent like this when William lost David and when her mom was dying.

"William, these folks are like no one we've ever known and still oddly familiar to me. I don't know if I felt connected to it because I knew or because I actually am connected to it."

"I don't believe that if you were stranded and wound up in that same bar knowing nothing, you would feel any relationship to these people at all. It's because you went in there knowing and looking for it."

"Maybe." She looked around her apartment.

William said, "Name one thing that was familiar."

"Okay. And I'll only admit this to you. If you tell anyone, I'll deny it, call you a liar, and haunt you when I'm dead."

"Your honesty is your most endearing quality."

"I really liked the Irish music that Nellie was banging out on the old piano."

"Yeah." He nodded gravely. "I'd deny that too."

"Do you think music is one of those primal things that come from centuries of your ancestors listening to the same sounds? And that it leaves some kind of chemical imprint, and so you're attracted to the musical sounds of your heritage?"

"What other possible explanation could there be for bagpipes?" he asked.

She kicked off her shoes and pulled her tired legs up under her on the sofa. "I felt I knew these songs, but how could I? Could there be a genetic memory for music? How else is Mozart possible, and then what else? What else are we drawn to unconsciously?"

"Ilana, stop driving yourself crazy. I've got no room for you on my schedule. Surely you saw how little you actually share with these people in Albany. And, surely, you can't believe that you are being totally controlled on an unconscious level and your decision-making is not your own."

"There are diseases that are genetic. Right?"

"Right."

"So, they are in us when we are born."

"And?"

"And they are there waiting, and then, they emerge at some preprogrammed time and kill us."

"Yeah?"

She continued passionately, "Our own end may be imprinted

in every single cell of our body, but we go along with no conscious suspicion at all. What could prove our minds to be more clueless about who we are than working and planning for a future that every single cell in our body knows isn't coming?"

"Knows? Come on. Are you suggesting awareness on the cellular level? Are we really talking about a form of panpsychism here?"

"Awareness is cellular. It's brain cells and sensory receptors. It's a material thing. I don't know if rocks and trees have some kind of consciousness, but the brain is made of neurons and cells that create knowing. Some of those things we are aware of all the time, like the temperature in a room, our name, or where we're sitting. Some things we are aware of only if we try, like a childhood phone number or long division. And other things we are always unaware of, like what our liver is doing or the word I'm going to say next. William, we don't even know what we're going to say until we've said it. I hear it when you hear it. Surprise, surprise."

"Ilana, it's not all programming. You may have a genetic disease, but you are a lot more likely to eat too many Big Macs and die of a heart attack, catch the flu, or step out in front of a bus. Do you believe your genes made you step out in front of the bus? Were you programmed to step off that curb?"

"No, but what if kids watch their dad get hit by a bus, and they're traumatized? Is that chemically marked inside of them in some way? And do they then bear children who find themselves inexplicably afraid of buses? They walk around bus stops. They have bus nightmares."

"Bus nightmares?" He smiled at her and tried to lower the pitch. He could see her spinning. "Ilana, you aren't really saying that your life belongs in a barroom in Albany with a day laborer who never thinks past the present moment."

Her argument collapsed along with her energy and face. "No. No, no." She looked away and answered with a lost softness, "I don't think that." Her eyes filled with water she did not think she had. Fatigue and sorrow leveled off at the rim of her. She didn't want it to spill over into William's lap, but it was unavoidable. Her seeping melancholy was as impossible to pile neatly inside of her as grains of sand. She was miserable, miserable and confused, and miserable because she was confused.

William handed her a tissue to wipe the reddened edge of her nose, dissatisfied that this was all he could do. He squeezed her hands and asked in a troubled whisper, "Ilana, tell me. Why are you so unhappy? Please tell me. What is it? What is going on?"

Her voice was raspy. "I've worked so hard to get where I am, to be who I am."

He teared up, too, hurting with her. "I know."

She pleaded, bewildered and spent, "I'm successful."

"You are."

"I've done all the right things. I went to the right schools, I got all the good grades, I studied, and I worked and got a great job."

"Yes, Ilana, you have. All good."

"I am thirty years old and—" The only tear left slid down the side of her face. She paused.

"What?" he asked with gentle affection.

With her eyes lost and wide, she said, "Every move I've made was biased, and every choice I've made has limited my choices, and it's all now so narrow. I feel like I woke up inside of a tunnel that I didn't know I'd been walking through for decades."

He hugged her for a long time and then left her asleep on the sofa.

The next morning, she went to work because work was waiting. She rolled out of bed, showered, dressed, and left exactly as she always did, without thinking. She looked forward to the reliable distraction of her job. She thought it was best. She sat in the opera rehearsal, exhausted. The mayhem of the weekend had accomplished what countless nights of round-the-clock meetings and rehearsals could not: physical dominance. It was an effort to raise her arm, to use the keyboard, or to answer the phone. She hid all of that.

Several years ago, the scenic department constructed a wide board for Ilana. It laid across the tops of the armrests and the chair backs in the theatre, creating a mobile desk for her. On it, she positioned her laptop, calculator, little laser light, and cell phone. She could return emails and rework the budget as she monitored the rehearsal (and kept an eye on the jokers in the brass section). She was so unfamiliar with exhaustion that she feared she was coming down with something. She never coddled illness, and it frustrated her to be sick. Her father had always recommended natural remedies first, so she started chewing garlic, which may or may not be valuable but had the consequence of making Ilana smell like gnocchi in a room full of singing Italians. The tenor asked three times for a lunch break, and it was only 10:30 a.m. She relied on her personal power to get through the morning, and she had to admit that being in her usual routine was calming.

Off to the side of the rehearsal hall, Glen Sammis entered, escorting the formidable Isabella Wharton on a private backstage tour. Glen started at the opera as the director of development two years prior, making him the chief fundraiser for the company. He was an unnaturally colored male: his face too tan, his teeth too white, and his hair highlighted like a zebra. Glen was a consummate consumer in a city willing to accommodate. He spent on dinner what others spent on rent. He considered himself a nihilist because he wore last year's Zanella suit and didn't think most people were concerned enough about their shoe leather. He craved only what he did not have. Ilana was careful with his ego because he was responsible for bringing in the money, and she knew better than anyone else how critical donors were to the financial viability of the company. Nevertheless, standing near Glen always gave her an itch on the back of her neck as though the legs of some insect were crawling there. He reminded her of a praying mantis.

Ilana had read the Isabella Wharton bio that Glen had circulated last week. It was a subtle brag, the only subtle thing about him. Now, here they were in the rehearsal hall. Ilana made sure to keep her head down. The last thing she needed was a fake hello with Glen, although a stolen glance did reveal that seventy-five-year-old Mrs. Wharton was uncommonly beautiful.

Ilana could hear Glen turning it on, and she noted it was a little gross for him to be flirting with this elegant elderly woman. He was not nearly as suave as he believed he was. Glen was Glen's greatest fan. Ilana wished they were standing further away because she could hear him emphasizing the architecture of the stage, and she needed to focus. Out of the corner of her eye, she saw Mrs. Wharton. She had seen her at other events, but this was the first time Ilana really noticed her, which felt different. Their eyes met very briefly. Isabella raised her white soft palm to silence Glen. Her outstretched arm had a floating quality. She looked lithe, deboned. Glen stopped talking. She spoke very slowly, massaging every syllable.

"Who is that?" Mrs. Wharton asked Glen.

"Our production manager, Ilana Barrett. Brilliant at her job. Runs the opera like a—"

"I will lunch with her tomorrow."

Glen's smile had a tight, botoxed look that complimented the alarm in his eyes. This was a very bad idea. Ilana wasn't politic. She was not interested in the solicitous care and feeding of philanthropists. That was his job, and Ilana was extremely clear on that when she hired him.

"As luck would have it," he said, winking at Mrs. Wharton, "I'm available for lunch tomorrow. Ilana isn't actually in the development department and—"

"You mean other departments don't get lunch?"

Glen's face went blank. Had she turned him down for Ilana? Really?

A quiet force emanated from Mrs. Wharton as she smiled. It was the expression of someone certain they would always get exactly what they wanted because that is what her kind of money bought, exactly what she wanted.

Glen ran his fingers through his coifed hair. He reached taller with his chest. "I was thinking, you and me, I actually have a contact at a new members-only restaurant on the Upper West. I could get us in tomorrow."

"Ilana, you said?"

"Yes, Barrett. It's only that we're in rehearsal, and she is responsible for so much. Ilana doesn't usually take lunch."

"Still." Isabella Wharton let her eyes rest on him. She did not retreat. The "still" hung in the air between them until the discomfort was too much for him.

"Because it's you, though," he responded, "I'm sure she'd be delighted. Exceptional people are the exception, you know. Now, Ilana is one of those people really invested in her job, though I've never heard her talk about anything else, so I don't think, you know, conversation-wise, it's going to be all that scintillating," he said cheerfully. Her imperial expression did not change.

"A risk I'm willing to take." She turned her eyes back to Ilana and watched her jump up from her seat and walk to the stage. There, she pulled aside the first violinist, and they spoke privately.

Isabella Wharton had an overly sensitive instinct for turbulence in others. She watched and sensed the turmoil beneath Ilana's façade, that hint of a hazardous edge an inch away from the surface. And finally, she thought, someone not to type. Finally, someone interesting.

Isabella turned to Glen. "I'll send my car for her at noon."

"Oh-kay. Yes. Uh-huh, sounds good."

Half an hour after Isabella Wharton had been escorted to her limo, Glen intercepted Ilana in the hallway and got what he'd anticipated.

"Glen, I don't do donors. I don't even do lunch. That's your job."

"It's Isabella Wharton. She has agreed to underwrite a new production. And I don't have to remind you that her participation in our annual fund and in the gala is mission critical."

Ilana detested small talk and the obsequiousness that was required when taking out donors. It made her feel embarrassed and inauthentic, and she already had more feelings than she could safely control.

"I'm not the right person for this."

"I know. But you are who she wants."

"Why me?"

"Believe me, I do not know," Glen said with honest, derisive bewilderment. Ilana bit the sides of her grin. She looked at the floor as she considered if there was a way out of this. Glen continued, "Hey, look, I tried to talk her out of it. The last thing I want is you or anyone messing with my donor. I've been angling a meeting with her for a month. I know the old lady likes me, and so I can't figure out what she's thinking. I'm much better conversationally than you are. I mean, maybe I've said too much here, but it's not like you're into this kind of thing, and let's face it, Ilana, some people find you a little impatient." She looked at him, raising her left eyebrow. "Okay, okay, so maybe I didn't mean to say impatient. I don't know where that word came from. You know how a word comes out that you didn't mean?"

"Yes. I do."

"Good. Okay, then, do this. One lunch, and I'll take over."

"Fine."

He turned, stopped, and turned back. "Did you change your hair?"

"No."

"New suit?"

"No."

He studied her. "Something's different."

I'll bet.

Her phone vibrated. She reached for it. Into the phone, she said, "Hold on." She looked at Glen, silently asking if there was anything else. He thanked her and strutted away.

It was Adam on the phone. They'd had a couple of quick phone calls during the day where she had assured him that she was better and would explain things later. She did not think she was better, and the thought of explaining things was crippling.

"Hi," she chirped.

"That sounds falsely cheerful."

"Sorry, brass section's playing poker."

"Who's winning?" he asked.

"Unclear, but it seems the trumpeter bet the chandelier in the lobby, which I had to remind him he does not own."

"I wanted to remind you we're meeting at the Taj tonight. We have dinner with Courtney and Chris."

"Oh, no, not tonight. No. No. I don't really like them, Adam." She heard Cafferty's voice: *I don't set my alarm, and I don't eat with people I don't like.*

"Chris is my editor. This relationship matters. I need you."

"But they're so cold. It's like having dinner in a meat locker."

"No one expects a hug."

"Adam, I know you agree they're pretentious in that uniquely uptown way."

"They're a bit affected. Still, they've always been nice to us. We canceled on them last time. You can't really have anything against them."

"Her hair doesn't move."

"What? Her hair?"

Realizing how trivial it sounded, she added quickly, "Maybe it sounds silly."

"Maybe?"

"Okay, it *is* silly."

"Yes."

"But it's a solid piece. It's distracting. Sometimes, when she's talking, I can't concentrate on anything else. How on earth do you walk crosstown, with the wind in this city, without your hair moving? What's it made of?"

"Ilana, tell me you're not serious."

"Okay, that's really not it."

"What, then?"

"They're sour."

"Sour?"

"They use cynicism as an intellectual trench coat so they don't have to justify their opinions as they roll their eyes."

"Okay. Okay. I promise we'll eat quickly and get out of there. I can't wait to see you. I want to hear what happened in Albany, and I have something very important to tell you. I had an amazing insight, like a mirage, last night in Times Square."

Self-loathing was a sharp-nailed grip squeezing her throat, making it hard to swallow or find the breath for her words. The last thing she thought she could handle was a social dinner with people she barely knew. Or, then again, maybe it was all she could do.

"Adam, have you ever noticed how all of our friends look alike?" she asked him.

"No, they don't."

"Yes. They dress the same. They talk about the same things. They all went to the same five or six graduate schools."

"Well, Ilana, those are the people we like, I guess. People are attracted to people with the same interests."

"I don't know if that is true. Or if it is true . . . if it's good."

Too excited to focus, Adam continued with his own agenda, "Honey, I really can't wait to see you. I have something special planned. See you at the Taj.

No, not special! Please don't do special. I don't deserve special.

The Taj was a cramped Indian restaurant in Midtown, where the chairs touched each other and the dal bahar would melt your socks. Most people were okay with tiny, packed restaurants again, and Taj was busy. The Mumbai chef liked to punish American sophisticates who smugly said, "Spice it up." The smell of cumin, cardamon, and cinnamon permeated. The waiters had to slip sideways through constantly morphing open spaces. Arriving patrons had to physically negotiate themselves into their angular seats. It was never a straight shot to the table, and oversized people learned to dine elsewhere. Certain tables, for no discernable reason, had acquired a cachet. Adam ranked one of these. As his profile as a public intellectual was growing, these little perks were volunteering. When he entered, the maître d' called him by name.

Courtney, Chris, and Adam were already seated when Ilana arrived and maneuvered her body to the table. It was a testament to the supremacy of her political self that she could manage to smile pleasantly and exchange hellos.

Adam stood. "Here she is."

"Hi."

Adam reached over to hold out her chair. She caught his eye, saw his familiar expression, and disintegrated into a spec on the chair—a speck of lint, of dander, or whatever was more worthless than dander. She sat primly and sank behind her social shield. She didn't hold Adam's eyes. She didn't want to know what he was feeling or thinking.

Adam was relieved to see how composed she looked. He relaxed. He was sure now that she was fine. Whatever had happened in Albany, she had risen above. He had his own secret this night, and he could barely keep his smile in check. This was going to be the most important night of their lives. It was all planned this time. No silly spontaneity. The champagne was on his dining room table, chilling in a silver bucket on a lace tablecloth. He had covered his apartment in flowers: one hundred white roses. He would sweep her back there and into the world of beauty, safety, and lifelong affection that he was constructing for them. He was secure in the knowledge of their future. Moving his leg, he felt the small ring box in his pants pocket. He knew that his unconscious mind, as the manager of his love and life, had chosen Ilana and had chosen well. He was comforted to know he could trust himself this way and decided right then to write an article focused on this, on how loving someone is the most important decision—the least conscious choice—we make. We may or may not decide to marry or live with someone (the jury's still out on that), but the actual loving, the falling in love, the feeling of being in love, no one commands it, no one controls it; that is clear to everyone. Maybe that's the easy door to getting the public to reconsider the blurry line between conscious and unconscious decision-making. Everyone has experienced that. *Yes*, he thought, *I'll write that one. That will speak to the general public since it affects everyone. They get that; they have felt it. It could probably get placed in* The New Yorker *or* Atlantic, *outside the science journals.*

Chris said, "We ordered the usual."

"Of course," Ilana said. "Although I do have a craving for meatloaf."

"Probably the Albany influence." Adam reached for her hand.

Chris looked interested. "Business trip?"

"No."

Adam teased her fondly, "She needed a weekend away, and really, what is more away than Albany?"

Ilana responded, "Actually, Albany is very nice. I didn't get to see as much of the city as I would have liked, but perhaps another time." *Perhaps another time*, the words echoed. Was that only inside of her? Or did it echo with resonant throbbing throughout the room as it seemed to her?

Courtney smirked sarcastically. "You mean, having been there, you'd actually go back?"

"There is life outside of Manhattan, Courtney," Ilana said.

"Sure, it's just not worth living." Courtney tossed her head back with a laugh. Her hair did not move. It looked lacquered.

Adam saw and threw Ilana a private smile. He loved that they had private jokes. He said, "Albany has some fascinating buildings. We forget it's almost four hundred years old. The State Capitol and the City Hall are meticulous examples of Romanesque architecture."

Ilana listened to him talk. He was so smart and interesting. He was not boring, not at all.

He continued, "They have a few great old hotels restored with spectacular detail."

Chris turned to Ilana and asked, "Where did you stay?" All three of them looked at her expectantly. She went blank. Blood rushed to her face.

"Ilana?" Adam prompted her. "Where did you stay?"

Her mouth opened involuntarily, and words came out. "Different from Manhattan buildings, though. Have you ever noticed that you can't look out in Manhattan, only up? All of the buildings are attached and tall, and you can't see out, only up, and mostly straight up."

"It's their function to block out the bridge-and-tunnel people," Courtney replied. Everyone laughed. Ilana didn't laugh. Such an innocent, simple question—"Where did you stay"—could have been a disaster. She knew she was not prepared for this dinner, and her antipathy for Courtney was growing.

The waiter arrived with a bottle of wine, and Ilana lightly touched the rim of her glass, subtly indicating she would pass. She drained her glass of water and felt like she might sell what was left of her soul for an aspirin.

Chris said, "I've lived my whole life in New York, and I've never been to Albany. Although I think you had a trial there, Courtney, didn't you?"

"A few years ago," she replied. "Interesting case, double homicide, nice family, and the uncle did it. You never would have guessed. And, yes, Adam, he chose to do it, and, yes, Adam, he was completely responsible, and yes, Adam, he could have chosen to do otherwise."

Chris turned to Adam. "Courtney watched your panel discussion on ethics, the law, and the brain."

"I'm expecting some blowback from the legal community."

"Oh? You think?" Courtney added sarcastically. "Because you and your research buddies think no one is responsible for anything they do, and you're willing to challenge hundreds of years of intent and our entire legal structure?"

"We're not saying people aren't responsible. We're saying that responsibility is a social construct, not a biological property. People still need to be treated as responsible agents for the sake of society and as predictors of possible future behavior. We require a social system to live together, and for it to be viable, we must enforce its rules. We should, however, now that we understand the living brain better, make a distinction between punishment and custody."

Incensed, Courtney's voice got louder. "You don't think a man who rapes five-year-old girls should be punished?"

"Listen to how emotionally loaded you just became. Where is that passion coming from? Did you think it over and then decide to raise your voice and get agitated, or did it happen without your choosing?"

Courtney forcibly lowered her voice and challenged, "If you say that a criminal committed a particular act but didn't really choose to, he couldn't help it. You eliminate personal responsibility, and intent is a fundamental concept in our legal system. If you kill your wife in a car accident, or you kill her with a gun after lying in wait, it's the same result, but the intention is what matters to us, to the jury, to the system."

"Yes." Adam's eyes sparkled. "But if you later find that the man who killed his wife with a gun had a brain tumor pressing on the orbitofrontal cortex, where we know the governor of your behavior lies, then you are willing to consider it as a factor in his ability to choose. You present that evidence to the jury and expect mitigation. You do that for physical, structural defects in the brain. Why not for chemical or electrical impulses that emerge from a nonconscious level?"

"Oh, this is ridiculous." Courtney slid back in her seat.

"Listen to yourself, Courtney. Why are you so angry? This is a biology discussion."

"Adam, you are carelessly chipping away at what we believe we are as human beings and expecting no reaction."

"Yes, and your sense of panic is fascinating. I'd like to study that."

"Oh, yeah? Glad to fascinate you, Adam."

Chris shifted, clearly uncomfortable. "A very interesting area of future research."

Adam, not good at reading other people's nonverbal signals, ignored Chris's discomfort. "Of course, nothing is indisputable except the fundamental biology. I think of us like baked goods. Our genes are the recipe. Every recipe is different. Some recipes are deeply flawed, but you didn't choose your ingredients."

Chris said, "It seems to me we have an override system, and *that* is where we deliberate. You can choose not to do something. You can want soda and not drink it. You can want to punch someone and stop yourself."

Courtney said sarcastically, "I want to punch someone right now."

"I guess I should be grateful for your perfectly functioning prefrontal cortex, which is exhibiting self-control." Adam laughed.

Trying to draw the conflict away from Courtney and Adam, Chris turned to Ilana. "What's your take on this?"

Adam jumped in, "She's been listening to me for so long that she's half-scientist now. Right, Ilana?"

"I think we do things we can't explain all the time. I know I have."

Chris nodded. "I agree with that."

"I think Adam's right," Ilana said. "We make up stories and manufacture excuses. I'm no longer really certain that the me I think I am . . . is really the me I am."

Courtney chided, "You sound like Dr. Seuss."

Ilana continued, "I want to know how choices were made about me and for me and if I am freely living and in control or if it's only the illusion of control. Frankly, I am not at all convinced that my brain is an ally. We already know our brain lies to us."

"Only our left hemisphere!" Adam laughed heartily.

Chris jumped in, "Adam, this is an interesting book project for you! *Your Unconscious, Your Enemy: Is Your Brain Out to Get You?*"

"I like it."

They all sat back as the waiter poured their water glasses and dropped off popadam for the table.

Ilana speculated, "And maybe it's not this or that anyway. Maybe it's a continuum, a line, being conscious: you can be in a coma, semiconscious, deep asleep, or half asleep."

Adam added, "Focused, daydreaming, distracted, alert—they are all different states of consciousness. And we come in and out of all those states all the time. Sometimes we're fully conscious and choose deliberatively, and sometimes we don't, and we don't especially recognize the difference."

"Okay, I might buy this continuum thing," Courtney said. "Perhaps greater control is something we developed as we evolved. Now we're getting more control as our brains get bigger and more complex."

Ilana answered, "Seems like the opposite to me."

"How so?" Courtney asked.

"Used to be life was basic: what will I eat, where will I sleep to be safe and warm. In the 1500s, after dinner, there were two choices: go to bed or talk. Then, we created all these choices. Now we can choose from movies or TV shows, hundreds of video games, YouTube, music venues, poetry and lecture series, museums, parks, and restaurants. And then, what will I wear? My jeans, sweats, a dress? Which dress? Will I take a cab, drive, a bus, or the subway? It's proliferating exponentially. Maybe lots of things are being relegated to an unconscious level out of necessity."

"I like that, Ilana." Adam grinned. "Because consciousness is inefficient, and we can only attend to a couple of things. Are we becoming more automated? We're only at the edge of this research. This is where AI may help." Adam grabbed Ilana's hand. "But, seriously, does anyone *not* understand why I love this woman?"

Ilana said quietly, more to herself, "I'm not sure any of us are who we think we are."

"I know who you are, Ilana, and you're spectacular." Adam's eyes were full of her. Ilana turned red, which he mistook for a charming blush. It was actually shame.

Courtney jokingly slapped Chris on the arm. "Why don't you ever say things like that to me?"

For minutes, Adam loaded the conversation on his shoulders and carried it alone. Finally, he saw Ilana's exhaustion. He realized that he should not have insisted on dinner. It was inconsiderate. He would apologize later when they were alone. He furtively slipped his hand into his pocket to feel the small box that held their future. The engagement ring he purchased that day was a glory of white light and brilliance. Tonight, he would capture her with his vision of their tomorrow. He would release her from whatever was troubling her. He thought about where they would be in fifty years—old together, happy together.

Get out.

Ilana's mind repeated over and over, *Get out*, until she stood.

"Excuse me," she said, interrupting, and she angled her body toward the restroom.

Chris asked, "Adam, is she okay?"

"Not sure. Overtired, I think."

But she didn't turn toward the restroom as they thought. She stopped by the maître d' instead. "Please tell the others they should stay and enjoy their meal, but that I am not feeling well and went home." She walked quickly for the door, threw it open, and stepped out. The relief was instantaneous. By stepping into the outside world, the feeling of being hemmed in disappeared; once there on the street, no eyes knew her, and no one expected anything. Liberation. She decided to walk all the way home. She relished the repetitive movement and the solitude. Walking. Rhythmic walking. She was doing exactly what she needed to do. She forced herself to stay in the moment, to get a sanity break from her own thoughts and from what she knew lay ahead of her that night. It was difficult to keep her mind blank. She had to manhandle her thoughts to keep them on the city lights, the honking cabs, and the passing sidewalk beneath her moving feet. She stayed in the moment because she felt a gratifying relief in it. She noticed how cunningly her thoughts tried to work their way back to the problems at hand. She scuffled with herself. She needed breathing space, recovery time. Every time she found her thoughts slipping back, she recited aloud the names of the streets; she described aloud the people passing her. Luckily for Ilana, it was the city, so she was not the only person walking down Sixth Avenue talking to herself.

An hour and a half later, Adam put his key into her lock. He had not forgotten it. He walked in, certain he knew exactly how to turn the night around. He'd rehearsed the right words in the cab. He would wrap himself around her, apologize for pushing her to dinner when she was clearly exhausted, and tell her about his vision for their future together. What an idiot he had been to propose to her in a room full of their friends. This was meant to be one of life's most private moments; a commitment to forever was a solemn affair. He saw that now. He felt a gratifying exhilaration as he began this new phase in his life. After the proposal, he intended to sweep her up to his apartment, cover her in white roses, and guzzle champagne, and they would take care of each other forever.

"Ilana? Hey, are you feeling all right? I'm sorry. I shouldn't have made you go tonight. Forgive me because it's all about to get better."

No, it's not.

"Adam, I am sorry I left like that. It was rude."

"It's okay. Are you sick? Want me to make you some soup or something?"

"No. Thanks."

"I had planned for us to go back to my place tonight. I'd still like to."

"Adam, please, sit."

"Can't sit. I've got something important. Ilana. Last night, I was standing, believe it or not, in Times Square, and I had a premonition."

She responded distantly, with a small smile, "You told me once only people from Coney Island have premonitions."

"It was strange, but like it was telling me something I knew all along." He was shining. The words burst out with enthusiasm. "We're going to have children, a big yard, and a dog, and I love you. It's not that I didn't love you. I've always loved you. Suddenly, everything fell into place in a way I didn't know it could. I thought—"

Anxiety exploded inside of her. "Adam, I need to—"

"I'm so, I don't know, alive!" He grabbed her and, with quaking sincerity, confessed, "Ilana, I've always been less sure of things than I pretended. It never seemed manly to admit that."

"Adam." She was nauseated.

He barreled on. "I thought that if I laid it all out defenselessly, you wouldn't want me because I would appear vulnerable, and I was unwilling to risk it. But now"—he put both hands over his heart and reached out to her with his whole self—"don't you see? I get it. This was the reason you felt like something was missing. It was me. I needed to be willing to risk it all, to not hold back. I needed to be all in. I can't tell you what a relief it is to be this sure of something, of someone, of us." He hugged her joyfully, and then he held her far enough away to look into her eyes. He was ready to spend the rest of his life clearing the path for her to walk so she could step with ease. He was finally, totally, and blessedly all in. He was thinking he would never let go, and then, her face? Something was very wrong.

"Honey, what?"

She looked achingly at him. "Please sit." Her earnestness pressed down on his shoulder like a firm hand, and he sat. She continued, "I respect you deeply, and you know I would never lie to you, and not being completely truthful is the same as lying."

"Okay," he replied, coaxing her to unload. "Whatever it is, Ilana, whatever."

She trembled. Her knees felt watery. She sat next to him. *Say it,* she told herself, *you must. Say it.* "I spent the night in Albany with a man I met in a bar." She looked away. She could not look at him. If she could have looked, she would not have seen a thing because nothing changed, not the plane of his body, not the expression in his milky blue eyes, nothing.

Adam struggled to make sense of her words, words that surely must mean something else. For him, it was as though she had spoken in an unknown language. He recaptured the words from the air and played them back in his mind. *No,* he thought, *it must mean something else. I heard wrong, or she misspoke.*

She forced herself to meet his eyes and said softly, "I slept with someone else in Albany. I'm so terribly sorry. I can't really explain how it all happened. It just did."

With a swift, crippling pain, like a gush of poison into his bloodstream, he bent forward. He hurt. He physically hurt.

"Adam, I'm so sorry. There's no excuse. It is complicated. I didn't intend to. I didn't decide. It sort of happened. And I wish I—"

He raised his hands in front of him to deflect her words. It was a useless defensive gesture—like someone hoping to stop gunshots. He got up and stepped backward. She rose too. They stared into each other's eyes for a brutally long time as it all became real to him. Without turning away, he opened the front door and backed cautiously into the hall. He stood there with the doorway between them.

In a rush of desperation, she said, "Adam, I want to talk, to try and explain." Her mind searched frantically for something to say, for the right thing. His look silenced her. She had never seen a look like his. He reached out and closed the door with the gentleness of someone holding a glass that had cracked into a thousand thin white trails over every inch but was still intact and vulnerable to that final shattering vibration.

On the inside, Ilana stood staring at the closed door.

On the other side, Adam stood staring at the closed door.

They both stood on either side of the closed door for a long, long time.

Ilana didn't sleep. She shifted in the sheets. She got up and fixed them. She sipped water and stared at her ceiling. If only she could get an hour of sleep, one hour. But something inside her was howling all through the night. She tried to make sense of it, and when she couldn't, she tried to put it out of her mind: forget Albany, forget Fiona, forget Cafferty, forget the look on Adam's face, and forget the damage she had done. She couldn't forget. And Albany had not forgotten her.

❖ ❖ ❖

FIONA THOUGHT that what she felt now was like the time she got sunburned. She had discounted all the hysterical warnings about her fair Irish skin and had lain out with her friends in the bare sun one summer noon. She slathered herself in baby oil and sizzled sunny-side up with the other seven teenage girls (dressed mostly in skin) on beach towels by the side of the river. She felt the sun like warm hands. She dozed. In her dream, an enormous Teflon spatula came down from the sky and flipped each of them over, but it didn't, of course, and it was days before the burn cooled. She was constantly aware of it beneath the threads of her clothing, an ever-present reminder, which she bore in silence rather than give credence to the warnings she had ignored. This, now, was like that. She felt Ilana's presence like a burn underneath the fabric of her every day. She was aware of it each waking moment, and when asleep, she could feel the distress of the burn as it rubbed along the fitted sheet.

She began to walk, not little simple strolls, but rather long, fast-paced walks. Those who passed her could tell that this was a woman on a mission. They instinctively stepped aside as one would give way to a rushing person in a hospital corridor. Willow noticed the turbulence in her mother and inquired, but Fiona wasn't talking, not now, not then, not at all. She was uncharacteristically quiet. While her walks appeared desultory, they weren't. Any low-flying plane would have clearly discerned the decreasing concentric circles around the churchyard cemetery.

The rising eastern sun created white lines and gray shadows that striped the graveyard in black and white. Only the extremely devout attended mass on a weekday morning. The pious few stood around waiting for their god to unbolt his door. Fiona concluded her walk at her brother's grave. She kept the grave clean, even though Nellie told her it was foolish to tend a grave. Fiona didn't know why she did it, but she did. The crusty ground resisted her knees as she said a few words of greeting to Joey.

When Fiona stopped talking to God thirty years ago, she began talking to Joey. At times, when she was puzzled by something, she would sit there a while and always leave with a plan. She would not say he helped her (she was too much of a pragmatist for that), but there was some therapeutic value to sitting there knowing she had his complete attention. Today was different. She was not there to talk to Joey. Today, she dug her fingers into the brush and dirt on the side of his gravestone, and with vivid accuracy, she remembered where. She clawed her fingernails into thirty years of undisturbed ground and pulled out a stone, a small flat stone about the size of her fist. She stared at the unearthed memory yanked from its tomb; tiny chunks of dirt, a blade of grass, and a desiccated leaf fell through her fingers. Fiona stood with that flat stone clenched in her fist, and she began to shake. She struggled to keep the emotion under her skin. From a distance, she resembled any other graveside mourner. Then, she shot up, whirled around, and hurled the stone at great speed at the rectory window, which shattered. She experienced the shrill blast and shattering in slow motion. The pious faithful froze, aghast. A curtain moved upstairs, and the priest, Father Cummings, peered out, distressed. Fiona turned away and began a very slow walk home.

ILANA SANK into her work for the upcoming gala fundraiser. Inside the office, people shied away from her. Everyone could tell something was off. She seemed spring-loaded. She was startled when a limo arrived at noon to pick her up for the lunch appointment that she'd completely forgotten about. Isabella Wharton. She had to do this. She knew she had to. She had a clear view of the numbers, and the budget was very tight.

Once inside the car, she did not let her mind wander as the limo drove her to Mrs. Wharton's large penthouse on Central Park East.

She sat and watched the world go by.

Inside the elegant study, Isabella Wharton sat in absolute calm. Ilana always thought that absolute calm was like absolute zero: theoretical. Now she knew differently. Shrewdness lay on the older woman's face like a thin veil, untethered so as not to muss her hair, which was stunningly pure, clean silver. When she gestured with her outstretched arm, Ilana noted that floating quality. Her litheness and beauty did not distract from the intelligent worldliness in her eyes.

The study was lively but orderly and filled with unusual pieces impossible for her to place. She picked up a small china figurine and wondered about its origin. Then, she forcibly yanked her attention back to Isabella Wharton, who was speaking. Concentrating was strenuous. Earlier that morning, William prescribed Xanax, but she hadn't taken it. She didn't think she deserved to feel any better.

"Please." Isabella signaled for Ilana to sit. "I can imagine you were not so pleased when Glen told you I wished to meet you for lunch."

"On the contrary, I was delighted," she lied.

"Oh, I don't think so. Personally, I find Glen tedious and predictable, and I could see when you glanced at us the other day that you agree."

"Glen is brilliant at what he does."

"Yes, well, so is my urologist, but I wouldn't want to lunch with him. On the other hand, you looked like someone most unlikely to 'lunch' at all. Ever."

"I eat lunch. I don't make an event out of it. Usually at my desk." She smiled. "Except under special circumstances."

"You don't need to do that," Isabella told her. "Please be yourself."

And who would that be?

A wave of pain crossed through her eyes. Isabella saw it.

Trying to avoid the older woman's piercing gaze, Ilana rose and wandered around, looking at the artwork. She wondered what it would be like to be Isabella Wharton, who was still beautiful and astonishingly wealthy. Even in her distressed frame of mind, Ilana was captivated by this woman who carried herself with a blend of worldly sagacity and wry humor. There was nothing ordinary about Isabella Wharton. Ilana drove the conversation back to the opera.

"I know you've told Glen you're interested in supporting a new production, but before that, I did want to thank you personally for all your help with the gala this Saturday. We've got talent coming in from all over the world to celebrate Maestro Riconi."

"Yes. I decided to give myself two super gifts this year for my seventy-fifth birthday, and one of them was to underwrite the opera gala." Isabella let the sentence hang unfinished, and Ilana felt obligated to ask.

"And the other gift?"

"The other? Oh, yes, I remember, a new husband."

"Sale at Bloomies?" Ilana was stunned she said it aloud. "Ah, sorry."

The older woman's eyes approved. "I don't do sales, dear. Really, there's nothing more common than a husband off-the-rack."

And Ilana laughed spontaneously. She didn't feel she deserved to be happy in any way, but it was funny.

The door opened, and the housekeeper, Mrs. Grace, entered carrying a lunch tray of petite sandwiches. "I ordered a collection of finger sandwiches. I hope there's something you like." Mrs. Grace set the small table.

"I'm easy when it comes to food. As long as I don't have to think about it, shop for it, cook it, or clean up, it is exactly what I want."

"Then you're in the right place. Thank you, Mrs. Grace." The dumpy housecoated woman nodded and left. Isabella turned to Ilana. "I'm in the process of divorcing the current Mr. Wharton because I have four months of pictures of him in sexual gymnastics with Mrs. Grace."

Ilana's eyes shot up. "What?"

"Shocking, isn't it?"

"You mean that Mrs. Grace?"

"Precisely. Initially, I assumed he was just fucking her, which didn't concern me." Ilana didn't know Isabella Wharton well enough yet to know that astonishing people was one of her hobbies. "Now, however, it seems an emotional attachment has formed, and that is not to be tolerated."

"I see." Ilana tried to measure out exactly the right mixture of tone. "So, you had an open marriage?"

"From the start and in writing."

"Interesting."

"Monogamy is rather ridiculous."

"You think?" She was losing her bearings in this conversation.

"Certainly. An arbitrary social constraint that has proven quite unworkable and the cause of so much unnecessary pain. One insignificant sexual diversion has split up entire families with long histories, with lives and children together, an absurd overreaction. Why humans insist on joining sex and love, I will never understand. Many times, they do go together, but it's very often the case to have one without the other."

Speaking carefully, Ilana replied, "I suppose everyone has different needs."

"What I need is a way to quitclaim Mr. Wharton to my housekeeper."

Ilana felt comfortable teasing her. "He's not a piece of real property."

"True, there is very little real about him at this point—not his teeth, his hair, his left knee, his right hip, or his erection. He is more a collage of spare parts." Mrs. Wharton leaned over to the intercom and pressed the button. "Mrs. Grace, two mint teas."

"And she still works here?"

"She has a binding contract. And, good help, you know." Isabella winked at her playfully. "And perhaps it's a little bit fun having her bring me tea."

Ilana could see it was clear that retaining Mrs. Grace had nothing to do with "good help." This woman was a force. She was the queen on the chessboard. Ilana was spellbound, and she squirmed in her seat as the stubby sixty-five-year-old Mrs. Grace waddled in with the tea service. She stared while Mrs. Grace leaned over the small table, exposing her rolled-down stockings, her stout, unattractive legs, and black orthotic shoes. Mrs. Grace set down the teapot and silently left the room.

"Quite the spring chicken," Isabella commented wryly.

The image of the bloated, hair-netted Mrs. Grace on her back with her varicose-veined legs in the air reminded Ilana of a *Saturday Night Live* sketch.

Isabella continued, "Evidently, she has hidden gifts."

"Expertly concealed, I'd say." Ilana loved the strong mint tea. It was soothing, delicious, and new to her. "I hope the divorce goes smoothly for you. Now, about the upcoming season."

"I am hoping for a protracted and scandalous divorce." Isabella kept control of the conversation.

"Really?"

"I have a few comments about the construct of marriage that I'd like to make publicly."

"Like what?"

"Love is worth preserving. I'm not divorcing Mr. Wharton because of adultery, and I want to make that perfectly clear. I'm divorcing him because he breached his commitment to love only me. That was his failure."

"I don't think the state recognizes contracts made about emotional issues. Falling in love with someone else is not grounds for divorce, but the adultery is."

"I believe there are enough property issues to keep us busy with the court for a while. But I want the real reasons to be noted in the record and in the press and start a public discourse. I don't care what it costs. I have something to say about the distinction between love and sex. And I will find it all an entertaining way to pass the time, and time is all life is about, isn't it?"

"Odd." Ilana looked into the distance. "Someone else said something very similar to me."

"Oh? I hate to be redundant. Another wickedly wealthy old lady?"

"No. A carpenter in Albany."

Isabella's smile took a few seconds to reach its peak. "You know, my dear, if your pupils dilate like that when you speak of him, really, no mystery will be left at all."

Ilana glanced away, embarrassed. "Oh."

"A delicious man?" Isabella grinned.

"Not the right man."

"Pity."

Ilana felt exposed and was glad to recognize the aria playing softly in the background. "'Casta Diva.' Callas?"

"Yes. I love Maria and Onassis and everything about that all too horrid scandal. He traded the love of his life, his soulmate, to raise his fame profile. A great drama still not properly told. Perhaps I should commission that opera: "Maria and Ari: A Torrid Tale." They were two poor Greek kids who took on the world. Opera comes to life: love, sex, fury, lies, and betrayal, all dramatically played out to its tragic end. She was only fifty-three when they found her dead. It was 1977." Isabella spoke with mesmerizing serenity and undeniable authority. "I remember it clearly. The Rue Georges Bizet in front of the church was jammed for her. The crowd stood shoulder-to-shoulder in the most eerie silence when they carried Maria's body through the doorway. People were weeping, but there was no sound. Can you imagine Callas and no sound? You can watch the newsreel. There was an unearthly quiet as though all drama was over now because heartbreak had silenced Maria. Then, in the back, amid this haunting silence, one stranger began to clap, alone, at first, slowly *clap clap clap*, and then the entire crowd burst simultaneously into wild applause, shouting, 'Brava!' 'La Divina!' It was a moment of sweeping collective emotion. A moment I'm certain little Maria Kalogeropoulis would have loved."

Ilana mused, "I've read enough and seen enough photos to really wonder what she could have seen in Onassis."

"Ah. Well, everyone seemed to know." Isabella allowed a sly smile. "Ari was well known as a man with"—she searched for the right word—"talents."

"Must have."

"Oh, I've spoken to women who would know. I assure you. Have you ever heard, dear, the saying that short men try harder?"

"I think so."

"Ari was very *very* short." Isabella Wharton looked straight at Ilana, daring her to ask for details.

Ilana didn't. She reached for her teacup and then changed the subject. "So, then, you have always been an opera fan, Mrs. Wharton?"

"Please, call me Isabella, I insist. When I was growing up, my mother couldn't do anything around the house without an aria on her lips. She had a light, melodic voice, perfect for bel canto. She cooked with Bellini and vacuumed with Donizetti. I was spoon-fed mashed bananas and Rossini simultaneously. It turned out to be the greatest gift she ever gave me, albeit unwittingly. She was not singing for me. She sang because she was a brilliant woman, and it masked the tedium of her day. She eventually preferred sleeping to being awake. She actually slept herself to death. She should have had four or five children to keep her busy but was damned to only one. Personally, I was happy as an only child, but she was bored to the very marrow of her bones."

"I'm an only child. Adopted." Ilana surprised herself by speaking so freely.

"Did you miss siblings?"

"Desperately. Every year, I wrote to Santa to bring me a brother. I told him he could keep the bicycle, computer, party dresses. It was all I can remember wanting as a child."

"I never felt that. It made me feel special to be an only child. So, Santa didn't hear your pleadings?"

"When the letters failed, I tried bribery, but I was unsure of what he liked. One year, I left a huge pecan cookie and chocolate milk. The next year, I left a strawberry orange smoothie and a Chinese chicken salad. Then, I tried a mango, a five-dollar bill, and, in desperation one year, spanakopita."

Isabella laughed. "You must have been an interesting child."

"I felt like I was supposed to have siblings, like I was actually missing people. My parents would only roll their eyes and tell me they already had the perfect child. Eventually, I got old enough to realize it wasn't going to happen. In the schoolyard, though, when I watched the other children scrapping with their siblings, sometimes I would run into the girls' room and cry. I felt so envious."

Ilana's thoughts went back to those days. She thought it was selfish of her parents. It may have been their only selfish act. And now, now that they were gone, it is the one thing that she could never forgive, having to bury her mom alone.

It was unexpectedly effortless to be in Isabella Wharton's company, and Ilana slipped gratefully into the ease of it. She needed respite from the yelling of self-damnation that splashed around in the stream of her thoughts. She found some soft solace in the presence of this unique woman. She ate a little. She breathed a little. She was relieved to have this time to not think about Adam and what she'd done. She was happier not being alone with her thoughts. Adam was alone with his.

Adam is alone.

ADAM SAT at his dining room table surrounded by one hundred dead white roses and an empty bottle of champagne. The shriveled flowers had a pungent, acidic odor. White petals had fallen to the floor, where they were already curling into themselves and tipped with brown age spots. He felt older. Another time, he might have been stunned that the flowers had all died so quickly, except he couldn't be any more stunned. He was at the outer limit of completely stunned. He hadn't gone to the lab. He couldn't remember what he did. His mind was staggering around in a punch-drunk frenzy and smacking into dead ends. With both feet flat on the floor and his palms cupping the rim of the table, he waited for clarity. He ran the events over in his mind, searching for the flaw. He ordered the flowers. He bought the wine. He loved her. She loved him. What went wrong? He decided he would figure out what went wrong, and he'd fix it. All he needed to do was study it because he believed, like all of life's mysteries, there was a logical answer that was consistent with the natural world. And then, the thought of this other man would rage into his mind, possess him, and kidnap his deliberations. The muscles in his stomach would tense, his heart rate would leap, and his forehead would sweat. He would feel anger, then self-pity, then anger again. What was interesting to him, as a scientist, was that while he was experiencing it, he was observing it. While he was feeling and responding to the emotion and rage, he was also noting and commenting on how powerful and uncontrollable his rage was. It felt like a split-brain experiment or like subjects he had spoken to who had been in traumatic accidents and would describe the accident as something they endured but also something they had witnessed from the outside. He wondered if this was a neurological mechanism where, because of a sudden, unpredictable, traumatic event, the brain's two hemispheres, which usually worked in concert, started overworking individually, trying to organize this new alarming information and leaving him waiting for instructions or a course of action to be revealed.

Ilana had used his words against him. She had said she "didn't mean to." She said she "didn't decide, that it sort of happened." Those were code words for him now, and she knew that. It spoke to the heart of his research on personal agency and the biological genesis of thought. Ire started to rise and clutch his throat, but then it subsided because he knew that she wasn't manipulative, that she meant what she said. Did she really lose control of her conscious override? Did her deep-rooted biology make this decision, and if so, what does that mean for him? What if it were true? If she didn't "mean" to, if she had not "chosen," had not "deliberated," what does that mean to him in the real world, in real time, right now? Does he accept that? Must he? And if he doesn't, does he rewrite every article he's written, reject every panel he's spoken on, and his own research? Where does this leave him? It left him sitting, sitting with his feet flat and his palms cupping the table's edge, surrounded by the pungent odor of dead flowers and no understandable plans for tomorrow. Should he call her? What was she doing?

Ilana kept to herself and worked hard throughout the rest of the week. Everyone did. And then, finally, it was the night of the gala tribute. It was the crown jewel of the season. It rushed at her with formidable force. She had labored for many months, puzzling together the pieces for the event to honor Maestro Riconi, who was celebrating his ninetieth birthday. The company was recreating special moments from his critically acclaimed performances. They had pulled the original talent from all over the world. It would be the grandest party of the season, and they expected to make a profit thanks to Ilana's tight financial fist and Glen's ability to promote the event. Excited anticipation colored every face inside the opera house as they readied for the evening. The atmosphere was thick, as were the tensions that came with any event so long planned and with such exposure within the music world. Final sound and stage checks were in progress. She kept her head down. She did her job.

Ilana's office door cracked open tentatively. Martina Marone, a principal ballet dancer who was set to recreate her role in a pas de deux, shyly poked her head in. Ilana admired her. Martina moved like a cloud. Her arms and legs drifted with lissome grace. When she leaped up and out in a grand jeté, with her legs in an impossibly taut split, her feet stretched, and her thighs turned out, Ilana marveled to see Martina actually pause in midair. She alighted at the apex of her leap as though she had made some kind of bargain with gravity, which had agreed, perhaps from pure respect, to exclude her from its grip. And contrary to all the explosive power in her extended muscular legs, her arms, hands, and fingers floated, poised in an effortless gesture that even the thought of a breeze might displace. It was this contradiction between the granite potency of the legs and the supple quality of the arms that mesmerized Ilana. Had she ever told Martina this? She didn't think so. In fact, she didn't think they'd ever spoken to each other directly. Martina was never trouble. She found this to be true for the dancers (as long as the floor was exactly what they needed). They worked hard, and they kept quiet. They were competitive with each other and always seemed to be arguing about the temperature in the rehearsal space, but they never bothered her. They were not like the divas at all. She had heard rumors that Martina would be retiring soon. She would be sorry to see her leave the stage, but then, she was thirty-three.

"Ilana?"

"Come on in, Martina."

Martina entered and was careful to completely close the door behind her. She walked over and stood in front of Ilana. Her eyes dropped to her shoes. Ilana looked down and noticed how tiny Martina's feet were. She glanced up and saw Martina's slumped shoulders.

"Are you all right?" Ilana asked.

"I am not." Martina began to tremble.

"Tell me." Ilana thought she looked exactly like a hummingbird fluttering frantically against a windowpane.

"A number of years ago, I injured my left hamstring, and I reinjured it in rehearsal this morning." Her eyes filled. "I've wrapped it. I've had the shots. I've medicated. I've tried everything. It won't support me. Not tonight. It won't."

"Oh, shit." Ilana flew into gear. She grabbed the phone. "Who's covering you? We need to run it."

Martina's hands flew to her face, and she began to weep. Ilana stopped and returned the receiver. It would all wait a few more moments.

"Are you in pain? Do you need a ride to the hospital?"

"It's not that. I don't care about the pain. It's only pain."

Ilana could see she had something to say and waited for her to continue.

Martina continued, "I've given my whole life to ballet."

"Yes."

"No vacations. No college. No marriage. No children." She shook heartbreakingly. "I've taken class every day of my life. I've never regretted it."

"Yes, I know the commitment," Ilana said with fresh compassion in her tone. Martina was a little surprised to hear the swell of sympathy. Everyone knew Ilana was emotionally intransigent when it came to the opera house's business. Something was different about her. Martina felt safe, so she took it to heart and ventured out a little.

"Did you know the choreographer didn't want to hire me for this, even though I did the original role five years ago?"

"I didn't know that."

"I had to fight for my spot. They said I was too old."

"It's a short career, Martina." Ilana walked around the desk and sat on the edge. "You know that."

"There does seem to be a whole lot of empty life left after the dancing stops." She let her eyes wander out the window for a moment. "I'm not sure what I'll do. I was planning to quietly retire after this performance. I told my family and friends this would be it for me. They're all here tonight. I wanted my last night to be a night like this, a glorious night I could remember, you know, celebrate privately, for myself. But now, now, to have it all end like this! To not have that moment." Tears flowed. "To be shoved out injured. Exactly as they all expected. To be broken like they expected. My end will be a little white strip of paper slipped into the evening's program announcing a cast change. That's what they'll remember. What I'll remember. It, well, it's the worst possible end." Bereft, Martina's struggle to control her emotions only made her more sympathetic.

"Martina, you've been a beautiful gift to dance. You must feel good about yourself, about your career. You can't let this injury overshadow all of that."

Martina answered, "The miserable truth is that I could recover from this. I've done it before. I know what it takes: two months of hard work and physical therapy. I could absolutely do it, and then I could have another shot at that final performance, at that glorious last moment to dance me into retirement, you know, to know it is your final bow. But as soon as they hear I was replaced for injury, no one will ever hire me again, not at this age. No one. This is the worst way to say goodbye to the only thing that has ever mattered to me." Her cheeks were soaked. "This is the saddest day of my life."

"I'm so truly sorry." Ilana felt her devastation. They were so close in age. She could not imagine what it was like for life to feel over so young. She knew the devotion required to reach the height Martina had in the world of ballet. Most people go through life without ever having to make those kinds of sacrifices. And now, Ilana found that she felt the heartbreak of others in a new and profound way. It was the piece that Boney had deposited inside of her one night, weeks ago, in Albany.

"If you don't mind," Martina said, having regained her calm. "Could you announce it so I don't have to say it?"

"You haven't told anyone?"

"No. My partner is young. He's nineteen. He has been expecting me to fall. Someone told me he had a pool going with other cast members for when."

"A pool?" Ilana repeated in disbelief. "No."

"So humiliating. I don't want to cry in front of them, you know? I don't think I can say it without crying. I'll collect my stuff, nod as you replace me, and then I can leave quickly out the back, okay?"

"Of course. Sure." Ilana picked up the walkie-talkie. "Vincent, production meeting on stage, everyone for the pas de deux, five minutes."

"What's up?" came back the confused question.

"Five minutes." Ilana clicked off.

"Thank you." And with swift little bird steps, Martina left as quietly as she'd arrived, having made no impression on the carpet.

As Martina closed the office door, Ilana's eyes drifted down to the little bag left in the corner. It had been there since she returned from Albany. Inside was an unopened sewing kit.

Things thrown away.

Five minutes later, Vincent, the other dancers, the choreographer, the technical manager, and the conductor were all gathered on stage and speculating about what the problem could be. Martina stood a little to the side, a few steps from the back door, ready to bolt. She had washed her face. She looked composed, almost regal. Ilana barreled into the waiting scene. She locked eyes for a moment with Martina and then faced the group.

"Okay. I have some concerns about the operation of the lift apparatus and trap door in the pas de deux sequence," Ilana stated flatly.

"Concerns?" Vincent asked.

Martina looked at her, confused.

"The lift works perfectly," the technical director added. "I checked it myself. Hell, I built it myself."

"I have a problem with it, and so for safety reasons, I'm eliminating the pas de deux."

Martina's mouth dropped. A roar went up.

"Are you kidding?" the technical director asked.

Anger swarmed Ilana like bees. She stood firm and calm. "It's unavoidable."

"Ilana, I don't think this is necessary," Vincent said.

She laid her eyes on him with all the power she carried. "But my call."

Nonplussed, he replied, "Of course, your call."

"I realize it's short notice, and it's disappointing." Catching Martina's eye, she said, "There will be other shows."

"Let me show you how it's working," the technical director implored.

The choreographer stepped forward. "Maybe I can work around it."

"No time," she answered.

The conductor whined, "How will I change the score in this short time? What about the musicians?"

"It's only two minutes and forty-seven seconds of a three-hour and four-minute show. Lift it out. Make the adjustment. You're the best in the business. Make it work."

"Ilana." Vincent tried to pull her aside. "A minute alone. You want to talk about this."

"No, Vincent. There's no time for discussion. It's final. The two dancers can see me for their checks. Everyone, back to work. Thank you." Ilana turned and left the stunned group behind.

There were plenty of stage people who disliked Ilana; it was the nature of her job, but this surprised everyone. On the way out, she brushed eyes with Martina, whose expression was soaked with emotion. This was the kindest thing anyone had ever done for her, and again, her eyes were filled with an expression of hope and gratitude that Ilana would never forget.

Martina's partner in the pas de deux raced over. "Martina, can you fucking believe this?"

"No. No, I can't." Martina turned, exited, and blissfully rushed off to physical therapy.

After Ilana walked away, the unsettled group called her all the derogatory names creative people always call the suits who manage their world. Vincent stood for two minutes, wondering. Everyone else fell quickly into place and worked it through without that much effort.

He started a pool? Fuck that guy.

Ilana knew she had spent some hard-earned personal capital. An explanation would have to be forthcoming to the general director, but she knew he was busy and would be inclined to trust her. This was the first time she had used her acquired power in this way, and she smiled to herself all the way back to her office.

That night, The Lyric Opera sang out with orchestral beauty, stunning arias, and with operatic grace, but without the pas de deux. It was the first time Ilana felt good about herself since Albany.

❖ ❖ ❖

THE FOLLOWING few weeks passed in a fog. As she slid onto the bench at their usual restaurant, she asked, "William, the harder I work, the more work I have. Why is that?"

"You're in demand. Don't be so good at stuff. Drop a few balls. Miss a few meetings. Don't pay the brass section."

"Radical and risky."

"Hey, I spent the entire day in group with three bipolars, two OCDs, and a woman with nine personalities, none of whom are continent."

She raised her left eyebrow. "Remind me not to sit on your sofa."

"So," William led.

"So?"

"So, I ran into Adam yesterday."

"Oh." Anguish. "How's he doing?"

"Second-degree burns from the torch he's carrying. Have you spoken?"

"He hasn't tried, and I have no right to try, and I don't even know if I want to try." She felt ashamed. "He's right to stay away from me. He can't trust me. I can't trust me."

"He's been trying to work it all through. I think he's made a little progress. I agree that a little time apart may be good for you both. But considering everything, is this really a three-year relationship-ending situation? It was one errant night."

"I don't know. I went to Albany to take a peek at who I should have been, to try and get a compass reading on why I make certain decisions, and in an instant, I turned into someone else. Can you imagine how frightening that is? Do you want me to say I don't think about that night with Cafferty or to deny I'm having an actual sexual sensation at this very moment because I spoke his name? I can't say that. And until I can, I will not expose Adam to any more risk. It's not right."

"Do you regret it?"

"That's the problem. No. So much pain and destruction, and no, I don't."

"Oh. I see."

"If you understand it, please explain it to me." She could see William studying her. He looked perplexed.

"How about, instead, we have a nice dinner and talk about lots of nothing?"

"Sounds perfect. God knows I need the break from myself."

William wedged himself securely under the emotional burden that she'd been balancing on her own. His company was a relief, a chest-expanding deep gulp of air, because he knew her, and nothing needed to be explained. He had shared her life as she had shared his. The day he admitted to himself that he was gay, she was there beside him. She knew before he did. It had been a tricky journey for William. He told her it was like walking past a mirror one day when you're twenty-five years old and realizing you're Asian or bald. It was so obviously the kind of thing one should have noticed sooner.

He told his family, assuming they would be initially upset and then get over it. He was wrong. Homosexuality did not blend with their Bible, and even with all the pleading from the New Testament to love, to turn the other cheek, to not cast the first stone, it did not assuage their visceral disgust. Vile! They said it to his face. This one thing was suddenly everything he was, all he was, and all he would ever be to them. His two brothers and sister slammed the door on him with such apparent ease and with such finality that the sound of it had never completely left his ears. It banged around in his dreams. The wound it caused stayed open and raw even as the silence between them went from days to years.

William's father, Charles, had been the most offended by his son. It reflected on him somehow. He was a baker by trade, so he lived in a white world: white flour, white sugar, white salt, white life. He felt holier than others living in such whiteness. He felt righteous. Whenever William's mother would waver, he was there to remind her that her everlasting soul was at stake. Her everlasting soul.

When William heard that his sister had given birth to his first niece, he found a private corner and broke down. He wished he could be who they wanted to love, but this was how their god made him. He missed his family.

With the passing of each holiday, William would imagine them gathering cheerfully in his parent's two-story suburban home. He imagined them sitting around the big table sharing Christmas dinner, Easter brunch, and the annual Labor Day barbeque. He knew how loud it must be now with nieces and nephews. When he could stand the sharp sting of thinking about them, he allowed himself to question, *Did any of them, any one of them, ever wonder how I am?* And then he remembered vividly a story read to him as a child. It kept him awake as a small boy. It was about a little girl and a matchbox. She was out in the winter cold, freezing and hungry, trying to sell matches to survive. She glanced through a windowpane and saw a big, loving family eating their dinner in warmth and laughter, and she froze to death outside their window watching. That would not be him. He would rise above and have a happy life. They did not control his future—only haunted his past. He made a good life in the city. He had a successful practice. He had deep friendships. He had a world of colorful and interesting friends and at least one great love. He shared these thoughts with no one. But Ilana knew them anyway.

"Wine?" the waiter asked.

"The Heitz Chardonnay," William answered and coughed.

"Stop that. You know how socially unacceptable it is now to cough. One sneeze can clear out an entire movie theatre."

"Yes. I've gotten more than a few evil eyes."

"When do you go back to the allergist?" she asked.

"Next week. But truth be told, my dear, you look a helluva lot worse than me."

"I can always count on you for the ideal compliment."

"Seriously, Ilana. You're looking ashen. What are you doing for yourself that's positive?"

"I bought a membership at the gym."

"Good. Really, good. How often are you going?"

"It's on my list of things to do right after washing the car."

"You don't own a car."

"Damn it." She smiled.

"You never used those yoga lessons, did you?"

"I might still."

"You should go. Especially because you are kind of in flux right now . . ."

"In flux? William, is that a professional diagnosis?"

"This is an opportunity for you."

"An opportunity for what?"

"For reflection."

"Reflection is for sissies," she said, and William laughed out loud. He had a hearty, contagious laugh. People turned his way and laughed a little without knowing why.

So, they didn't reflect. They drank white wine and ate sloppy mussels in garlic and olive oil. They consumed two luscious desserts, one musty glass of port, and three after-dinner mints, and they had been far better fed by their friendship than by anything they'd eaten.

ISABELLA FOUND ILANA'S company tasty. She enjoyed people amid a personal struggle. She liked it when the emotional ante was high. She could sense that this was the case with Ilana, although she still didn't have all the facts. Ilana seemed to be in the clutch of personal drama meant to end in a great change, and for Isabella, change was oxygen. She could not be happy without it.

All her life changes drove her. She changed elementary schools four times, each time at her own insistence. She was a precocious child. She attended two high schools and six colleges, not capable or willing to follow a straight line. Her need to experience new environments was nearly pathological. It was a pressing urge, as inescapable as a sneeze. She was an experience junky, a culture interloper, a drama addict, and if she lived for an extended period without those heightened moments of extreme experience, then anxiety would crest inside of her and come crashing down. Contrary to appearance, she had not lived carefree but rather with meticulous care. Industriously, she had hunted the novel experience, no matter how foreign, no matter how filthy. It was nourishment when her friends or family exclaimed with confusion, "But why would she do that, or go there, or be with that man?"

Isabella would seek out uneven souls—the exalted, the wounded, and the hazardous. She stood in the crowd in front of the jail when Mandela emerged. She yanked off one of the first rocks the day the Berlin Wall fell. She bit the insides of her mouth as she watched Mother Teresa tell poverty-stricken mothers and their starving children in Calcutta that birth control was a sin. She worked in a pool hall and had strippers for friends. She dined with ambassadors, had been drunk with her gardener, and married well along the way a number of times, but always for love.

Tonight, she trolled her salon like a long-limbed Siamese cat. Even though she knew that *salon* was an archaic word, she used it anyway to describe her living room. She loved that it suggested a time past. It alluded to leisurely social evenings, when lively conversation was an art form, and it was common for people to entertain each other with wit and erudition. She hoped that it reminded her guests of Christopher Hitchens and Gertrude Stein. She did this purposefully so they knew what she expected of them.

The salon was a room with dark-red walls and heavy damask ivory curtains. One wall was decorated with ritualistic masks that Isabella brought back from Africa and New Guinea. On the wall by the door were a series of used bush weapons, knives, and machetes. Isabella enjoyed telling her genteel guests that the black flakes on the blades were the dried blood of dying Bushmen and that it was bad karma to clean it off. It was an exotic exhibit, lending theatrics where no more was needed. This was easily her favorite room. Isabella loved the night. She cherished the wide-awake hours while the world slept soundly around her. It made her feel indomitable. She spent many of those hours in this room.

Nights were different for Ilana lately. She longed for the dreamless sleep that came from dead exhaustion. Many nights these past few weeks, she met Isabella in her salon, where they had come to know and enjoy each other's company. Ilana was grateful for this surprising new friendship. This was someone who didn't know her, so she couldn't be disappointed. That's the good thing about new friends: the blank slate. Currently, what Ilana craved was constant absorption, and her psyche had found some rest, curled up within the turret of Isabella's epic distraction. She was striving to put Albany behind her. It lay-in-wait.

Ilana blurted out triumphantly, "What about *Salome*?"

Isabella's eyes sparked. "*Salome*." She thought a moment as she continued to pace around the room. "It would need to be performed the way Strauss intended, which means casting is a very serious concern."

"True. A completely nude soprano could be the most gruesome visual of the season."

"We'd need someone shapely and someone at the beginning of her career."

"I'll start a search tomorrow." Ilana sat comfortably. "How was your settlement conference with the lawyers yesterday?"

"Shockingly, Mr. Wharton rejected my very generous offer of twenty-five dollars and a one-way ticket to Timbuktu."

Ilana giggled. "Shocking."

"Shortsighted, really, Timbuktu is lovely this time of year."

Ilana added, "I wouldn't know."

"Are you not well-traveled?"

"I've been to all of the usual places."

"Oh, you mean the Paris, London, Rome grand tour?"

"Yes."

"Shame. That is so little and so very much of the same. Which languages do you speak?"

"I have two years of college Spanish. I know some Italian from the libretti. Oh, and I've almost mastered English."

"You should begin your education by traveling throughout Central and South America to grow your Spanish. You will find the Latin culture warm and exhilarating."

"Some of us have to work, Isabella."

"Dear, you're hardly living hand-to-mouth. Surely you can do some traveling."

"The opera world is unforgiving and twenty-four seven. I can say, though, that I've always wanted to go to Rio."

"Rio is a gem, and you'd look quite spectacular topless."

"I'm not the topless type."

"*On verra.* When you go, make sure you get out of the city and tour around the smaller, less commercial areas."

"I would love that. Still, it is hard to get away."

"You love your work more than anything, then?"

"I don't know if I'd say *love*, but I do like it very much. I know I'm very lucky to have it."

"Oh. Like is nice. Luck is good." Isabella pressed the intercom. "Mrs. Grace, we are ready for tea." Isabella turned to Ilana. "I love that she brings us tea. Don't you?" She placed her long, thin hands royally in her lap.

"So, did Mr. Wharton's counsel make a counteroffer?"

"Yes. They countered with the house in Arles, the Bentley, and

$85,000 a month in support."

"Oh, so, you're not that far apart then," Ilana teased.

"I'm sure he should get nothing. I'm not the one who fell out of love. He's in breach."

"Marriage is not a simple contract. There are social and moral issues."

"Ah, another American Puritan, how ordinary."

"I assure you, Isabella, I'm not a Puritan."

"You live in the United States, and so you have been inculcated by the cultural mores here, like it or not."

"And you haven't been?"

"I was. But then I shed them all one long, drugged night, forty years ago, in the Congolese jungle. A story I may tell you someday."

"Do I want to hear that story?"

Isabella's eyes bloomed. "Everyone wants to hear that story."

"Well, even though I haven't been to the Congolese jungle, I may not be as inculcated as you suspect."

"When I married, three times in fifty-five years, a fairly reasonable number as my first husband died quite young, I married men who agreed with me that sex outside of marriage was acceptable for pleasure."

Ilana said, "Okay."

"I truly loved my husbands, but I was aware that people have completely different sexual needs, and committing to sex with only one partner for an entire lifetime could be a formula for dishonesty, and that dishonesty could cause the loss of love, which is what I believe to be of value in the first place."

"I don't know." Ilana had just felt the harsh edge of honesty with Adam. "Sometimes honesty causes more pain than good."

"Historically, the concept of faithfulness was prized so that offspring could be accurately identified and cared for, and I'm in favor of that. While you have young children, monogamy may be the best course. When people were living to a ripe old age of thirty-five and experiencing at most twenty years with the same partner, I suppose it may have been tolerable. But now we live to eighty and longer, perhaps sixty-five years of sexual activity." Isabella's eyes flashed. "If you're lucky. But anyone who tells you physical attraction isn't perishable is lying. Contrary to the anniversary cards in the drugstore, it does not feel like the first time over and over with anyone."

Ilana countered, "I think the idea is to put effort into sex. Satisfying the other person is part of what being in love is."

"I contend sex has very little to do with true love." Isabella leaned in toward Ilana, cutting the distance between them in half. "A person can have world-shaking sex with someone they don't even like." She rested her elbow on the upholstered arm of the chair. Her sharp brown eyes pulled at Ilana. "True fidelity is emotional, not sexual. It is tied to friendship, respect, humor, lifestyle, and deep mutual affection. When Mr. Wharton fell 'in love' with Mrs. Grace, that was the moment he cheated on me." These last few words failed to hide the betrayal Isabella felt. Most of Isabella's words carried a cosmopolitan savior faire, but the tone changed ever so slightly at the end, and Ilana caught it. Isabella had been hurt, and Ilana was sure Mr. Wharton would pay.

Mrs. Grace entered with the tea tray and began the ritualistic setup. Ilana watched the obsequious Mrs. Grace, and she knew that even if she tried for her entire lifetime, she would never understand how a man could trade the fascinating and fearless Isabella for Mrs. Grace.

She asked Isabella, "Do you have children running around the jungle, Rio, or anywhere else?"

"No. I believe if one is going to be a mother, one must be a good one, and not all women are right for that job. I am easily impatient. I find childish questions irritating, not cute. I don't respond well to drool, piss, poopies, or vomit. I do not long to have a baby suckle from my teat, and I react negatively to loud noise."

"Doesn't sound like a recipe for motherhood."

"Exactly what I thought."

Isabella picked up an invitation from the divan and held it out for Ilana. "I'm having a cocktail party. Kind of a different crowd. You must come. You do have cocktail attire, don't you? Or do you only have those conservative straightjackets I always see you in?"

"I have a drop-dead cocktail dress that is sexy and gorgeous and looks spectacular on me."

Go shopping.

"Perfect. Wear it and bring your friend William if you like. I do love gay men. It has been my experience that many of them are more well-read than the average man."

"All right. He'll be ready to party. He's been down for three weeks with the twenty-four-hour flu. Everyone seems to be sicker longer now."

"Oh, shame, I'm never sick," Isabella answered plainly.

"Oh? What do you attribute that to?"

"Late nights, mint tea, and the critical realization that sex is aerobic. That is why the right sexual partners are so important. It is a serious health issue." She enjoyed teasing Ilana.

"Doctors do recommend half an hour of aerobic exercise every day to maintain good health and energy."

"Ilana, this must be why you look so fatigued." Ilana knew Isabella was baiting her. "But I suppose you haven't been flush in free time since you got back from Albany."

"True," Ilana replied. "But I'm not a big fan of free time anyway. It gets me in trouble."

"Do you have family in Albany?"

Ilana's brain screeched to a halt. "Um." Her words stumbled. "Not really."

Isabella allowed loose reins to her curiosity. "Not really? Hmmmm. Friends, then?"

"No."

"Oh." Isabella stroked a modern art piece of shiny, crafted marble sitting on her coffee table. Smiling, she said, "I remember one time you mentioned a carpenter?" Ilana noticed the mischief in Isabella's expression.

"Did I?" Her body's soft tissues plumped.

THE DAY TURNED night sooner, the stifling heat was a memory, and the edges of autumn were now crowding in around the frame of the city. This morning, very early, when Ilana took a shortcut across the empty stage at the deserted Lyric Opera House, she stopped abruptly in the middle. She had taken this shortcut for years, and she had never stopped before. Did she hear something? Ilana turned and looked out at the vacant theatre. Thousands of seats with their jaws dropped, long carpeted aisles that narrowed and then disappeared into darkness, light pods of red from exit signs shining with subtle alarm, this way out. She swallowed a gush of anxiety. It was completely silent, and she was completely alone. Her arms fell to her sides. She felt bare. She was more alone than ever: her mom was gone, Adam was gone, William must have a new boyfriend. She felt the ghost of Albany standing behind her, over her shoulder, close enough to feel it breathing on the back of her neck. All the questions. The consequences of that trip had not been fully realized, and so it hung in the quiet moments of her life, lingering. She felt something brush her cheek. She shivered and then darted across the stage and into the wings, panting. The janitor looked up, startled. She nodded and moved on as quickly as seemed appropriate. Ilana was connected to her body in a new way, trying to learn to live with herself. She felt like she was two people; she couldn't figure out how to bring her two selves together.

Saturday nights were easiest for her. There was so much required of her pre-curtain that it was hard for her to think about anything else. Now, with the stage set and the performers primed, Ilana peeked out and examined the audience. Her eyes ran up and down the rows. The audience members were entranced by the orchestra, and they peered into the pit as they took their seats. Reviewing the glossy rows of patrons, she wondered for a brief second how many pretenders were sitting there faking their lives like she was. How many were following rules they didn't even acknowledge? Nevertheless, she was relieved that the evening was laid out so well. Then, she saw the paramedic at the stage door. She walked toward him, determined but not rushing; that was the difference between perceived and actual authority.

Glen caught up with her, and she asked, "What?"

"Chorus master slipped on the stairs."

The paramedic looked uneasily at the cluttered, chaotic backstage. "Is there a more direct route?"

Glen and Ilana answered together, "No."

Ilana asked Glen, "What do you think of the audience?"

"C-plus."

They graded all audiences. When she first began in opera, Ilana saw the audience as individuals, each carrying the baggage of their day with them to the theater, but she learned after her first season that audiences became a single entity once the lights went down. The members were susceptible to each other in mystifying ways. The company didn't know what to expect until the curtain rose. The exact performance on two different nights could be greeted completely differently, and it wasn't the show; it was the audience. There were times when the audience came with an agenda, either they disapproved of the casting, or they had been primed to be either ecstatic or hostile depending on the reviews. Some of these instances were notorious moments in the history of opera, which included the countless nights of openly partisan whistling and the throwing of vegetables so common with the La Scala opera-goers. Ilana knew the audience was the wild card. It was the one thing over which she had absolutely no control. The mood of the audience could make or break any performance. William called it a dysfunctional codependent relationship.

They passed Vincent as they hurried backstage. Ilana asked, "Time?"

"Three and a half minutes to curtain," he replied.

Ilana turned to the paramedic who was following her and warned him seriously, "Stay very close." And she took off straight across the stage. Heavy backdrops fell silently and with great speed from thirty feet above. Pillars were being constructed by stagehands in hard hats speeding around in motorized forklifts. Props people were scurrying around moving furniture. A ground cloth was attached in sections. It was a coordinated chaos. Flying pieces of hefty scenery missed them by a hair as Ilana walked with complete confidence across the floor, and the worried paramedic couldn't get close enough.

At the bottom of the stairs, a small group watched the chorus master's ankle swell. The paramedic knelt down to examine it.

Ilana felt Glen hovering behind her. He'd been trying to set a meeting with her all week. She knew his jealousy over her growing friendship with Isabella was ripe. The paramedic wrapped the chorus master's ankle.

"So, with Wharton," Glen dove in, "how goes it? Is she interesting?"

"Exotically so."

Glen's friendly interest was like that of a hyena hanging slightly back from the pride, grinning in camaraderie but mostly waiting.

He commented, "She's so well-connected and so wealthy—it's unimaginable. I checked, and fortunately, she has no children, so we have a good shot at an estate donation."

Such a pig.

Glen said, "You wouldn't believe some of the stories I've heard about her."

Ilana turned from the paramedic and faced Glen. "Actually, I would believe every story you've heard."

"But she's elderly now," Glen added.

"Not by any definition I've ever known."

"How does she strike you?"

"She strikes me as a woman who would ride a llama bareback through a burning building in a pair of crotchless panties if she damn well felt like it."

Glen cued up his smile, the synthetic one manufactured "as needed." He wanted Wharton. Wharton should be his contact. Ilana returned his smile with exactly the same level of faux warmth. Glen was always on the hunt. He was irreplaceable, but no matter how hard she tried, she couldn't make herself like him. The chorus master stood tenuously and was led off.

"Okay?" Ilana asked.

He nodded and hobbled off.

A voice came in over Ilana's headphones. "Curtain, thirty seconds."

An intern came up from behind, touched Ilana's arm, and held out a cell phone.

"Who brought a phone in here?" she asked.

"It's yours. They had me bring it down from the office. You have a call, and they said it's important."

Over her headphones, she heard, "Twenty seconds."

"Oh, good grief." Ilana paused, distracted. She looked quickly around the stage. Everything seemed to be in place.

"I should get rid of this call, then?" the intern confirmed.

"Who is it?"

"Someone named Fiona."

And it was like plunging into a swimming pool. Her ears stuffed, and her eyes blurred. Ilana felt detached as she watched her own hand reach out and take the phone. People were talking to her, but she did not hear them; she saw their mouths moving but heard nothing. In a trance, she crossed out of the confusion, walked down the stairs, opened the door to the backstage ladies' room, entered the stall, locked the door, and sat down.

"Hello?"

"Missy?" Fiona's voice sounded so familiar.

"Yes. Hi."

"Hope this ain't a bad time for you. Not busy, are you?"

"Not at all."

"Good, 'cause that rude guy tried to give me the brush-off. You left your card and all, so I told him it was okay, you said."

"Yes. I'm glad to hear from you." A long pause followed. Neither woman knew what to say.

"Patrick is leaving for NYU, and since you're the only person we know down there in Manhattan, Shea thought you might, you know, take him under your wing. You know, so he had someone local to call if he got arrested or sick or in some kinda trouble."

My little brother.

Emotion peaked. "Oh, yes, yes, I'd be so happy to, Fiona, happy to." Her hands were trembling. She gripped her slipping phone.

"In fact, gee, I had an idea on the spur here," Fiona continued, and Ilana noted how false it sounded and how whatever she was to say was most likely mauled to death in her mind. There was nothing spur-of-the-moment about this. "How about, I was thinking, maybe you could come up tomorrow for the going-away party? Yeah, how about that? You could get to know each other a bit. You know, I'm saying, if you want to and you're not busy."

"I want to."

"Okay, then. Good. Yeah, good."

"Good. I can take the two o'clock."

"Okay."

"Okay."

They hung up. Ilana heard the orchestra upstairs but stayed in the stall for a long time.

Up in Albany, Fiona walked to the church cemetery. She stood for a while, looking at the rectory. The window she had shattered was boarded up. She didn't know why they hadn't fixed it. When she was a devout young girl, comforted daily by the church she loved, she thought the windows were the eyes of God, and through its glass, he watched his community of people with kindness. Now it seemed right to see the window disfigured by a cast of ghastly wood and duct tape. A blind eye. Yes. God was blind. He cannot see her standing there precariously perched on the possibility of a conversation that had been stalled for thirty years.

"Fiona?" The voice came low and soft from behind her. She turned slowly, not sure what she would see: her dead brother, some other restless soul, God himself?

"I hope you are here to talk because the church can't afford another broken window," Father Cummings said.

"Not sure yet."

"Oh. I see. Whenever you're ready. I'll wait. I've been waiting."

He turned and walked to the church steps, and she watched him struggle to get up them. The moist and young of Father Cummings had been left out too long in the hot sun. His skin was cracked, his hair white, his gait uneven; time had been unforgiving. It was inconceivable to her that only seven years separated the two of them. It looked like decades. She hadn't heard that he was sick and wondered what afflicted him. He opened the church door and entered, leaving it ajar. Fiona hadn't stepped a single foot inside the church in over thirty years. She was ready.

Fiona had always felt deeply affected by the solemnity of the church. She recognized this church as a *thin place*. Her mother used to tell her stories about thin places like Roslin Glen in Scotland. It was a place where the partition between the divine and earthly was thin, where the separation between the material and the spiritual was diaphanous, where the passage of time was erratic, and where one could sense an odd energy and lose their bearings. She had certainly lost hers.

As she entered, the statues' hands laid their lean, possessive fingers on her. She knew the audible hush was decades of softly whispered prayers—prayers spoken in hope and trapped inside wooden walls, waiting for the ears of their god. At the center aisle, she planted both feet and took a hard look around. The nave was so tiny. It had loomed cavernous in her memory.

It was the scent of the room that triggered her most visceral memory, the burning wax from candles that were lit with purpose:

candles that burned for broken hearts, for damaged families, for lost souls, and one candle that burned for her every single day since *that* day. Standing there, she felt the warmth of the quiet and the relief she remembered that came with utter peace. She had missed this stillness most of all. Hesitating there at a doorway to her past and peppered with memories, she realized she was not that girl anymore; the freedom from that acknowledgment felt luscious. She saw Father Cummings kneeling in the first pew. She walked the aisle with confidence and sat down next to him. She waited for him to finish his prayer. He sat back.

"I was thanking God."

"Because I didn't break another window?"

"Because he has finally guided you here."

With a touch of sarcasm, she said, "And you've been waiting?"

"Every hour of every day."

She looked away, suddenly uncomfortable by the unanticipated vulnerability on his face.

She remarked, "Not one thing has changed. Even the crack in the altar is still here."

"I opposed all of the changes. I wanted it to stay exactly as it was."

"Why?"

"The walls, the stained glass, the pews, they are all witnesses. Fiona, I have always wondered why you didn't come to me. Why you didn't tell me."

"Tell you what? You're a priest. I was sixteen."

"Sixteen. Sixteen." He wiped his nose with the cuff of his vestment. "I can't believe it. Even as I say it. Back then, it didn't seem as young as I know it is now. It was you and me. And you paid an enormous price because of me."

"It was both of us. I pushed you. I can't pretend I didn't. I believed I was in love. I was in love."

"It was my job to stop. My place."

They sat in silence. Fiona looked at her fingers and chipped off a bit of her nail polish.

"How did you find out?" she asked.

"Your mother came to confession that summer."

Fiona was stunned. "She did? My mother?"

"It was the only time she ever came here. I sat behind the screen, listening to her confess my sin. It was clear you had not told her who. I figured you had a reason. I asked if you were going to come in, and she said you'd gone away. The pain was so acute, I couldn't leave my bed for weeks. The diocese sent doctors, but no one could figure out what was wrong with me. How could they? How could they guess the heartache, the shame, the worry for you, the destruction of everything that I held sacred, everything that mattered to me." He dropped his head in his hands. "What I had done."

"What *we* had done," she corrected him. "You were young, too. Twenty-three is young."

"Not that young. I tried hard to find where you went, but no one knew. I know it's no excuse, but I want to say that I'm a man. Just a flawed man who fell in love when he wasn't allowed to." He looked at her beseechingly. "I have dedicated my entire life as penance for that one moment."

"Everybody around here always said what a great priest you are. At first, I got angry, and then, I had to laugh."

"Rightly. Rightly. I am laughable." Emotion choked his next words. "I failed you. I failed my vows. I failed my God. For that, there's no penance. I feel the disgrace today exactly as I did thirty years ago. There has been no relief. I've allowed no relief. Not a single day has passed that I haven't risen before dawn, knelt on the cold stone, and prayed privately for you and for the child. I know it isn't much, but it was all I could think to do."

"Oh, Frank." She said his name. It felt good. She allowed herself to look at him unguardedly. They searched each other's eyes for the people they had been, for the young two, locked in one forbidden moment of love thirty years ago. "It was all so long ago, Frank."

"It was yesterday."

The devastation of his life was so complete, so real, it reached her. This man who sat beside her was irreparably broken.

"I saw our girl."

"A girl?"

"Yes. She's a woman now. Pretty. Whip-smart."

"I have waited a long time for you to come to see me. I don't know if this will help now in any way, but I always wanted to tell you." He turned his body so he faced her fully. "Fi, my love and affection were genuine. It grew slowly over the months we worked closely here together. I had no right to fall in love, but I truly did. And if you would've stayed, if you would've told me, I would've made my life with you."

A small smile crossed Fiona's face. "Yeah, actually, it does help." Fiona felt aloft. "It helps a whole lot."

She saw the statues of the saints smile generously and open their arms to her. She heard the heartbeat begin anew in the church all around her. She felt its rhythm with her own. She looked at the destroyed man beside her, whom she once loved with all her heart, and she felt something for him she never thought possible: mercy. Yes, mercy, because there had surely been enough suffering to go around.

Father Cummings watched her leave. She still had that little hitch in her right hip when she stepped. He felt the urge to smile, but he had lost that recipe. He had seen the dawning of forgiveness in her eyes, and with fervor only possible in the profoundly religious, he thanked God for this sweetness. Throughout the years, many of his parishioners had spoken of how life seemed unsuited to Father Cummings. He was too frail for its ordeals. He seemed excessively affected by the cold, by the heat, by the passing of the days. Still, he had been a faithful cleric, always at the bed of the sick, always collecting for the poor, and while there was some sense of warmth within him, it had always been completely inaccessible. Even so, they knew Father Cummings was available for confession twenty-four hours a day. He knew what it was like to nurse an injury to one's soul. He had never confessed his own sin. He had not tried to relieve the burden of it. This Sunday, at long last, he will go to confession. This Sunday, he will receive absolution for a sin that he had carried for thirty years. He believed that Fiona's coming was a sign from God. Perhaps it was forgiveness? He wondered about their child, who was now a woman. He prayed that she was Catholic.

After Fiona closed the church door, it wasn't Father Cummings who lay down on the pew with grateful relief; it was Frank. It was Frank who had been chained in pain for all these years. It was Frank who lost control that night, and now it was Frank who put his head down on the wooden bench, surrounded by everything dear to him, sleeping in the rapture of tranquility he had not known for decades. And 150 miles away in Manhattan, Ilana couldn't know how the events that she'd set in motion had cleared the path for one man to heal after a lifetime of remorse and self-rebuke. She would never know that to the man who gave her life, she returned the favor.

AT ILANA'S APARTMENT, she hurriedly packed her overnight bag, although the haste was needless because she had time. The haste was inside. It was excess emotional energy that made her rush. It was an internal force that drove her, an impulse she attempted to restrain even as she felt it carry her off. She sensed her groundlessness, but she did not stretch her toes down to reach or try to balance. Instead, she packed and packed again. The Albany story wasn't finished. It was a book half-read, with the characters poised in midsentence, a novel left open in the middle of her life. Everywhere she went, her mind tripped over it. She felt compelled to finish it. This time, however, she was in control. Expectation was on her side. She was done being surprised.

A knock on her door surprised her. She walked over and swung open the door. Adam stood on the other side, carrying a small cake box.

He held up the box. "Mario's caramel cheesecake. Your favorite."

"Thanks. But, actually, Adam, while I would definitely like to talk to you, I'm in a hurry to the train station."

"I'll ride along."

"No." Too strong. She tried again, softly. "No, Adam."

"I've been thinking about it all," he said with a self-deprecating chuckle as he entered and closed the door behind him. "Now there's an understatement."

She smiled sadly and admitted, "Me too." What she meant was that she had been thinking obsessively about Albany and everything that goes with Albany.

Adam thought she meant him. He felt heartened and said, "Look, I understand that a lot of what's gone on is connected to the death of your mother. I know you're still grieving, and it has thrown you off balance. I want to help." His eyes filled. "Ilana, I love you."

This admission salted the wound inside of her, and again, it began to bleed. How could she be the source of all this sorrow? She knew it would be a long time before she would unsympathetically judge another human being because much of what she thought was immutable, even about herself, turned out to be wrong.

She looked at Adam's face and could see his feelings were controlled by a short rein. She could make him happy. She had the power on the tip of her tongue. She could blow off Albany. It would be easy, but it would be wrong because then they would need to begin the process of separation all over again. Looking at him right now, she was only certain of one thing: she could not marry Adam. It would be dishonest. Adam was the future she'd been chauffeured to by circumstance, by social expectation, and by the world she was raised in. All she learned was that she didn't know what she wanted.

"Adam." Her voice failed.

He sensed the way her sentence was going. "Ilana, I don't know what went on in Albany, and I don't want to know any details." He took a deep breath. "I forgive you. Let's forget it and move on."

"No. We can't."

"If I'm willing to let it go, surely you should be. I get that it is all wound up with your birth confusion and genetics, and maybe I talk too much about motivation and intention and all that, but the bottom line is that it was a mistake. Humans make mistakes. It is our nature. We can try and understand it together." He put the cake down on the coffee table in frustration.

"No."

"Can you love me for three years and then turn it off like a faucet?"

"I haven't turned it off. I still love you, Adam." She turned to him fully and completely and said the absolute truth. "I still love you. It's different now."

"Why can't we try to fix this?"

"We've had a comfortable love, genuine and caring, but—"

"But what?" Incredulously, he repeated, "But what?"

"I don't think I want comfortable." She tried so hard to make it better, or at least easier. "You deserve someone who is completely and passionately in love, who wants the kind of life you want. I don't even know what I want. I have been blindly following models all my life: the good girl, the good student, the good daughter, the career woman, all models I have never questioned and never examined. There has been so much hidden training. I feel . . . I feel like a marionette."

"What the hell are you talking about?"

She took a slow breath. How could she explain this to him when it was still so unclear to her?

"Ilana, listen to me," Adam said with severity and power that was not conducive to discussion. "Hear what I am saying. You are having some kind of nervous breakdown due to the death of your mom. You can take control. Calm your brain and take conscious control."

"I don't want to marry you, so I must be having a nervous breakdown?"

"I'm not saying that."

Her voice rose. "I'm not having a breakdown," she said with a conviction she did not actually feel. She turned back to her overnight bag. "Right now, I need to get to the train station."

Exasperated, he asked, "Where are you going in such a hurry?"

"Albany."

"Oh, god!" He threw his hands up and began to pace.

"Fiona called me, invited me. It's what I need to do."

"What about what I need?" He took her arm and made her look at him. "What if I said I needed you?" He stood on the edge of an irretrievable loss of dignity. She didn't want the responsibility for his pain. She was flailing around for answers. All she wanted was a switch for her brain—to turn it off, to turn it off, to get a break.

Her voice shook. "Fiona reached out to me."

His voice rose in anger. "You're going to see that guy, right?"

"Wrong. I'm going to see her. To talk to Fiona. It's what I wanted all along."

He yelled at her, "Ilana, get a grip. It's me. I know you better than anyone. We were meant to be happy together." Emotionally, he continued, "We have a world and a life. What are you doing to us? *Why* are you doing this?"

Ilana hesitated. She stared at him, momentarily paralyzed and experiencing a crippling confusion, wondering if he was right. Her eyes swam. Bewildered. Tremulous.

Adam hovered. His face was red. His eyes were demanding an answer she didn't have.

Be honest. Be honest. It was her only guide. She went with it.

"I'm not sure what I'm doing. I need to hear what Fiona wants to say. You must protect yourself. Stay away from me. I don't know where this is going. All I know is that I have to play it out, play it to the end."

Angry tears filled his eyes as he put it all on the line. "Even if it's the end of us?"

A moment, a hesitation, then she said, "Yes. Even then."

Adam backed away from her, turned, and walked out.

On her way to the station, Ilana reran the conversation on a constant loop. She had shared a significant part of her life with him. He had been a support, a friend, and a lover. He held her during the darkest hours of her life. Memories were catapulted to the front of her mind, powerfully vivid. Her mom had always liked Adam. Ilana considered the real possibility that she had just made the biggest mistake of her meticulously planned life. She got on the train anyway.

Meanwhile, in the corner of her mind, Isabella Wharton sat in a prominent chair. Ilana knew that Isabella had lived her life outside the lines with no regard for the social model and customary norms. She was a woman who had seen things, who had been hard, soft, and heroic, and who had not shied from life's extremes. The more time Ilana spent with her, the more she admired her, and the aperture of Ilana's world widened.

Sitting on the train, the coarse fabric of the seat scratched her thigh. She crossed her legs, then uncrossed, then crossed again. She got tired of staring at the geometric pattern on the indoor/outdoor carpet and focused out the window. Her life felt exactly like the scenery flashing by. She was going along, but she was not the engine, not even the navigator. Sounds grew acute—steel wheels, baby cry, newspaper shuffle, a man's cough, computer clicks, phone ring, briefcase open—life got loud around her. Should she be running toward Albany or away? She understood on a fundamental level that no matter what anyone might speculate about how the conscious or unconscious motivates decisions—or what the underlying frayed tapestry of human nature was—something subliminal was driving her. She could call it curiosity, but that was too unintentional. She wondered about what we label curiosity. Where does curiosity come from? Is it evidence of an unseen, unconscious guiding hand?

The headline on the magazine she spied on the train's floor asked readers how they spent their free time. She'd never had an off switch. Her whole life, she'd simmered, planning and prepping, and it took every second she had. There was the elite preschool at two years and nine months, where she prepped for the entrance exam for the private K–12. Next, she began the serial school preparations where quizzes led to chapter tests, which led to unit tests, then midterms, and then finals. In high school, she prepped for the SAT for college. In college, she prepped for the GMAT for business school. After the MBA, she prepped for the interview for the right job, and then she hit the ground running and never slowed down until now, until right now. She had a 401k, a pension, a life insurance policy, and the wrong life. But then, painfully, she had to admit, no, she had exactly the life she'd prepped for.

Ilana sidestepped her way off the train platform and into the terminal tube, navigating through the rolling bags. She remembered the way to the taxi stand. A hand jutted out from the crowd and grabbed her carry-on bag. She jerked back, ready for a confrontation.

Cafferty.

She let go of the bag. They said nothing. She followed Cafferty to the parking garage. He held open the door of his pickup truck. She climbed in. They drove. She squirmed. She tucked her hair behind her ears. She broke the silence.

"Fiona called you to get me?"

"Yup."

"Thanks for picking me up."

"Yup."

Ilana studied him. He was not really handsome at all. His body was overtly muscular. He had a tough, angular, and indifferent face. This was a man she would avoid at a party. She couldn't imagine why she was attracted to him.

A moment passed, and she said, "I've arranged for a hotel room. Could you please drop me there so I can change?"

"Hilton?" He chuckled, and it sounded derisive.

"Marriott."

"Serious?"

"Yes. I came to see Fiona and Patrick."

"I know."

He yanked the car to the side of the road and jammed it into park. He turned to her. "I make a good breakfast."

"You do." She tugged on her hair as her pulse shot up. His eyes were intense, and she noted how satisfying it felt to be wanted with such raw force. She answered too politely, "I think a hotel might be best. But thank you."

"But thank you?" He leaned in. "You've confused me for someone in your other world."

"Unlikely." She breathed in. The smell. Wood. Moss. Green. Earth. She tried to hold her ground while her body mutinied.

"So, I have to figure out what you want? Figure out which is true. Your words, or your body? One of you is lying. Seems to be a habit of yours."

"Lying?"

"Lying."

"Maybe, maybe because I don't know what I want anymore."

"I can help with that." He slid his hand underneath her skirt and slowly dragged one finger up the inside of her thigh. "When was the last time someone took you limb-from-limb in a car?"

"Never." A shudder.

He ran his tongue up the soft underside of her bare arm.

"I do have some self-control."

"Are you sure you wanna use it? Like right now?"

His hand entered her panties. Her head dropped back.

AT THE PUB, the hometown crowd drank in the night in their usual spots, but the piano was silent because Nellie was late. It waited, looking cranky and dilapidated, the white keys yellow and the black keys chipped. It seemed incapable of music without Nellie. Ilana knew legions of musicians who had anthropomorphized their instruments, but here, it felt as though the piano actually had an attitude. It sat peevishly. Nellie Shannon was late, and the piano knew it.

Willow hung gaudy streamers that she had shredded into thin strands so there were more of them. A sign reading "bon voyage" lay on a table. Shea was pouring drinks behind the bar when Ilana and Cafferty entered.

"Hey, Missy," Shea yelled and poured them both a shot.

"Pop, her name's Ilana." Willow smiled. "Decorating for the big shindig tomorrow night." With all her eccentricities, Willow had a lovely quality that engendered affection.

"Hi, Willow. Beautiful sweater."

Willow winked at her. Ilana smiled back. Cafferty wandered away and began a game of darts with two men whom Ilana would have crossed the street to avoid if walking alone. She had learned that feeling threatened was more a function of what you're used to than actual risk. She knew this thought would please Isabella.

The locals stirred around in the pub, all the usual ingredients of the community stew. It was a collective living room. She recognized a few people from her last visit and noted they were sitting in the same spots.

"Hey, doll." She turned to see the drunken man lick his hands and then flatten his unruly wirehair to spiff up. "Lonny Day here." She looked. He continued, "So, wha d'ya doin'?"

She teased, "I am pursuing a path of intellectual inquiry on the questions raised about my life choices, especially considering the biological genesis of thought, epigenetics, learned bias and norms, and the sneaky slippage between conscious and unconscious decision-making."

A pause.

"No, fuckin' shit, me too."

Ilana laughed. "What are the odds?"

Shea slid over toward them. "Hey, Lonny, leave her alone."

"We's talkin'."

"Missy, if he bothers you, hit him over the head with a bottle. That's what we do." He landed a bottle on the table next to her.

"Thanks for the tip."

Shea added, "Gotta hit him kind of hard too, 'cause he's real stubborn."

Lonny nodded. "Yup, that's true."

"Shea, where's Fiona?" Ilana asked.

"Been hard to keep track last few weeks. Been walking around like some kinda whirligig. Tongues have been wagging around her. Married all these years, and she still surprises me."

"Did you and Fiona marry very young?"

"Nah, we were ripe and ready. Got pregnant with Willow on our honeymoon."

"Oh." A pause. "I was adopted." She searched his face for some sign of knowing.

"That right?"

"Yes."

"Never known an adopted person before. Wait, that's not true. Lindy Baines was adopted. Yeah, I remember her. Used to blender-up all her meals and eat them through a straw. She was a strange one."

Ilana grinned, and one eyebrow went up. "Like me?'

"Aw, you're not strange. Different, though. Like someone you could have known but didn't. Know what I mean?"

"Yes."

"But I'll tell you what. Fiona was something when I met her."

"Yeah?"

"So innocent, sweet, pure like an angel. I remember she'd been out of town for a spell, and then she came back, and she looked beautiful. She was fresh, you know? I saw her trying to get a job at the dress shop on Third. She's always been a snazzy dresser. Still is. I was delivering UPS then, before I got the pub, and I watched her fill out the application real slow, like she thought so carefully about every word. I knew right there that was the girl I would marry. I knew exactly who she was that first moment. Sure, now she's a pain in the ass, but I gotta tell you, I love that witch."

"And would you love her no matter what?"

Shea's eyes locked onto Ilana's, and his playfulness dissolved. For a split second, she saw an edge in his face that seemed perilous. Slowly, he took the cigar stub from his lips and answered with sagacity she did not expect. "No one loves anyone no matter what, Missy. It all matters, especially in love."

Later, Cafferty's dogs jumped all over her. They welcomed her back to his home like a lost traveler. Their gusto made her happy. She had never received such a dramatic greeting. Her family was more of the genuine smile, light kiss on both cheeks variety, reserved, with only the appropriate amount of fuss. These dogs were in sync with the natural state of their surroundings.

"What's this?" Ilana asked.

"Fish 'n chips from Stop 'n Go."

"Looks pretty greasy."

"Yeah, I thought it looked good too." He took a bite.

"Okay." She nibbled.

"What? You don't like fish?"

"I like sushi."

"You eat that?"

"You eat this?"

As they ate, Cafferty casually asked her about her life in Manhattan. He was trying to be polite because he genuinely didn't give a shit about Manhattan. It did seem like the right thing to ask.

With vivid detail and breezy enthusiasm, Ilana launched into a monologue about Isabella Wharton, and that led to stories about the opera. She mimicked a hot-tempered soprano who, in a fit last season, began screaming at the audience in Hungarian. She told a tale about a particularly nasty row with the orchestra after someone put Crazy Glue on the maestro's baton. She felt compelled to give Cafferty the details of her successes because he didn't seem to know who she was by her title and her address. This was the way it worked in Manhattan. You said hello and then you said where you lived and what you did, and it triggered a precise platform of data, including salary level, education completed, and presumed connections. Ilana could not relax until she was certain that Cafferty was at least a little impressed. She spread her achievements out all over the room.

She was grateful to crawl in between his sheets and arms. She knew she was leaving the next day, and so she let go and gave herself permission to be with him in the moment. She held off from judging herself for this one night. And as sleep closed her in, she imagined that maybe Cafferty would visit her sometime. She could show him her favorite restaurants, her Broadway tickets, and Central Park. So fun. Then, fully relaxed, warm, and physically sated, in his nest, she slept. When she exhaled, he breathed in. There was a rhythm to them.

After Ilana's eyes closed, Cafferty studied her. He had let her ramble on. She had reaffirmed all his reasons for disliking Manhattan. All this talk about folks married many times, of sex as an activity like bowling, of grown people gluing other grown people. Ilana's world sounded like a mix of the immoral, the unnatural, and the pointless. Good that she was here now. He was relieved to have her asleep in his arms. The contour of her body curved precisely up against his. He would peel away that silly city. He knew what she needed. She needed to sit down and soak her feet in the river. He would take her to Miller Pond. And then, he, too, slept.

IN HIS EAST VILLAGE apartment, William stood and shivered. He regarded all his things. His gaze fell on the Oriental rug, and he remembered when he and David found it at a garage sale on their drive back from Maine. Some wretched older couple had laid their insides out all over their front lawn for everyone to pick over. Their discards told a long story: five TV tray tables, two dial telephones, an 8-track tape player with thirty-five homemade tapes including Isaac Hayes, a car phone with antenna, *The Jane Fonda's Workout* video, a half-assembled Total Gym, a typewriter, a fold-up bridge table with four mangled decks of cards, a circular poker chip holder (the chips long gone), a pet rock, a VCR with *Billy Jack* stuck in the mouth, and this Persian rug. William, who knew about these things, had insisted on telling the warring suburban couple that the rug was authentic and worth much more than they were asking. He felt like he was stealing. David was furious with him. David believed that everyone had to own their flaws. These people were clearly stupid. They didn't know the value of their own rug. They probably didn't know the value of anything else in their lives, including each other. William insisted on paying more anyway. Later, David would tell their friends that they purchased the rug from the cast of *Les Misérables*. For seven years, William and David had been a couple. They had enjoyed an easy, committed, and loving relationship. When David died in an accident, it was devastating.

William glanced around and understood that the apartment itself didn't matter; it was walls, nothing more. The things inside were the souvenirs of his life. These were the things that traveled with him. Perhaps it was time to let the apartment go. It was time for the footprint of his life to be smaller or somehow different. He felt cluttered. He would reorganize. He liked cleaning out the closets; for months, it gave back satisfaction. He had let the chores slide recently. The rooms no longer had that fastidious appearance he found ideal. Dust had crept in. David used to say that dust would be bold if given an inch. It was not that William didn't see it anymore; he saw it, but he found it too hard to get to. He sat feeling exhausted and seriously considered not answering the door when he heard the knock, but it persisted, so he got up and answered.

"Hey. Sorry. You probably hate surprise visitors."

"Not a bit," William replied, and he motioned Adam in because even feeling sick like he was, William wouldn't close his door.

Adam sat down pathetically. "She went back there. To Albany."

"Oh."

"William, you know her as well as I do. She might even say better. You must tell me how to drive her back to her senses."

William took a quiet breath and walked to the wet bar. "Bourbon?"

"Sure."

William wanted to read a book or take a nap, but Adam was despondent, so he poured them each a glass. Then, he did what he did best: he listened. He felt deeply sorry for Adam because they both knew where it stood. Adam's fingers gripped the glass so hard that the tips turned white. He took a shaky sip.

He asked, "How did you do it?"

"What?"

"How did you go on without David? I can't imagine my life without her."

With raw honesty, William replied, "I looked so damn hard for another option, but suicide seemed melodramatic." He rubbed his eyes. "All loss is bloody." William knew this. He knew intimately the demon that Adam now faced. In the beginning, the loss will sit like a stone ruthlessly on his chest day and night. There was no winning, no beating it back. It had a course to run, and it would run all over him. William truly did understand loss. He was glad he had opened his door. An hour later, with no answer, Adam thanked him and left for home. William crawled into bed so fast that he was asleep before Adam even got in the cab.

After leaving, Adam couldn't decide. He couldn't decide a thing: not whether to stand or sit, whether to eat or not. He couldn't decide if he should answer his phone messages, take a shower, or open the window. He couldn't make himself decide. He kept trying to decide.

He was suspended. Later, he would describe this state as compulsory and say it felt like hovering, as though he were waiting for a message about what to do next but from an outside source. He stood forestalled as his brain attempted to process the trauma of this derailing of his future. In this blurred state, his brain was striving to create a story that made sense, a story to explain what had happened. He knew this was what brains do. He waited. It was a difficult task for the storytelling part of his mind to piece back together some semblance of a future.

When he finally did sit down, it was in the soft leather chair that he had brought home from the office because it rocked. Something about the rocking—rocking back and forth. Then, he began the replay. He replayed his last scene with her over and over, considering what he said, rehearsing what he should have said, changing the tone and altering his movements, repeating, reworking, reviewing. His mind chewed and chewed, searching for solace. And then, he thought of his middle school crush again; for some reason, Esther Ann Holiday popped into his mind.

ILANA WAS on the phone with the musician's union when Cafferty woke up and came into the kitchen. Since then, without pausing her phone call, she had breakfast, got dressed, and climbed into Cafferty's pickup truck. Cafferty heard that money was overdue for something or other, and Ilana was very heated. He thought about how silly her job sounded and how senseless to be upset over something like that. He was confident he could fix her.

Half an hour later, Cafferty pulled the truck off the asphalt and onto a curved dirt road. They tunneled along through a swirl of tire-kicked dust and stopped in front of a fence. He got out, went around, and opened her door. She was in mid-sentence. He grabbed the cell phone from her hand and turned it off.

Irritated, she asked, "What are you doing?"

"Bad cell area."

"Cafferty, that was important."

"Follow me or stay here alone. Up to you."

She looked. Woods wrapped around the truck with powerful, thick, domineering old trunks. The dust had not yet settled, and the sun, which shimmied through the branch canopy, created thick lines of light alive with frenzied particles. He shoved her cell phone carelessly into his pocket and walked toward the fence. No way would she stay here alone. She would feel more at home in the subway at midnight. She got out of the car. He boosted her over the fence. Then, he stood atop the *No Trespassing* sign to get himself over. They walked farther into the woods.

Fifteen minutes later, they arrived. They scrambled together to the top of a huge stone pile. Ilana watched mesmerized as Cafferty carelessly tossed off his clothes. He stood stark naked on the top of a huge rock and jumped off into the clear lake water below. She watched him plunge down and sensed the pool's depth, more deep than wide. He surfaced, stroking the cool water. This was a pool designed by nature, fresh rainwater caught in a trough of granite. She wondered how anyone would know it was here, but Cafferty grew up here, and children knew these things. She knew that children live in the natural environment in a way that is never shared by adults and with an interconnectedness that adults never know. No place was like where one ran loose as a child. She thought adults could show the fastest route to the highway and the closest ATM, but only a child knows which hedge has the secret crawl space, which alley has the wooden ramp to the broken fire escape, and which rock in the old wall is loose enough to remove and peek through into the neighbor's yard.

"C'mon," Cafferty encouraged her from below.

She was hot from the hike. It was sticky, not much like autumn at all. Her skirt clung to the back of her thighs. She looked at the promise of chilled refreshment below. Her eyes scoured the surrounding area, and it was deserted. Should she do this? And then, a thought, Isabella. Isabella would be the first one in. Isabella wouldn't care or think twice. Self-consciously, she began to shed her clothes. She thought about the local headlines: Naked Opera Manager Arrested for Trespassing and Indecency. She kind of liked it and knew lots of good lawyers in the city.

Everything off. Once naked, she glanced around again and then stood straight up to take her leap. And it was not until then, not until she stood, with her legs slightly parted, with her arms straight out from her sides, that she felt it and stopped. There, up high, completely bare, she felt the sun over every inch of her skin. She felt the breeze touch her in all her tender places. She closed her eyes. She tilted her head back. She experienced the union of the warm granite with the soles of her feet. Cafferty looked up and watched, drawn in. The forest seemed unusually quiet, and everything felt balanced on the tip of something else. All things waited on the slim, raw woman, standing motionless in a single instant of utter elemental harmony. And then, she fell forward. She did not open her eyes. She allowed herself to fall naturally in a moment of immaculate trust. She fell to the lake, and the liquid enveloped her body. The water touched her with the same intimacy as the wind. Fluid air bubbles ran along her unwrapped body, in between her legs, and along the tips of her nipples. No matter what happened to Ilana, for the rest of her life, she would never again be fully contented swimming clothed.

Later, at O'Hollerans pub, the party began early. Nellie was banging out a song. The music jazzed the locals, and folks sang along. Patrick was being toasted and slapped. A few had brought him gifts.

This time, Ilana arrived in sync, and she felt the difference. This was a room of people who expected everyone who entered. She recognized most of the faces now. It embarrassed her to realize how blatantly she must have stuck out that first time. She would have never entered if she had known that this was not really a public place. She wondered how many bars there were like this across the globe, active community living rooms.

Ilana relaxed on one of the black stools beside the piano as she waited for Fiona, who had been conspicuously absent. Ilana listened to the rousing music. She loved the characterized sound that came from the out-of-tune keys. She almost felt she knew the words, but that would be impossible. A number of people came over and talked to her. She was an accepted anomaly now. She was that opera lady.

"The pub is not the same when you're not playing, Nellie." Ilana smiled fondly at her grandmother. "It's like the room isn't awake."

Nellie held a conversation without ever missing a note. Her fingers knew where they were going.

She eyed Ilana mischievously and asked, "I heard there was a murder at the opera?" Several others around the piano leaned in, fascinated.

Ilana began, "There was a murder at the Met in the summer of 1980. A young violinist lady never returned to the pit after intermission. They found her body the next day. She had been killed by a member of the stage crew while the opera played out front." Those around the piano exchanged glances, and Nellie banged out an ominous chord. "But the whole time they played that performance, all the musicians knew that something horrible had happened because her violin was left on her chair. Musicians never do that."

"Damn right." Nellie said. "I take this pianie everywhere I go." Laughter punctuated Ilana's story. "What else, Missy? True stuff."

"There is the story from January of 1988 when, during a national broadcast of *Macbeth*, an elderly man dove from the top of the highest balcony at the Met, five stories straight down, committing suicide."

"No shit," a man commented, amazed.

"Damn," someone murmured.

"Then, in 1996, and this one I remember, the tenor Richard Versalle sang the line 'Too bad you can only live so long' and then fell over with a massive heart attack and died right on stage."

"See," Nellie exclaimed. "I told you opera ain't boring. Hey, Shea, you cheap bastard, fill me up." Nellie raised her shot glass. He waved that he would get to her. Nellie looked at Patrick. "Hey, Paddy, nothing sadder than an old woman with an empty glass."

Patrick took her glass and headed for the bar.

"You know." Ilana mustered as much nonchalance as she could. "I was wondering, Nellie, are either you or Fiona afraid of the ocean?"

"Naw, born in a seaport, Sligo. Always loved the water. Swam like a fish." She played while she spoke.

"Okay."

One theory down.

Nellie added, "Now, my ma? She was batty 'bout water."

"Yeah?"

"Most of her whole family drowned in a fishing accident. Wasn't even a stormy sea that day, flaccid as a drunken sailor." The old woman winked at her with a knowing grin. "Whole town went looking for 'em as the sun went in, but all they found was a board from the boat and a floating tin of bread pudding. Ma wouldn't get in the water for love or money after that, same with my brother, Ethan. That's how I knew she wouldn't come after me when I hopped a boat to America."

"Oh. Isn't that interesting?"

"Naw. Everyone has bad fishing stories like that one where I'm from."

Willow joined them and announced, "I've decided to take a college class. I know I have some hidden talents. There are other things I must be good at, you know, besides cooking. But what?'

Ilana responded, "Perhaps you should look into environmental studies because you're interested in waste and conservation."

Willow sparked. "I could start a think tank."

Ilana smiled. "Okay."

"Here at the pub."

"The library might be more suitable."

"Oh, I love the library. Grandma, I'm going to start a think tank."

"Girl, your tank's been empty for years." Several patrons chuckled.

Willow endured good-naturedly. Whenever Willow had an idea, she made lists, and most of the time, ecstatic intentions aside, the only thing she actually accomplished was the list.

Ilana could see that Willow was so clearly happy and at peace in a way that made her envious. She wondered if she would ever feel happy the way that Willow was. For over an hour, she studied her while she secretly waited for Fiona. She found her effortless smile charming. She watched the way she engaged and listened to others. She saw the twitchy joy with which she served, and she noticed the subtle discomfort when people paid her too much attention. She felt a pang watching Willow because she had never felt the kind of relaxed glee she saw alive in her radiant half-sister. Ilana's life had been calculated. Glee was not written into the American program for sophisticated professionals. Glee was, well, déclassé. If Ilana had run into Willow in Manhattan, in the normal course of her professional day, this fidgety, seemingly juvenile woman would have been dismissed. Ilana might have rolled her eyes in a silent expression of judgment. Here and now, she recognized Willow as the only truly harmless person she'd ever known. She was a person without guile, unskilled at the art of disdain, and Ilana chafed from the rub of her own ugliness. She learned she wasn't qualified to judge others because her assumptions were biased. She recalled Isabella claiming that a person only accepted what was part of his or her own cultural field as valuable. Manhattan was a culture. It was a big, small place. And she wondered if the silken contempt that clung to everyone that she knew was better than the lightness of life in Willow. If life was only about "passing the time," was being smarter more valuable than a gentle heart? Ilana thought that smart was better. In fact, she was sure of it, but why did she think this? How many truly happy people did she know in her professional world? Why was she certain that being smarter was better? Better for what?

Everyone is the exact same amount of dead.

She tried to wriggle her fingertips under the skullcap of certainty that dictated what she'd learned was valuable. She felt the cap there, tight, unforgiving, and spouting the unambiguous agenda of her class and her education. That little voice inside her head was an installed post-birth software program. She liked thinking about it that way. She wondered why she had not seen the rigid boundaries of the program all along. Contrary to what she had been told about her life's open options, her choices had always been defined by others. The inevitability and expectation of an advanced degree and a professional career were so pervasive that she never questioned it. The privileged children of doctors become doctors, architects, or scientists; they rarely consider every lifestyle option. One of the powerful elements that drove her choices was the expectations in the faces who leaned over her crib and said, "Good girl." Ilana felt her toes on the edge of the track that she had been on her entire life. Gingerly, her toes stretched out beyond the rim, and there was nothing, open space; was it a few inches down to something solid, or was it an abyss? Was there freedom in the emptiness, or only emptiness? She wanted to look at Willow and at herself without expectations. She wanted to weigh their existences with a blank slate. She wanted to ascertain real value. Was there even such a thing? She concentrated, and for one exhilarating second, she saw the solid cage around her. Everything in the room blurred. With all her intellectual might, she continued to pull away from what she thought she knew so that she could see it for what it was. She wanted free thought. She was close enough to see its shadow on her hand, but she couldn't grasp it.

She needed some air. Ilana left the pub and walked the backyard path along the river. She wanted to walk the river again, to recapture the sensual lyricism of that first night. The evening waved a calming palm along the top of the river and turned it to glass. She wished for the magic she felt the last time. She breathed in heartily. She smacked the blood-sucking mosquito who feasted on her elbow. A little red bump of reality appeared and began to itch. She thought about the swim. She stopped walking and closed her eyes. She summoned up the sensations from the morning: the warmth from the baked granite radiating under the soles of her bare feet, the invasive breeze between her parted thighs, the fall, the plunge, the bubbles fingering every part of her, the underwater sex where, in the end, she had to hold her breath and thought she would explode, the release was so violent, and then floating limp and weightless, sated and fluid.

"Ilana?" She spun around, startled and embarrassed to be caught in an erotic reverie. Her face was flushed. It was Fiona.

They stood. Face-to-face, the resemblance was undeniable. They both stood with their weight shifted to the right leg, and they both regarded the other with the same penetrating expression. Fiona lifted her left eyebrow. Ilana lifted hers. The consanguinity of animals, the scent of your baby's skin, and the link between them existed in every cell of their bodies, and there was no denying it. They did not approach. No familial hug hung in the air. It was enough that these two women could stay poised as they poignantly acknowledged that they shared what they were made of.

Fiona whispered, realizing she felt scared and sixteen years old, "Hi."

Ilana answered anxiously, "Hi."

Words were going to be difficult. Ilana's stomach churned, and her body shuddered. This time, she would let Fiona lead.

Fiona looked out at the water. "I always like the river this time of day."

"It does have a special charm."

"Yeah. That's a nice way to put it, a special charm. But you're probably really good with words." A long pause, and Fiona asked, "Where do you live?"

"In an apartment in the West Village."

"Oh. Never been there. But that's probably got some charm too."

"Of a different kind."

They both looked at the river for a moment. What was not being said was getting loud inside the silence.

"I'm sorry that my coming here before upset you," Ilana said with plain honesty.

"Took some getting used to."

"I'm sure. I should have realized that."

"I was actually looking for you just now. I wanted to tell you a story about this girl I knew."

Ilana swallowed hard. "I love a good story."

Fiona plopped down on the ground. Ilana sat down too, two feet away and thirty years apart.

Fiona began, "So, I didn't know this girl all that well, but she seemed like a nice girl with a really great figure."

Ilana's heart pounded. She felt it in her throat and temples, and she heard it in her ears. She was excited. She saw that the cause of her recent body-numbing fatigue was not the long work hours but the steady emotional pounding she'd been taking. She'd been under siege for months.

Fiona continued, "Anyway, so this girl, who will be nameless, worked at the church for a couple of hours after school every day for months. She was sixteen."

"Very young."

"Yeah. And as it happened, this brand-spanking new priest came to the parish. He was educated, handsome, kind, and real young too."

"A priest?" Ilana listened intently.

"Yeah. They worked on this charity thing together, very long hours, and they really put their hearts into it 'cause they both really cared. Anyway, after a time, the young girl couldn't help it, and she fell in love."

Barely audible, Ilana said, "Oh."

"She really didn't mean to at all and wouldn't of if she could've helped it."

"Of course."

"So, one night, one time, in the church when they were alone, nature kinda overpowered them, if you get my drift."

"In the church?"

"Third pew from Saint Frances."

"I see."

"Now, this young girl, who obviously had the worst luck on the planet Earth 'cause it was only one time, got pregnant. She was sent away for a while to have the baby, give it up, and never tell anybody."

"Oh, dear." Ilana's tongue felt thick. "She told no one whose it was?"

"Never. Never told a soul who the dad was, no matter how much she got threatened to tell the truth, confess, bare her soul, clear her conscience, yada, yada."

"Because she loved him?"

"Because she was ashamed and scared shitless."

Ashamed?

This was the hardest conversation of Ilana's life.

Ashamed?

She didn't want to hear this. It was so deeply painful. Maybe there truly were things not meant to know.

"Ashamed?" Ilana asked, not sure she wanted to know.

"She figured God must hate her. It seemed the worst sin in the world. For a long time, she figured she might as well get packing for hell."

Ilana breathed heavily and said, "That must have been really awful, especially for someone so young."

"It was no walk in the park, I can tell you that."

"Didn't she have anyone she could talk to or confide in?"

"Nah." Fiona shrugged. "That's why she got close to the priest in the first place."

"Right."

"And after, she hated the priest most of all."

"She did?"

"Yeah, because she thought that she had suffered but that he went on his merry way like nothing happened."

"Is he still a priest?"

"Yeah, in the same parish."

Ilana flinched, visibly stunned.

Here? He's right here?

Fiona continued, "She never went back to church, though, never saw him. Then, something happened, and she went to see him."

"Oh?" Ilana looked down, knowing that something was her, and she prepared for more pain because of her.

Fiona continued, "She hadn't talked to him, or to God either, in thirty years. But she went, and when she did, she was floored."

"She was?"

"She found out it wasn't what she thought all along. She had it all backward."

"How?"

"See, she went on with everything, you know? She moved on. She made a good life for herself. She got a good man and a family too, although she knows they would *never* forgive how she kept a secret like that from them all these years. Some people not that forgiving. But the priest, you know, he never got past it." Profound emotion crept over Fiona. "He never got forgiven, you know? He still lives it every single day." She looked into Ilana's eyes with heartbreaking sadness. "He's a ghost of a man. Not really even there anymore."

"Oh, no." Ilana burned with grief for this man she did not know and for the teenage mother who'd lived this.

"You see, so this girl had it all wrong. All this time, she thought she was the one who had done all the suffering, but turns out, his whole life has been one long suffering." Fiona looked miserably out at the river. "She feels sorry for him now. His punishment seems so much worse, plus he's got that eternal damnation thing to deal with."

"Yeah. That's a tough one."

Fiona managed to hold the catch in her throat because she was determined to continue. "I know for years that girl had dreams about what happened to her baby."

"Did she?" Ilana began to shake inside, and her throat tightened.

"The girl felt so scared, you know, leaving her baby girl there and walking away like it didn't come from inside her. It's not easy to walk away from your baby—doesn't matter how old you are. It cuts you in a way that never heals." Fiona repeated wretchedly to herself, "Never heals." Fiona needed to take little gasps to continue. Her words came out in short bursts, but she was determined, and she kept going. "And she always knew when it was her baby's birthday." She looked Ilana right in the eyes. "She always knew that. And in secret, she counted the years, wondering all the time whether she was dead or alive. Was she sick, was she happy, was she hungry?" Fiona tried to suck back the tears. It was impossible. She pushed on. "So, finally, in order to move on, she had to put it all out of her head, you know?"

"That was the right thing to do." Tears poured down Ilana's face as she tried to stay casual for Fiona's sake.

"It was the only thing." Fiona struggled with the emotion she could no longer hide. The practical reality of what happened to her thirty years ago gave her no solace, not then, not now.

Ilana said with consuming emotion audible in every syllable, "I think she deserves to know the baby was so happy."

"Was she?" Fiona's eyes shot to her with desperate hope.

Ilana noticed that the eyes beseeching her looked like those of a scared sixteen-year-old girl. There was no longer any possibility of containment. Tears openly drenched both their faces, but they did not move. They maintained a false air of calm even though they were utterly abandoned to their feelings, and they had never looked more alike than they did at this moment.

Fiona continued, "Even though she never got to play with her little toes, feed her, or smell the top of her head, she was still her baby, you know?"

Trying to relieve Fiona's pain, Ilana said, "The baby was so lucky. She had wonderful parents who loved her very much."

"What were they like?"

"They were older. They couldn't have children of their own. They loved her thoroughly and gave her a wonderful life. She misses them a lot, an awful lot." Ilana turned her eyes to the river, swallowed hard, and finished her thought. "Especially her mom."

Fiona said, "I heard she turned out great, smart and pretty, and with a really great figure. And now this girl was thinking maybe she didn't have the worst luck on planet Earth. Maybe it was a blessing instead. Yes, she thinks now it must have been a blessing of some kind."

The onslaught of emotion rendered them both silent. They sat in their own minds for a time. Ilana couldn't say for how long. And then, Fiona stood. Ilana followed.

"Thanks for the story, Fiona."

"I wouldn't repeat it, though; it would hurt a lot of people who don't deserve it."

"I understand. I promise."

Fiona looked at the grown woman before her. This was her daughter, this exquisite, intelligent, whole person. It was excruciating that she didn't have the chance to know her. No matter what the social circumstances or the religious taboos, she was made from love, and she was so beautiful. All the emotions that she would have felt every day while raising her, Fiona felt right now. For the rest of her lifetime, Fiona would never receive another gift without the thought of this one. This was the greatest gift of her life.

Fiona took a breath. "So, don't be a stranger around here."

"I don't think I belong here."

"No. But you're welcome, you know. You're welcome is all I want to say."

"Thank you. That means a lot to me."

Fiona turned away, took one step, stopped, and turned back. Then, in a very quiet whisper, almost too breathy to be understood, she said, "I would've named you Lynne."

With a quiet quiver, Ilana whispered back, "Lynne is nice."

Lynne.

Fiona walked on, and Ilana knew they would never talk about it again. But they would both know. Ilana thought about the terrified teenage girl, impounded, alone, devastated, and afraid that her God hated her when, instead, she should have been going to the high school dance. She felt the emotional cost of leaving her baby and then carrying that secret alone for thirty years. Ilana's heart broke for her. She wished she could comfort that teenage girl. What a sweet relief it would have been if the girl could only have known then that it would all turn out all right.

Ilana strained her eyes to watch Fiona as she disappeared around the bend. Fiona was a formidable woman. She was sensitive, strong, and colorful. But she was not her mother. Of course, she was not her mother. Of course, Ilana had known all along that she was not her mother, and with reborn strength, she stared down the truth.

My mother is gone.

Fiona walked the long way home. She crossed behind the Haney's backyard shed. She remembered when she had a crush on Buddy Haney. He had gone off after high school to make his way in the world. Her world was here. Everything she needed to make her happy was within ten miles of where she was born. She descended heels first down the crumbling bank. She searched for a small space under the aged cement walkway. Lots of children had secret spots, and her's was here. She crept inside for the one and only purpose of being totally certain that not a soul knew where she was. It was similar to what she felt when she snuck into the church basement and thought only God could see her. Even God couldn't see her in there. She thought she must have been a silly child, believing she could hide from God. She would spirit away half a box of Oreos, slip soundlessly out the back screen door, and run like crazy to this special space.

She searched for that secret safety somewhere underneath decades of unrestrained growth. She pulled the vines away. And it was there. She crawled inside. It was a tighter fit now than when she was a girl. She looked out at the world, and when she was completely certain that not a soul could see her, joyfully, she cried. She sobbed with tears generated by the glorious release from thirty years of wondering. When Ilana was born, Fiona was allowed to hold her for a few minutes. The tiny newborn had closed her fist around the teenage girl's pinky finger and held on with alarming tenacity. That feeling on her finger had never completely gone away. Fiona had adapted to its grip. She had no idea it would feel this good when the little fist let go. And in a moment of blessed reconciliation, she was deeply thankful.

Twenty minutes later, a passerby would be surprised to see a grinning middle-aged woman with a wild set of auburn curls and a now dirty, striped spandex dress crawl out from under the walkway and give him a big hello.

Next Sunday, Fiona would be at mass. She would take back the church she loved, and it would nestle back in around her. She would get a smile from Father Cummings when she received communion. He would pass her the host with his hands trembling from profound gratitude, and they would both be released from pain. She would have the answer she craved when she stared up at the night sky, the answer to why, and he would savor the sweet peace of forgiveness.

ILANA WONDERED ABOUT the priest as she walked toward Cafferty's. Should she see him? No. Enough. So much had happened. She had been touched by Fiona, Willow, Nellie, and Boney. She had been intimate with this outside man, and she was profoundly changed.

Distractedly, Ilana climbed the back porch steps to Cafferty's home. She placed her hand surely on the screen door and began to swing it open. She stopped. She pulled her hand back.

What am I doing? I don't live here.

She stood disoriented because walking in felt wrong and knocking felt wrong. Trapped in indecision, the dogs barked wildly. Cafferty whipped open the door, turned, and moved back to the stove. He stood barefoot in his work jeans and T-shirt.

"Talked to Fiona, huh?"

"You saw?"

"I saw you when I took the dogs out. What're you talking about?"

"Nothing much," Ilana said.

"That'd be some bullshit right there. Want some chili?"

"Chili? No, thanks. Not much of a chili eater."

"I can change that."

No. No, you can't.

Ilana leaned up against the kitchen wall. She looked around and saw how foreign it all was. She let her thoughts go and knew that nothing here was home for her. She was not a chili girl. She was not a pickup truck girl. She was not Lynne.

"So, okay." She shifted her feet. "Well, then . . ." She looked around the kitchen with the kind of finality that dawned on someone, realizing they didn't recognize where they were. "I need to go home."

With uneasy deliberateness, Cafferty put down the spoon and turned to face her. "This is as good a home as any."

"Yes. It is. But it's not my home." The room stretched. She felt awkward standing there, as though her arms and legs were too long, and her body was somehow out of proportion.

Cafferty watched her through narrowing eyes. He cornered her in his mind and studied her intently. He knew bodies don't lie that lay that way. Never had a pairing been clearer. Inside of him, a fuse began to burn. Life was simple. Cafferty knew this. Life's only commodity was time—time and what you did with it. He knew folks wasted the few moments they get to be alive mired in indecision about things that made no difference at all. Everyone gets dug into the dirt and forgotten. His fuse flared.

He asked, "When are you coming back?"

"I don't know if I am." Her evasiveness was all the oxygen his flame needed.

"You're done? When this is obvious."

"It is not obvious. It's impossible."

"Impossible?"

She spoke quietly. "Cafferty, I have a career and an entire life someplace else, a life I've worked very hard for. I'm sorry for being so confused and dragging you into my confusion, but I don't know where I belong."

Cafferty's agitation quickened. "You belong in my bed."

He stepped toward her. She took a step back quickly. She couldn't let him get closer. He knew why, and so did she.

"I have a lot of people depending on me. I have friends who I care about, and I have a job that I'm committed to."

She shifted her feet and glanced out the window, unnerved by the toxicity in his look. He was not a man who asked twice. He was not a man who would forgive her and show up with cheesecake. With unmasked intensity, he picked up his spoon and turned back to the chili on the stove. Stirring the pot should have been an innocuous gesture. It was not. It was a winding and winding, tighter and tighter, a repetitive act, a pressure cooker. Ilana realized it was the most aggressive gesture she had ever seen.

When he spoke, his tone was rife with warning. "You're not who I thought you were."

"You can't seriously expect that I would walk away from everything my life has been about. I'm sure you never expected that."

Ilana knew that SHC (spontaneous human combustion) was nonsense, of course. The idea that humans could generate so much internal energy that they could set themselves ablaze and incinerate their surroundings was absurd. It was fertilizer for the tabloids, but opposite Cafferty, right now, she could swear she felt actual heat on her skin. She tried to reestablish calm.

"You don't understand." she said.

"'Cause I'm a hick?"

"I didn't say that."

"You think it."

"I don't."

"Liar."

His eyes flared up. She felt singed.

He continued with biting hostility, "I understand plenty. You're a screwed-up fancy woman who would throw away or sell every minute of her life for a ritzy office and flashy title."

"That's not true." Ilana was offended by his analysis.

He raised his hand and replied, spitting distaste, "You're a mistake. I thought you were someone else. Some people work for what they need; for other people, work is what they need."

"It's not about the work. It's about belonging. It's about identity. It's about human nature. It's about making decisions free from influence and about living a full, chosen, meaningful life."

"There's no big meaning." He looked at her like she was a moron. "It's this. This is it. This day, and then the next day, and then the dirt. The rest is bullshit stories people tell themselves."

He ignited every passion inside of her, and that passion so easily flipped to anger.

"Perhaps I think there is more. Listen to you. I do what I want. I sleep when I want. I work when I want. You call it free. I call it self-serving."

His voice boomed. "It is bad enough when someone wastes your time, worse when you waste your own time, and you do both."

An urgent silence parted the room, and they stood on opposite sides polarized. Their bodies reached out, but they could not cover the distance. She knew if she only took a few steps forward, he would envelop her, and she would be still, she would be warm, she would be calm, but she would not be home.

Antipathy tinged his words. "I'm gonna walk the Pacific Crest Trail, swim naked, and play with my dogs, so you better get going 'cause your shoes are probably going out of style."

Acerbically, she said, "A good pump never goes out of style."

Throughout her life, in the years to come, Ilana would always remember that statement as the most ridiculous response she ever uttered. It was a response from the program. She didn't see it coming; it escaped from her mouth like a sudden wet sneeze, unexpected and embarrassing.

His lips thinned. His eyebrows rose. "Don't let the door hit you in the ass."

With a fury, she whirled around and yanked the door open. She exited, slamming it behind her. A ladle of chili flew after her and slammed in a red and brown rage against the closed door. Cafferty stood and listened to the footfalls as she stomped away from him. Cafferty had never been denied before; most women wanted to be with him, and other women would have been thrilled to know he wanted them. He watched the dogs joyously feast on the chili. He wondered for a moment if he had been too severe. He decided, no.

THE OPERA SEASON proceeded with its lyrical bloodthirstiness performed in perfect pitch. Ilana was charmed by Figaro, watched Louise flee, and buried Mimi (seven times in one week). There was a hush in her life. It would have been a sweet solace to still have Adam, to lie inside the arms of his affection, to have him back to eat with and to talk to. William had been busy with patients; consequently, Isabella had been her only real friend outside of the opera house, and they had grown very close.

Some nights, she had to leave her apartment and walk the Village streets to keep from calling Adam because she knew it would be selfish. She would not chance hurting him further. She would give him the time he needed to heal and move on. Ilana was certain of fewer things every day, but she was positive that she and Adam would be friends at some point. Perhaps when he found a new love, that door would open for them. It was only a matter of getting there. Their relationship had weaved a strong, long thread through both of their lives, and she couldn't imagine any other ending for them. She was certain that there was too much good to throw it all out. *Surely*, she thought, at the very least, *there will be friendship at the end, with time, when he is ready and can forgive me.* Surely, he, if anyone, would understand how little real power she had had over the past few months and how she had never intended for it to work out this way.

When the peregrinations of Ilana's thoughts carried her to the pub, Willow, Fiona, or Nellie, she smiled with a softhearted appreciation. She was glad she had such eccentric blood somewhere inside of her. She could not deny some connection existed or that she had been changed by them. She had spent hours trying to analyze whether she created the connection or uncovered it. She had come to believe it was there under the skin somehow, a life larva. No matter what, she never allowed thoughts of Cafferty. Those thoughts were pruned at the root.

Walking had become her late-night companion, a quiet friend who held her hand without getting clammy and whose breeze was the soft zephyr of a close conversation on her face. Ilana didn't cab anywhere anymore. She coveted the walking. Her step on the sidewalk was a metronome for her thoughts, pacing her with safe constancy. The feeling that something was missing, which had originally driven her to Albany, had opened new doors to more questions. She knew she was unraveling and that the walking was a part of it. She allowed her thoughts to wander, and they spread out wide. If everything she saw, everything she read, everything she heard, and everything she learned came from inside one culture, how could she ever hope to have an objective thought? Why was it that when a person had a religious vision, they only saw images of their own culture? Why hadn't a Buddhist ever had a vision of the Virgin Mary and wondered who the hell she was? Isabella had liked this question.

As predicted, Isabella Wharton's divorce proceedings had been ecstatic fodder for the tabloids. Her attorney had argued quite persuasively that years of extramarital sex on both their parts had absolutely nothing to do with commitment, love, or marriage and should not be considered when attributing fault or allocating financial distribution. The attorney cited instances from the animal kingdom and from other successful human societies with different social constructs. He found a wealth of examples to support Isabella's contention. He assured the judge that there was only one person at fault, only one person in breach of the prenuptial contract, only one person who cheated, and that one person was Mr. Wharton. Mr. Wharton cheated when he fell in love with Mrs. Grace.

Isabella's desire for a public forum had been achieved. Everyone was talking about it. How natural *was* monogamy? Were sex and love always related? News broadcasters ran internet polls asking the public how many sexual partners they'd had and whether they had engaged in extramarital sex. Had it affected their real love for their spouse? The numbers were staggering and clearly supported Isabella.

The subject incited emotional and poignant defenses of the status quo. Isabella had been characterized in unflattering cartoons as a threat to decency, motherhood, the family, and even apple pie. When asked by a reporter if she would like to answer these charges, she responded forcefully, "I'm outraged. I love apple pie."

Isabella had achieved the two things she desired: first, a freewheeling cultural examination that engaged her in conversations of substance, and second, an invitation to every chic dinner party in New York. Isabella was an obsessively social animal at peace only in a crowd and a woman known to throw a hell of a party. Ilana had never enjoyed reading the papers as much as she had during the Wharton divorce proceedings. The stimulation was manna and could not have come at a more opportune time.

The evening arrived for Isabella's cocktail soiree, and Ilana decided to startle her. For the first time in her life, Ilana consciously decided not to blend, not to wear the conservative black dress or blue silk suit. She shopped quite seriously for an outfit that would knock Isabella off her game. It was fun. She wanted something sexy, wild, out of character. She'd found it.

William had agreed to accompany her, and he was flabbergasted when Ilana's cab pulled up.

"Some outfit," he said.

"Yeah, it's new."

"I'm sure. Nice material."

"Thanks."

"Shame they ran out before the top was finished."

"Backless is in," she corrected him. "The tattooed salesgirl said so."

"Oh, good, an authority," he said.

"And besides, it came with the skirt."

"I thought that was a belt."

"Hey," she said, "I've got good legs."

"And plenty of them," he remarked.

She grinned fondly at him and complained, "I haven't seen enough of you lately."

"Busy."

"You look tired."

"Thanks," he said sarcastically.

"And a little yellow."

"No, really, stop."

Sitting in the cab with her skirt required strategy. William kept looking at her bare legs and chuckled all the way uptown. She nudged him repeatedly. She knew he didn't know the half of it. The skirt was so tight over her ass that the salesgirl talked her into a thong, which she wore for the first time in her life. This was how Ilana found herself standing in the doorway to Isabella's salon, wildly dressed and barely balanced on an aerodynamically improbable pair of silver spike three-inch heels. She noticed that even though she was physically tortured, she had never felt better and secretly wished she had done something more Medusa with her eye makeup.

Isabella's salon looked enchanted. It was so exotic that even the worldliest of invitees breathed in lusciously upon entering. The dark red walls were illuminated by hundreds of lit candles engaged in an erratic dance of light, creating a cloistered tribal ambiance. Ilana had been in this room many times, but this was the first time she understood the peculiar choice of colors. *Like no other room*, she thought. William and Ilana exchanged a quick look and then allowed their eyes to roam unreservedly around the visual dessert.

Bamboo trays of intriguing hors d'oeuvres were being carried by what looked like Sherpas, not men costumed as Sherpas, but Sherpas. A bartender in the corner poured flutes of champagne. Many of the guests were not in Western attire. While not unheard of in Manhattan, where the United Nations was a busy fixture, it seemed extraordinary to see such diverse kinds of traditional clothing in the same room. Several languages were spoken, some completely unfamiliar, some a series of clicks and grunts. In the background, Verdi's rich and haunting "Va, pensiero" played, creating a mystical undertow in the room. An organic exchange of culture and people was taking place. Ilana recalled the homogeneity of her last dinner party, which seemed like years ago now. She remembered telling Adam how all their friends looked alike. He scoffed. She was right. Ilana recognized that she was the most common person in the room.

"Was this a costume party?" William asked.

"Oh. I believe these people really are from those places."

"Very cool."

"Very. Important you stay alert."

"Are we in danger?"

"I am. I could fall off these heels and break my ankle."

"Definitely a weapon's grade spike."

"Ilana?" Isabella approached, eyeing her with exactly the kind of surprise Ilana had shopped for. "Fashion risk, my dear?" Isabella kissed Ilana on both cheeks with a European flair. "And you must be William." She offered her hand. With idyllic gentility, he leaned over and kissed it. It was suddenly the only thing to do, a lovely out-of-time gesture and something William had never done in his life. With all his city style and sophistication, he was still a boy from the Midwest. The enchanted quality of this night, the candlelight, the haunting music, the jungle ambiance, the machetes, the blood, the masks, it all released him to be dramatic.

Isabella said, "William, Ilana speaks quite a bit about you, so I imagine she must speak of me some."

"She does."

Damn, this thong is uncomfortable.

"And what does she tell you about me?" Isabella questioned.

"All the gory details, I'm afraid."

"Oh, good. Then we understand each other." She looped her arm intimately inside William's and walked him toward the bar. Isabella continued, "I lived for a time in a gay commune in Sweden."

"Really? Are you a lesbian?"

"Only briefly."

Ilana watched with a knowing appreciation. These two might be great friends, and that thought made her truly happy. She tried covertly to tug at the invasive thong.

"Champagne?" A glass sprung up in front of her face.

"Oh." Ilana turned. "Thank you."

"Mitch Heller, remember? My wife Ellen and I met you at the Riconi Gala."

"Yes. Of course." Ilana turned bright red. Not donors, not in this outfit. She adjusted her posture and tried nonchalantly to yank down the hem of her tiny skirt. "So nice to see you both. You're friends of Isabella's?"

"For many years." Mitch continued, "Ellen and I were discussing her unconventional divorce case."

"It does seem to have created a lot of discussion." Ilana tried to rub her thighs together to adjust the thong; she couldn't concentrate.

Mitch asked, perplexed, "Do you agree with Isabella on this?"

"I believe people should be free to make whatever lifestyle choice works for them." Frustrated, Ilana yanked at her skirt and almost fell off her heels. She grinned and continued, "I don't think the government should be in the business of telling people who or how to love."

Ellen asked, "And morality doesn't exist?"

"Isabella would say morality is only what any group of people agrees it is. We know that is the truth because morality varies from culture to culture, from past to present. An eclectic group crowds the moral high ground, and each of them is certain that only they are right."

Mitch said, "Some rules are universal, like, don't murder."

"Are they? There's capital punishment and honor killing."

"So," Mitch asked, "you think people should have sex with whomever, whenever, regardless of marriage?"

"I wouldn't say that. People should know who they are and embark on honest relationships based on understanding and mutual respect. But lifestyle commitments are not one-size-fits-all."

Mitch said, "Society *must* have rules to lift us above the animals, to function."

Ilana's eyes flashed. "Are any set of rules all right, or just yours?"

"Mine?"

"When you say society must have rules to function, that is what you're saying, isn't it? Your rules, right? You're certainly not advocating for the rules that condone ritualistic homosexuality in Melanesia, or the rules allowing polygamy in Saudi Arabia, or the rules of a society that lacks marriage altogether, like the Moso of China. You want your rules, right?"

"We are in America," he replied.

"Land of the free as long as they're your rules."

Ellen said, "There are plenty of us with the willpower and fortitude to devote our lives to one person, to achieve fidelity of affection and the physical. No greater or more successful social unit than that of the nuclear family has ever existed. It is a goal worth striving for, worth teaching our children to strive for, worth protecting. Nothing can compare with the love or connection that comes from one man and one woman sharing a lifelong commitment."

Ilana pulled herself back as her anger rose. These were donors. She had to control her emotions, didn't she? She answered carefully, "And I respect your desire to live that life, to love one man, to create a family unit. Wonderful." Passion began to seep into her voice, and she knew that she spoke not only for Isabella but William and, yes, even herself. "You are lucky to be living the life you choose in a society that approves of your choice. But please, Ellen, explain to me why you feel you must force—or punish—individuals who want to live their lives differently."

"Because having ideals matters, and there is such a thing as right and wrong."

Ilana's passion spilled out. "It seems to me that no *one* group, like monogamous heterosexuals, should be allowed to define love in only their terms."

Mitch responded, "So, you reject traditional marriage then?"

"Not at all! I don't reject anything. I believe that's my point. History, current events, and human nature have proven that love and sexual attraction cannot be legislated, and the world would be a kinder place if everyone were allowed the freedom to make their own individual rules for their own happiness."

Isabella joined them. "Ilana, Ellen is a theology professor." She grabbed Ilana's arm. "So behave yourself."

Yeah? Well, my father's a priest. See ya and raise ya.'

"Why don't I follow your lead?" Ilana responded coyly to Isabella.

They all laughed, but it wasn't a free, comfortable laugh; it had a murky tone.

Ilana abruptly stomped her foot. "Toe cramp," she explained. She stomped again as pain shot through her foot, and the thong slipped into a more uncomfortable area. She needed to get that shoe off, but there was no bending in her skirt.

"Excuse me. Very nice talking with you." She hobbled to the restroom.

Once inside the bathroom, she slipped off the shoe and pressed back the cramping toe, relieving the acute pain but leaving a residual ache. She massaged the toe and was shocked to learn that the thong could actually feel worse when she bent over. And she had had enough. She slipped off the thong, balled it up, and mashed it into her evening clutch. Having nothing on could not possibly be any more distracting than dealing with that full-time wedgie. She strapped back on her sandal and exited the bathroom.

The pleasurable evening stretched into the morning hours for most guests, but not Ilana and William. Reluctantly, around 11 p.m., William gave Ilana the ten-minute signal. A lifelong asthmatic, it was not unusual for William to cut out early, especially with people smoking.

Ilana saw the signal and knew to conclude her conversation with the Chinese UN ambassador. She had worked twice as hard to be taken seriously in her attire, and she promised herself she would stuff the outfit down the trash as soon as possible. One thing was clear: this was not her. She was glad she'd stepped out of her usual clothing, but she would make a beeline for her super soft Vuori sweatpants the moment she got home.

The ambassador continued, "The Beijing Opera has much to offer the world."

"Yes, I've heard that."

"It's a shame you have not been." The man spoke with an air of delicacy that felt genuine and ancient. Ilana was taken by his composure and elegance.

"Someday," Ilana responded, "I do hope to travel to China."

"You would be my most welcome guest. Allow me to send you a formal invitation."

"That would be lovely." She beamed.

"Do you have a card?"

"Certainly."

Ilana smiled graciously, reached into her tiny evening handbag, and pulled out her business card. The lacey thong, which hooked on the edge, came flying out with the card and landed on the floor between them. They both stared at the frilly lavender thing as though it might start talking. Ilana's face turned the color of dried cranberries. The ambassador went completely ashen. They stared at the undies with neither one of them knowing what to do or say. Completely paralyzed, Ilana's eyes were glued to the thong. She couldn't imagine picking it up. She couldn't imagine leaving it there. They stood. Dumb. Inert. Suddenly, a hand reached down and lifted the thong as though it was the most natural thing.

"Thank you, dear. I'll take those, and I'll get the ambassador another drink." Isabella strolled away. The ambassador bowed and excused himself without another word.

In the cab on the way home, William's eyes drooped, and his head laid back. She sensed the muscles in his body let go as he sank into the seat. He coughed. William was wiped out and clearly coming down with something. It was time to put her best friend to bed: no work, no conversation, rest, rest. She looked forward to nursing him. She loved him and was happy to have a way to show that. She would buy soup and keep track of the last time he took aspirin. She wondered if this was a budding maternal spark. No, she suspected this was how all true friends behaved. She had trouble helping him out of the cab and was grateful that, for once, the elevator was not temperamental.

Safely inside his apartment, she put William to bed. She used her palms to punch down his pillows and gently lifted his legs. She pulled up the sheets. She grabbed something she could change into from his closet, looking forward to getting out of her party attire. After saying good night, she closed his bedroom door.

William let his mind wander. Tucked under the covers, he knew that he had done too much. He was deep-tissue tired, his eyes were dry, and his chest felt too heavy to lift for breath. He was reminded of when his mother would tuck him in.

His mother and he had appreciated the same things: hush puppies, sea turtles, bake sales, and *General Hospital*. Growing up, his siblings had accepted that he was her favorite. He theorized that it was his strong feminine side that allowed him into her heart in such a uniquely intimate way. His world was a safe place with her. He never worried about telling her the truth, any truth. He hadn't believed a statement existed that could render him motherless. He was wrong. Her rigid, small mind overpowered her humanity, her heart, and even her instincts. The shock of it all could easily have explained her initial revulsion. But time passed. The situation stripped her down to her raw essence, and in that glaring emotional nudity, he looked at his mother and saw no one of substance.

She would not be surprised to learn he was sick; she expected him to suffer. It was the meal her god dished up to sinners. It had been eight years and two months since he lost his entire family in one moment of naïve honesty, but it was not until this moment, not until his kindest friend tucked him in, that he finally knew what sort of people his family was. He realized it wasn't true that you couldn't pick your family; he had picked Ilana, and he had picked well.

In the living room, Ilana settled down on William's sofa. She was too tired to go crosstown. She would get up early, check on him, and then go home to dress for work. She loved William's apartment, where she felt at ease. Her thoughts drifted as she fell off to sleep.

As a child, when Ilana walked in the front door from a day at school, she experienced an endorphin-style rush of happiness. It was the "ahh" feeling of safety and belonging. All day long, she maneuvered around the sharp prep school as though the environment was pointed; caution was required for even a small move. When she walked in the door to her parent's apartment on the Upper West Side, she could drop her backpack in the foyer, kick off her shoes, and slide into the kitchen parquet in her socks for the ritual glass of nonfat milk and two Mallomars. Her mother had created a satisfying, nourishing home. Ilana was acutely aware that her apartment did not have these characteristics. This apartment gave her that "ahh" moment. It was a New England autumn of burnt colors and sun-muted fabrics. David had been a genius with color. He did all the painting himself. He gingerly painted tender green vines around every doorway, no two alike. As her eyes closed and she became drowsy, she remembered the morning she came over when David was doing the leggy green lines around the kitchen molding. This apartment became his progeny. He left so much of himself behind on the walls, the stenciled window ledges, and the artistic bathroom mirror. She was so very comfortable. And she slept.

Colors returned with the morning light. Ilana woke up slowly, happy to remember she was at William's. His sofa was more comfortable than her bed. She got up, carefully folded the blanket, and peeked into William's bedroom. His breathing was slow and his eyes closed, still asleep. She padded soundlessly in a pair of his socks to the kitchen. Odd. Dishes in the sink? So unlike him. She pulled out the coffee pot and reached up for the cabinet door where she knew he kept the coffee and filters. She swung it open and stopped moving as she took in the sight. The cabinet was filled with prescription bottles—twenty, maybe more. Methodically, she pulled down the jars and read the labels: used Z-pacs, steroids, amoxicillin, every conceivable antibiotic, and all of the dates were in the last two months.

What the hell?

With jars cradled in a scoop of her sweatshirt, she whirled around and ran into his bedroom. He was sitting up. He looked sallow and exhausted.

"Good morning," he said with forced cheer.

"What's happening?" she demanded.

She dropped the jars and packages onto the bedsheets. She held her breath. He looked at the evidence. She needed the truth. She reached for his hand. It was too hot.

"You're hot."

He winked at her. "So I've been told."

"Stop that. Tell me."

"It'll be okay," William assured her.

"Tell me."

"I will, but on our way back to the hospital."

"What do you mean *back*?" Fear rose from the core of her. "What do you mean?"

"Ilana, it's a bacterial infection. We're working on it. But my fever is up, so I should go back."

"Why didn't you . . . never mind. Get dressed."

On the way to the hospital, Ilana cursed the traffic.

"How long has this been going on?"

"A few weeks."

"William, do you have a good doctor? Who's your doctor?"

"I'm handling it, Ilana. I have very good medical, and I'd prefer to do this privately."

"There's no *privately* between us, and you know that."

Ilana learned that he had been in and out of the hospital for weeks. She listened impatiently while he explained. "I got this flu, and then it progressed to a secondary infection, and that didn't sit well with my asthma." He was breathing with difficulty.

"How could you let me run around feeling sorry for myself, talking incessantly about my adoption and my stupid choices, when you were this sick? William, you needed me."

"It was what I wanted, Ilana."

She was genuinely mad. "I may not forgive you for that, William."

"Sure you will. You can't stay mad at me. I'm too cute."

Ilana blew into the hospital like a hurricane. She filled out the forms indicating she was William's sister, although that didn't feel close enough for her. It was unsettling that a few of the nurses knew his name and that several orderlies said hello. His doctor ordered another chest x-ray and immediately put William on an IV of antibiotics.

"Your fever is climbing, William," Doctor Grant said as he entered, looking at the chart. "This time, please stay put."

"Oh, he'll stay put, or I'll kick his ass," Ilana said.

"Doctor Grant, this is my sister, Ilana," William said.

"Hello. Good, I was beginning to think you didn't have any

relatives. So, then." Doctor Grant turned to her. "Perhaps you can persuade your brother to stay in bed."

"If I have to break both his legs," she said matter-of-factly.

William added with panting breaths, "She's a bit unconventional but extremely effective."

"Works for me," Doctor Grant said. "Tomorrow, we'll need to go into the chest and insert those drains we spoke about. We have got to get some of that fluid out of there."

"Are you sure? You know I'm a guy who does love fluids."

"William, lie down and get better," Ilana instructed.

Ilana followed Doctor Grant into the hallway. "Doctor? What are your expectations?"

"Expectations?"

"Honestly."

"He's got a perfect storm of issues here."

"In what way?" she asked.

"As you're aware, he has asthma, so his lungs started out compromised. When he got this antibiotic- resistant bug, it has been hard to get ahead of it."

She replied with a mixture of confirmation and hope, "But you will."

The doctor regarded Ilana and considered his next words carefully. "We've already thrown everything we have at it. All I can offer is more of the same."

Ilana shrunk back, crippled.

What? What did he say?

Her throat was so constricted that her voice came out high-pitched like a little girl. "Oh. No. You need to fix him."

"I'm sorry. This is tough. We'll put in drains tomorrow and then see."

As the doctor turned and walked back down the hall, Ilana stood still as stone, heavy on the floor, and with a soft, powerful whisper to no one said, "Fix him."

The next day, Doctor Grant inserted two drains into William's lungs. When Ilana called the nurse, she told her it went okay, but there would be no visitors because the surgery was tough, and he needed to be in the ICU. The following day, Ilana arrived, lugging flowers, cookies, and chicken soup from Zabar's.

William was hooked up to oxygen, but his lips were still blue.

Holy shit.

The truth planted both feet defiantly in front of her and would not budge. She couldn't step around it. He was sick. Way too sick. She couldn't go through it.

I can't do this.

"Hungry?" she asked him pleasantly without a touch of worry in her tone.

"Starved. They're big on Jell-O here. Jell-O and surveillance. I'm being watched like a lab rat." His words were forced, dry, with long pauses in between.

"You look better," she lied because she knew how important a positive outlook was to good health.

"Hey, when you're as good-looking as I am, well." His voice faded out. She opened the thermos and poured out the soup. She placed the cup onto the metal rolling table, and it made that clinking noise that went right through her.

"Zabar's? How did you get it here still hot?"

"I brought my own thermos, muscled a pack of old ladies out of their cab, and gave the driver a twenty."

"That's my girl."

She felt like she was going to lose it. He looked. He knew her too well. He saw her caving in. He saw that she understood what was happening to him. Reality leveled off in both of their eyes.

With profound compassion and struggling for breath, William said, "Ilana."

"No." A convulsive emotion welled up in her.

"It's okay."

"Don't you dare die on me, William."

Calmly, he said, "There are worse things."

She buried her face in her hands. "No, no, there's not." She felt bloodless and weak.

William said with his smooth, trained voice, reaching for breath but with an ethereal serenity, "Ilana, I knew this guy when I was growing up."

"Oh, William, for Christ's sake."

"Listen." His breath forced the words out in fits, so it took a while and completely exhausted him, but still, he told her, "I was a kid. His name was Yanni. He was the manager of this big shoe store in town. He talked to me a lot because I helped out there on the weekends for extra cash. All he ever talked about was how excited he was about retiring. He would travel to Poland. His whole family was from there, and he had pictures of Warsaw taped up all over. His bookcase was filled with years of collected guidebooks and road maps of Warsaw."

Ilana wondered what the hell he was talking about, but she listened because she could not have talked if she cared to.

"For the eight years I knew him, he planned the trip to Warsaw to leave the day he retired. When the day came, we gave him a huge retirement party. We all waved goodbye. He bought a first-class ticket to Warsaw and then dropped dead in the airport lounge of a massive coronary."

Whining like a child, she asked, "Why are you telling me this?"

"Because that was worse than dying. He missed out on what truly mattered to him, on appreciating his time, his life, and I haven't, Ilana. I've lived well and on my own terms. I have no illusions. And no regrets." There was loud breathing as his breath caught up with his words.

"But we are going to grow old together."

"Sweetie, I'm way too vain to grow old."

She looked quizzically at his smile. It was genuine.

"The two of us . . . the best part of me is who I am with you," she said.

"No, you are you, even without me." He was panting but

determined to make his point. "Ilana, I'm not afraid. And I'm not angry. If this is it, then that's that. But how you deal now and later matters to me. You're the only family I have. More than anything, I need to know you'll be okay. Do you understand that?"

"Yes."

And she did understand. This was what she would need if the situations were reversed, and so inside of her, a fierce and potent well of strength was tapped and came pouring in. Now she knew; she must laugh, she must tease, and she must be playful. Later, in the dark, when no one would know, she would cry so very quietly. And in the shower, the tears would mix so completely with the cascading water that no one would see. Because after all is said and after all is done, grief is the ultimate private affair. Ilana and William sat silently, holding hands for a profoundly long time, composed within the intimacy of each other's thoughts.

William knew how excruciating it was to be the one left behind managing the loneliness and loss; surely, it must be easier to be the dead one. He had no clear notion of what death was. He had no particular religious belief except a belief that if there was some kind of god, then a god created him too. He did find it implausible, though. He speculated that the more likely scenario was that contrary to Homo sapiens' bloated self-regard and belief in their meaningfulness, when considering the vastness of the universes, humans were most likely some insignificant biological by-product of no consequence at all.

Later, alone, William tugged on the sheets with fatigue so deep, it rendered his muscles unresponsive. He noticed that she had turned on the radio before she left, so thoughtful. He laid quiet, appreciating the rest, and unable to attend to even his slightest need; even an itch on the side of his cheek couldn't be reached; too hard, too tired, his arms and legs were deadweight. The only thing that kept him going that afternoon was his commitment to help Ilana through the shock. He saw her flail blindly for footing in the beginning, with her tears hidden by the fabricated smile. He marveled at her lock-jawed control. Then, he watched as she edged herself back from the lip of the unbearable. Finally, in the middle of her rushing emotional stream, she found a shaky stone to balance on. It felt safe to let her go, and he lay grateful for the cool, clean sheets. It was a sweet comfort to lie motionless in fresh sheets. Daily sheet changes was the one thing he liked about the hospital.

When Ilana left the hospital that evening, she took a cab home because, for the first time in months, she was too tired to walk. It was an exceptionally tranquil early evening, with no city breeze, no traffic wind. She looked out the window and saw nothing. Once home, she turned her shower water to extra hot and stood under the torrid force until her head dropped forward in pure submission. She did not have an ear out for the phone. She was not thinking about her meetings the next day. She was not strategizing about the upcoming talent negotiations. She was not thinking about Albany. She let the water subdue her, hard and hot, as she stood immobile. She didn't want time to move on. She wanted time to stop. She was suspended with her knees locked, her feet planted, and she pressed back with all her might for yesterday. The water was ice before she got out.

She was at the hospital early the next morning. Ilana found that William talked with greater ease, but he didn't look any better. Isabella's food and flower baskets came daily, not only for William at the hospital but also on Ilana's doorstep at home.

"Nice to have rich friends," William told her.

"Can't argue that. What's better than having a yacht?"

They answered together, "A friend with a yacht."

They enjoyed this. She poured him water and walked around straightening his bedsheets.

"Ilana, listen, after I'm cremated—"

"Oh, William, I swear, if you start with the death talk, I'll suffocate you with this pillow and be done with it."

"While that's a very appealing offer, what I wanted to say was, I've decided where I want to scatter my ashes."

"Oh." She sat down seriously next to him on the hospital bed. "Okay. If that were to happen, and should you die first, which is by no means for certain, where?"

"All over my parent's front lawn."

Knowing he's not serious, she said, "Oh, is that so."

"Between the hide-a-key rock and the plastic lawn flamingoes."

"Who doesn't love a good lawn flamingo? You're exhausted or drugged."

"I love multiple choice."

She looked at him, and it rushed out in her words. "I love you, William."

"I love you too." He took her hand. "What was your name again?" She laughed. "You know, Ilana, I have always believed that people don't change."

"Color me fascinated."

"Seriously, listen up. I'm sparking intellectually."

"Oh, I'd hate to blink and miss that."

"You have changed, or you are changing, or maybe you're becoming. You know how things become something else, something completely different, but that thing was dormant in them all along? Like a caterpillar or a tadpole?"

"I'm a frog? William, you're the one who's green."

"That's it, though. You're becoming. I could tell you pretty closely where everyone else will be in ten years, but you? I don't know about you."

"You know, I always thought I knew, but I don't think I do anymore."

From the very depth of William's heart, he warned her, "Ilana?"

"Yeah?"

"Ilana."

She looked.

"Don't wait for Warsaw."

Softly, she replied, "Yeah. Okay. I won't."

His next word was faint and slipped out matter-of-factly a moment before he gave in to unconscious sleep. "Cool."

She caught herself. She looked at her friend asleep so fast. She saw him openly at this moment. She looked at his face and at his body, knowing she could look plainly because he was asleep and she needn't pretend. He was so thin that she could see the veins underneath. His skin was yellowish, and his lips were an odd color she couldn't name. She did not need to hide the look in her eyes. She felt rage. Pure, unadulterated rage. Rage at everyone. Rage at everything.

WHY?

THE NEXT FEW weeks of relentless exertion were physically ruthless. The opera season carried on. The ripped costumes, the broken scenery, the complaints, and the backstage dramatics that used to send her blasting off like an action hero were all trivial now. She dealt with it without thinking and, surprisingly, without caring. All the drama she could ever stand was inside of her. She was cooking all of William's meals and carrying them to the hospital because food mattered to him. Still, he got thinner.

Word of William's worsening condition and Ilana's inexhaustible dedication traveled. She heard from so many people; even lost college friends sought her out to offer what solace they could. She knew she was lucky to have so many friends, but she also knew they felt sorry for her, and that pissed her off because it was such a futile feeling, so useless when there was so much to be done. She had also heard from people she would not even characterize as friends, barely acquaintances. Some called so they could feel good about themselves for calling; others called with a voyeuristic agenda that disgusted her. She practiced being polite.

Adam had come by the hospital several times to help. Mostly, she sent him to the market to restock William's refrigerator so she could continue to cook and bring fresh meals. It was so hard to find things that William could keep down. When Adam and Ilana wound up together, they stepped on each other's words and endured long, irritable silences.

One afternoon, when Adam was dropping off groceries, they arrived in William's apartment at the same time. They moved cautiously around the small kitchen, putting items in their places. It felt a little like old times, being alone doing something domestic with Adam, and it was soothing to her. She thought that perhaps this was the beginning of their friendship, a friendship she sorely needed. Adam turned to her with a box of oatmeal in one hand and a jug of ice cream in the other.

"Ilana?"

"Yes?" she answered with hope.

"I want us to be clear. I don't want to see you, not even as friends, and by that, I mean ever. Ever."

It stung. "Oh, that's too bad," she replied painfully. "Because you're such a great friend to have."

"I really can't stand being around you, and sometimes I get this surge of antipathy for you that's overwhelming."

"Oh. Okay." His words made progressively deeper cuts into her already wounded world. She said quietly, "You don't need to come by here, Adam. I appreciate it, but I can do it without your help."

"I'm not here for you." He shot back. "I'm here in spite of you. I'm here for William."

"Right. Of course," she said quietly.

"It took me a while to realize you aren't the person I thought you were."

Cafferty's voice echoed those same words in her head. She turned to Adam to reach out one more time, to try and explain one last time. "As it turns out, I'm not the person I thought I was."

"Talking in puzzles was never your style. Your confidence and self-awareness were your most attractive qualities."

"I must be one ugly broad now."

"You said it."

Hurt, she turned back to the bags.

This is my fault.

Quiet unpacking ensued. But she couldn't leave it this way. She didn't want it to be this callous.

"Adam, I feel like I'm struggling to wake-up from some cruise-control existence where I've made no free choices at all."

"Yeah? Well, you'll wake up alone, Ilana."

He looked at her, and she saw in his eyes the truth. The final, irreversible truth. They would never see each other again. They unpacked. They parted.

When Ilana wasn't at the hospital, she focused only on work. Still, anyone could see the curtain was down in her eyes. She was returning from a particularly icy meeting with the conductor's new agent when an agitated assistant stopped her in the hallway outside her office. The woman was practically hyperventilating.

"Ilana."

"Yes?"

"I don't know *how* he got into the building at all, but—"

"Who?"

"He marched right passed me as though I wasn't talking to him. Like I wasn't there."

"Who?"

"There's some man in your office."

"And you left him alone in there?"

"I was afraid to stay. He's . . .security's on their way."

"Okay."

Ilana cracked open her office door and peeked inside. Cafferty stood awkwardly in the middle of the room. His blue work jeans were torn at the knee, not designer torn but really torn. His dark plaid flannel shirt was thin and velvet soft from so many washings. His hands were shoved into his pockets, and his shoes were dirty. He was a large, roughly honed, handmade figure, out of place in the middle of this scrupulous finery.

She turned back to the assistant. "It's all right. I know him."

Ilana entered and closed the door behind her. He turned, strode over, grabbed her by the forearms, lifted her up, and covered her mouth with his with such force that she feared the door would collapse. A moment, and then he pulled away.

"Er, sorry, I guess," he said.

She flattened her skirt. She took a breath. "Okay."

They held each other in the palms of their hands and inspected: so much there, so much missing.

His eyes traveled up and down her body. "Looks like you haven't been eatin' breakfast."

"I actually had a Ding Dong at three a.m.," she replied.

"Most important meal of the day."

"Cafferty, what are you doing here?"

"Visitin'. Someone told me this was the most sophisticated city in the world, but from what I've seen, it sucks. It smells. There's garbage piled up on the sidewalks."

The door burst open. A large officer entered, yelling, "Security." The two looked over calmly at him.

Ilana said, "I'm fine, Jack. This is a friend of mine."

The security guard looked suspiciously at Cafferty. Ilana nodded, indicating he should exit, which he did, and then she closed the door.

Ilana knew the rumor mill would grind up a tart blend today. She had lived contentedly around here as the predictable one, but not this time. She knew the gossips would be driven to distraction attempting to figure out who Cafferty was and exactly what "friend" meant. She had never felt the surreptitious exhilaration of having people wonder, people who were convinced they knew her. She liked it. Isabella had rubbed off on her more than she realized. There was something fun about unpredictability.

Cafferty smirked. "Folks around here wound a little tight."

"Efficient."

"I came to see if this is where you're supposed to be."

"And?"

He studied her office. He ran his hand along the desk and the chair. He looked out the window and then examined the sash. She watched his body, which was uneasy out of its usual space. In a moment of humbling lucidity, she saw herself walking into O'Holleran's pub that day, fresh off the pavement, blinded upon entering the darkness, expecting anonymity in her eight-hundred-dollar linen pantsuit and five-hundred-dollar shoes, thinking she could blend in anywhere, believing she was worldly.

Cafferty sat down in her big leather office chair. "Good chair. 'Cept your ass is too light to break it in properly."

"Thank you."

"Another reason you should be eating breakfast." His hands examined the wood desktop. He raised his eyes to her. "Crappy woodwork."

"I know that now."

"Want me to make you a real desk?"

"Maybe." Ilana walked around to the window and looked out. Carefully, she kept her distance. "How is everyone? Fiona?"

"Good, yeah, all good. Surprised everybody all of a sudden started going to mass on Sundays."

"Really." Ilana kept her smile to herself. "I'll bet Shea was not too happy about that."

"He's got a few things to say, but no different there, huh?" Cafferty got up and walked around the room, touching everything, and looked like a hawk flying recklessly around a room filled with the finest crystal.

She asked, "So, is Shea still throwing people out of the bar?"

"Every day."

Ilana leaned back against the wall. She felt happy to see him. She asked, "And now that you're here, what do you conclude?"

"'Bout what?"

"My belonging here."

"All pretty fancy, and you're pretty fancy, so I guess it goes. How about you strip down, and we make *some* good use of this piece-of-shit desk?"

"We don't do that here at the opera." She smiled at him.

"You tellin' me no one gets screwed at the opera?"

"I definitely didn't say that. Tell me, Cafferty, hypothetically, could you leave your work, your friends, your home, move, and be happy living here?"

To his great credit, he gave this a moment of serious consideration and then replied, "I wouldn't *be me* here."

"Right."

"Yeah, I get that," he said. "All I wanted to say was that maybe I was a little hotheaded before. Didn't want that slammed door and flyin' chili thing to keep you from visiting 'cause my dogs really like you."

"Visiting?" She ran the idea over in her head.

"Yeah."

"Okay. I can do that."

"Good." He walked to the door. He put his hand on the knob and turned back to her. "See ya then."

"See you."

He nodded and left. She heard him comment as he walked past the assistant standing right outside the door. "I'd loosen that bun, honey. Got your ass all uptight."

ON WEDNESDAY, the garbage trucks banged through the early morning streets, callously loud; the lights were out again on Madison Avenue, leading traffic into gridlock; the alley cats prowled back to their lairs to wait out the day; the transit workers threatened another walkout; William died.

His friends were astonished by how conscientiously Ilana had cared for him. The past week had been hellish. She struggled valiantly with medicines, nurses, and red tape. She used every conceivable ploy, every pleading, and any threat to get William what his body required, which was some small semblance of relief at the end. She excelled at it. When her mother was dying, Ilana was not able to help. This time, she was determined to use every pulse of her enviable energy to make William comfortable. She got a reputation in the hospital as a woman who did not take shit, who did not understand the word no, and who evidently needed no sleep.

Several nights before, when William was too weak to stand but had too many bedsores to lie down, he looked at her with sarcastic cheer and said, "Well, aren't I a fucking mess?" She had plowed through the nurse's station until she obtained the painkillers he needed to rest, and now, thinking back, she realized those were his last words. *Well, aren't I a fucking mess?* The bacteria had moved into his bloodstream and won.

She sat on the side of his bed, stroking his bluish hand and wishing there had been some transcendent moment or wishing he had thrashed out or even looked at her, but he didn't. He left quietly. A gentleman. She was prepared, but she was not ready. She would feel chilled, blank, and lost until the anger set in again and warmed up her blood. It would take years to work it through, and the only person qualified to help her was now gone. In the core of her, a quivering began and would continue until it exhausted her.

That last week, without telling him, she let his family know. She wanted them to have a chance to redeem their damaged selves, to reconcile in some way, to say something, anything. She was desperate to do all the right things, and since she was unsure, she did everything. The phone call was truncated and pointless. No one responded with kindness. No one visited. No one sent a card or a flower. She admitted she knew nothing about the soul, but should there be a god (anyone's god), she was sure he did not collect souls of ice; no one could want the souls of these people. For a day, she seriously considered scattering William's ashes all over their front lawn, but instead, she decided to scatter them somewhere breathtaking and exotic, what he deserved instead of what they deserved.

The following couple days were a year long. Back at her apartment, she did all the appropriate things. She made the expected calls and ordered the food trays. When the flowers arrived, there was no place to put them all. The phone rang incessantly. She noticed how orderly it all was, so orderly, so painfully practiced. The virus of 2020 had taught everyone how to do this. People were well-schooled in death. All day, people arrived. They hugged. They cried. They ate. They shared a memory. They left her to her thoughts. She felt disengaged and like she was watching them from some distant fringe place.

When her mother died, it was a uniquely personal desolation. Her mom was a private woman by choice, a reader, and a loner with very few friends. As an only child, Ilana felt her loss so heavily because she bore all the weight single-handedly. She was the sole repository of the memories of her mother's life. Alone, she carried all the events and all the emotions. With William, it was different. He thrived as a socially popular member of a large and vibrant community. He was a man who generously gave himself to people who needed him. His loss was felt by many grieving. She was relieved that William had left others with minds full of him. She was thankful for the eclectic array of humanity that gathered here in memory: school friends, ex-lovers, other psychiatrists, workers from the various clinics, children, university students, and the lonely patient standing in the corner talking to the light switch.

Someone tried to make her eat something. Someone wrapped her in a sweater. Someone suggested she get some rest. Someone cleaned up. Everyone whispered. These were expert mourners. They knew the territory, and they fell into the customary routine. Death needs ritual.

All day, Ilana was aware of the touch of others on her. They brushed by her on their way to the food trays. They rubbed her lightly as they passed by for the bathroom. She sensed that every time a hand connected with her or laid a finger of brief wordless consolation on her shoulder, a subtle energy transfer occurred, one living organism shedding cells of plump sympathy to another. These random infusions transferred a few molecules of strength. Some university did a study once and found there was an actual therapeutic value to hugging. The afternoon wore on like an endless play in a foreign language: words, images, movement, the bare outlines of coherence, but no way for her to follow along.

"Ilana?"

This voice reached her. She turned. Isabella graced the doorway. Her navy silk suit was draped with a black scarf. They hadn't seen each other in weeks, but Isabella had kept track. Ilana had barely thought of her with everything she had been doing. Isabella carried herself effortlessly into the room.

"How did you know?" Ilana asked.

"Glen," she replied. Ilana looked at her as though she had never heard that name before, and Isabella helped her. "The opera?"

"Oh. Course," she answered distantly and added on autopilot, "Thank you for coming."

"Ilana, Ilana, give me one minute."

Ilana turned her face to her friend and tried to pay attention. "Okay."

"I am not going to bore you with Hallmark clichés."

"I wouldn't expect it."

"Platitudes don't ever placate."

"Right."

Isabella surveyed the room. She saw the perfectly displayed food trays and the redolent floral arrangements. "You've done a lovely job here, Ilana. William would approve." Ilana could only nod. Isabella continued, "In a few days, I must leave for Jakarta. I have business and perhaps pleasure."

I don't care. I don't care. I don't care. I don't care. I don't care. I don't care.

"Why don't you come with me?"

Dimly, she said, "Come? No."

"Come somewhere there are no expectations." A long pause. Isabella waited. "Travel. With me? Or on your own? Somewhere you've never been. Meet me somewhere in the world for mint tea. Go anywhere with no plan. It's what you need."

"I'm tired." Weepy from exhaustion and grief, she said, "I'm so *so* tired."

"Yes, I know. But, after a brief rest, Ilana, what holds you here?"

"I have a job. I have a lease." With a child's voice, she said, "I can't leave."

"Can't you?" Isabella looked into Ilana's eyes and whispered as she tried to get past the fog and reach inside. She leaned in closely. "Look around. Closely. Consider your life. Your time. Your choices." She reached out and squeezed Ilana's arm. She spoke with a knowing warmth so deep, it soothed Ilana. "My dear, I believe you're done here."

Isabella kissed Ilana's cheek, turned, and moved with a poignant gentility to the door. Ilana watched. The older woman stopped. She turned back. Her heart stretched out across the space, and she mouthed, "I am so sorry." Ilana's eyes filled. She nodded. She heard her.

Am I? Am I done here?

The burial was nice. Everyone said it—nice, so nice, a beautiful day with blue sky, clear air, and fresh flowers. Many friends, no family. *Except me*, she thought. She knew Adam was there. He did not acknowledge her. She expected that. Friends spoke lovely, heartfelt words about the meaning of William's life. Ilana didn't know what it meant. Ilana didn't know what any of it meant. She said nothing. She thought that maybe someday, maybe some years from now, she would travel back to Albany and ask her biological father if, after a lifetime of theological study, he could explain why all the wrong people die.

And then she slept.

❖ ❖ ❖

ILANA HAD PROMISED her mother she would not be one of those morose Sunday morning visitors who hovered in an excessively respectful silence and replayed their yesterdays over a gravesite. It was not conducive to moving on. Her mother and father were alive in her mind, and staring at a mound of dirt was impractical, futile, and too damn hard. But on this day, she went.

Unsure of the cemetery protocol and therefore leery about stepping in the wrong place, she trudged around the long way until she found them. When she arrived, she found her spirit lifted to see her dad next to her mom. She loved her father the way you would love a tender stranger or a sought-after infrequent houseguest. Ilana smiled to see him beside her mother, finally side by side.

"Hi, Dad." She pulled a colorful and exotic plant out of her bag. Her father was wild for unusual flora. She placed it on his grave. She sat down next to her mother. She breathed in the cool air, and she felt calm. It was the calm that comes from resolution. It was that sweet ending major chord the orchestra played at that last moment of the finale—a moment before the curtain came down, you got up from your seat, and moved on.

"Hey, Mom, I'm sorry about Adam. And I'm sorry about Cafferty. I remember when I would complain about Dad never being around, you would tell me it was a miracle to find one good man, and here I found two, and it's not right with either one of them. I need to open my world beyond what I know for certain." She smiled sadly. "I've been wondering about what freedom feels like." She took a long breath and pushed the hair away from her face. She played with a blade of grass as she sat quietly in the middle of rows and rows of people who were memories in someone else's mind. "So, Mom, I'm escaping. I want to feel what it's like to have a real choice with a whole world of possibilities. I want to get outside of me if that makes sense. Clear. Clean. And I know I cannot trust my brain to make a truly free choice because it has an agenda and a lifetime of hidden biases that I don't consciously control. What would it feel like to have no plan?

How would it feel to be totally ungrounded? Would I be free? Would I be scared? I want to see, or at least. I want to try."

She reached into the bag she carried and took out the empty Tupperware tub with "Mom" scrawled across the lid in thick black marker. She opened the top and whispered inside, "You were a great mom. Wish me luck." She quickly snapped on the lid, airtight, holding in her words. She put it down on her mother's grave. She stood. She looked around at the manicured lawn and noticed what a sunny day it was. She left the cemetery slowly, knowing it would be years before she returned, if ever.

One month later, having quit her job, walked her lease, and sold her furniture, she left for the airport. Ilana arrived at the international terminal with one carry-on bag and no ticket. She walked up to the big board listing all the international departures for the day. Without reading, she turned to a random stranger walking past.

She asked her, "Give me a number between one and twenty."

The woman looked at her oddly, then said over her shoulder, "Eight."

Ilana counted down from the top of the flight listings: one, two, three, four, five, six, seven, eight! She read the destination, bought the ticket, and smiled all the way to the departure gate for Warsaw.

THE END

ACKNOWLEDGMENTS

In my endeavor to create a traditional fictional narrative infused with themes of neuroscience and the ongoing debates surrounding free will and decision-making, I am deeply indebted to neurophilosopher, scientist, and author Patricia Churchland. She volunteered many breakfasts to stop this non-scientist from stumbling too grievously. Her sage advice, spirited personality, and thoughtfulness is a great gift.

Gratitude is owed to two exceptionally talented novelists and first readers: Anastasia Zadeik and Elizabeth St. John, whose patience and insights were an inspiration.

I'd like to thank Terrie Boley who read an early draft of this book and whose positivity was so genuinely appreciated.

Thanks to my editor at Koehler Books, Miranda Dillon, to the excellent design team there, Danielle Koehler and Suzanne Bradshaw, to Adrienne Folkerts for her patient assistance, and to John Koehler for his support.

To my large gregarious family, and especially my partner, Larry Goldenhersh, thank you for lifting me up every day and encouraging me to be seen.

Milton Keynes UK
Ingram Content Group UK Ltd.
UKHW041042181024
449742UK00030B/160/J